KU-743-974

EIGHTEEN COUPER STREET

Anna Campbell's life is dedicated to raising her six foster children. A pillar of the community, her door at Eighteen Couper Street is always open, for advice, treatment for all sorts of ailments or for a cup of tea and a chat. But despite caring for those around her, she is soon embroiled in family problems. When Bella becomes pregnant by Gus, Anna is horrified. And as well as confronting Bella's delicate and scandalous condition, Anna must also contend with the ever-present bane of her existence, her beloved Rachel's father, Gabby. Anna wants revenge, but at what cost to Rachel and her family?

EIGHTEEN COUPER STREET

Eighteen Couper Street

by

Millie Gray

Magna Large Print Books
Long Preston, North Yorkshire,
BD23 4ND, England.

KENT
ARTS & LIBRARIES

KENT
ARTS & LIBRARIES

British Library Cataloguing in Publication Data.

Gray, Millie
    Eighteen Couper Street.

    A catalogue record of this book is
    available from the British Library

    ISBN   978-0-7505-3710-0

First published in Great Britain in 2012 by
Black & White Publishing Ltd.

Copyright © Millie Gray 2012

Cover illustration © Gordon Crabb by arrangement with
Alison Eldred

The right of Millie Gray to be identified as the author of this
work has been asserted by her in accordance with the
Copyright, Designs and Patents Act, 1988

Published in Large Print 2013 by arrangement with
Black & White Publishing

All Rights reserved. No part of this publication may be
reproduced, stored in a retrieval system, or transmitted in any
form or by any means, electronic, mechanical, photocopying,
recording or otherwise without the prior permission of the
Copyright owner.

Magna Large Print is an imprint of Library Magna Books Ltd.

Printed and bound in Great Britain by
T.J. (International) Ltd., Cornwall, PL28 8RW

AUTHOR'S NOTE

This story tells of one family's life in Leith in the early twentieth century. Although it echoes some of the writer's experiences and personal feelings, the characters portrayed in the book are wholly fictitious and bear no relation to any persons, living or dead. Many of the street names, localities and other details from that period in Leith's history have been preserved however.

For my mother, Mary Steel McIntosh, whose life and times inspired this book

ACKNOWLEDGEMENTS

Thank you to Gill Marple, Leith Library Librarian; Noel Cochrane, Leith Storyteller; and Celia Baird, a true Leither, for your assistance in researching for this book. Special thanks also goes to Mary Gillon and Gordon Booth for your general assistance and encouragement. And finally, thank you to Kristen Susienka at Black & White Publishing for your meticulous editing skills.

1

GOODBYE, MY FRIEND

Reluctantly releasing the hand of her friend who was lying in the hospital bed, Anna rose quickly and grabbed the coat sleeve of the retreating minister. 'Please, please,' she begged. 'Just wait another half hour. He *will* come. He said he would. He just has to!'

The Reverend Hamilton shook his head in resignation. 'You said that yesterday and the day before.' He now looked down at the semi-conscious woman whose laboured breathing confirmed his thoughts that if Gabriel Forbes did not put in an appearance tonight there would be no requirement to come tomorrow. His attention now turned to the diminutive woman tugging insistently on his sleeve and he was moved to pity. 'Look,' he said, firmly removing Anna's hand from his jacket. 'I have two other wards to visit before I leave but I can, and will, come back in half an hour. But if the ne'er-do-weel hasn't put in an appearance by then I will have to leave.'

Anna sighed and nodded with relief. It was vital to herself that her friend Norma, who was now close to death, should be married so that she might meet her God without the heavy burden of having to beg His forgiveness for having mothered three children out of wedlock. Throughout her life Anna had believed that the good outweighed the bad. She now smiled, thinking how great an advantage it would be for Norma to be married tonight and yet not survive to live in holy but acrimonious wedlock with a waster like Gabby Forbes.

Anna had just decided to leave the ward and make her way to the entrance of the Leith Poorhouse and Hospital for the Sick, which had been opened just a year earlier in 1907, when she became aware that one of the Poorhouse inmates, who was judged well enough to work, had come behind the screens and was pouring the plateful of thin gruel-like soup that had been left to feed Norma into an old tin can. Anna's look of disgust had the thin bedraggled woman mutter, 'She's no gonnae eat it, is she?' Anna nodded in agreement. 'So I'm just as well tae hae it.' The woman then lifted the tin mug to her lips and gulped down its contents.

Looking around her surroundings, Anna shook her head. 'Have you been here since this ... palace for the destitute opened last year?'

The woman sniffed as she ran her hand over her shaven head, which Anna knew

14

would always be kept shorn so that there might be some control of the head lice that thrived in that charitable environment. 'Aye. Me and my auld man were ordered in here last year.' She sighed and shook her head. 'And d'you ken? Husbands and wives are kept separate...' Sniffing as a sly smirk crossed her face, she continued confidentially, 'But they *do let* me see him on a Sunday afternoon. And mind ye this,' she continued with a cheery cackle, 'getting this wee job gathering up the dishes in aw they wards here, with so many aboot to meet their Maker...' and she gave a quick look about '...means am gettin' right well fed. Might even get a bit fatter and I could get oot o' here.' She hesitated and looked furtively about her before whispering, 'And get a wee place near the docks for just my Tam and me.'

Anna smiled woefully, thinking that if the poor soul considered she was fat now what on earth did she look like before she was ordered in here?

A movement from the bed and a flicker of Norma's eyelids reminded Anna that she should be out looking for Gabby and dragging him to Norma's bedside.

Making her way to leave the long, bleak ward that was never free from the wheezing and gasping of its residents, Anna offered up a silent prayer that Gabby might come.

15

Flying down the stone stairs, bordered by their cold, soulless iron railings, she was dismayed to find the entrance deserted.

Standing outside the doorway she glanced up at the substantial stone plaque that was carved with the Leith coat of arms. Anna smiled to herself as she thought, *Oh aye, the people of Leith are so proud of their new Poorhouse. Our betters tell us, they do, that this place is such an improvement on the two that were closed down after being deemed unfit for human habitation.* Shaking her head in resignation, she asked herself, 'Why should people whose only crime is to be born poor be sentenced to imprisonment inside these walls and hidden away from the world so the wealthy don't have to believe anything other than that the inmates, securely locked behind tall imposing gates, are being suitably looked after?'

Raising her voice, she shouted towards the coat of arms, 'Believe me, you sanctimonious bible-bashers that congregated here to open this establishment, if I have only one wish left in this world then I would use it to ask that this,' she now spread her hands wide so that they included the whole frontage, 'is the last such degrading *institution* to be built in the whole of Scotland.' Little did Anna know then that her wish would most certainly be granted.

'Right,' she continued. 'Time to look for a

16

reluctant bridegroom.'

She turned and began to struggle down the glaur-sodden road towards the over-high gates and was about to slink past the mortuary building when she became aware of the unmistakable voice of a drunken Gabby singing tremulously:

'Come leave yer hoose in Couper Street,
And flit to Sunshine Square,
That's the place where merciful b-l-o-o-o-
    o-d-y Jesus lives
And all are happy there.'

He paused as his rasping smoker's cough engulfed him. Once the spasm abated he spat out, to Anna's disgust, the dislodged phlegm, which landed on his jacket sleeve. Not bothering to wipe away the mucus, he continued:

'Call the boys, call the boys,
Call the B-O-Y-S.
And to the girls,
C-O-M-E, and be stupid enough,
To T-R-U-S-T in Him
To make them H-A-P-P-Y!'

'That's blasphemy, you drunken sod,' hissed Anna as she pulled him from the wall and began to steer him towards the main hospital building, even though he was reeking of alcohol and pipe smoke.

Right there and then she was ready to give him a right sherracking but had to bite her tongue since she didn't wish to give him any excuse to turn on his heel and so leave Norma unwed.

Entering the ward, Anna and Gabby made a bizarre pair. Gabby, as instructed by Anna, was dressed in his threadbare Sunday best. The suit had seen too many years of wear and showed unmistakable signs of its owner having rolled over the ground on numerous drunken occasions. Nevertheless, Gabby was still a handsome man, even although his blonde curls were now unruly and lay like a thatch on top of his head. For those like Anna who had known him for years, his bonny face was clearly beginning to show the results of a decadent lifestyle. Careful scrutiny revealed that his Roman nose was beginning to turn mottled and pockmarked. His saving grace was his most attractive feature – his two bright-blue twinkling eyes. Those eyes had immediately enchanted Norma and unfortunately still had the capacity to beguile.

On the other hand, when you looked at Anna you were faced with a perfect lady who had all the grace and demeanour of a duchess. Her appearance was enhanced by being dressed in a long smart black coat and a wide-brimmed hat – the now superfluous clothes of a woman she had recently laid out for burial. However because she was small and comely, when she entered the ward it seemed as though she were on skates. And no one would have suspected that she was now forced to dwell at 18 Couper Street – a slum tenement that had been knocked up from heaps of rubble that weren't good enough for toffs' housing. Moreover, numerous families lived there and, unlike Admiralty Street, lacked the luxury of a lavatory on each landing for the sole use of only forty people. In Couper Street they had only one lavatory at the rear of the ground floor, albeit for the exclusive use of eighteen families.

Gabby dutifully followed Anna towards the screened-off bed. The Reverend Hamilton was already there and as soon as Gabby had taken his place at Norma's bedside he began the wedding ceremony.

Anna never heard a word of the vows made by Gabby, too drunk to stand, or by Norma, too weak to sit up. She did witness Norma's nod of consent and the cross she made on the certificate when it was put in front of her, but in reality her thoughts had drifted back to the time when she had first met Norma.

The single-end house opposite her on the first landing of 18 Couper Street had become vacant after old Annie Thom died and her body was being removed for a pauper's burial when Norma, one of the few Jewish women Anna had ever met, had arrived, along with Gabby. Anna acknowledged that there was something unusual that attracted her to Norma. It wasn't just her bonny face, framed by a mass of golden red-tinted hair, nor her large blue eyes that seemed to mesmerise you. No, it was her grace and her innate intelligence.

Anna realised immediately that Norma, like herself, had known a better life. It was also evident that because of their identical hair colouring Gabby and Norma could have passed for brother and sister. Anna had also noted – if she judged correctly – that their first child would be born in the next two months. Freddie did arrive as Anna had predicted and a year later he was big brother to Robert. A smile came to Anna's lips as she remembered how, two and a half years ago and to everyone's delight, Norma gave birth to her beloved daughter, Rachel – poor little Rachel who was now in the charitable care of the Poorhouse. Anna gave an involuntary shiver at the thought but she argued she had been quite unable to take on the care of the toddler.

Her eyes pleaded as she looked up at the green painted wall. 'Oh,' she wailed inwardly, 'Norma, please try to understand that because I had just taken on looking after my brother Willie's three motherless bairns and wanting to do my best to nurse you,' she sighed, 'until you were admitted here, I just couldn't.' Then she might have added, 'And if Gabby hadn't done what he was now expert at, and abdicated all responsibility – which meant I also had to keep an eye on Freddie and Robert as well – I just might have managed something.'

Anna was unaware that a full half hour had passed since she started reminiscing until she heard a voice say, 'You'll need to go now so we can get her ready for the paupers.' A pitiful cry escaped her when she realised that Norma had passed away and that the minister was long gone.

Rising slowly Anna went over to speak to Norma's lifeless body. Important it was that she should vow yet again to Norma that she would go and rescue Rachel from the clutches of the Poorhouse just as soon as she was able. She cried out, however, on stumbling over an obstacle, which proved to be Gabby who had slipped off his chair and was now lying in a drunken stupor on the floor.

As her tears flowed freely, she mumbled to the nurse, 'No need for you to wash her. I'll do it. I've done so many in my time. So please let me do this last service for her.'

The assistant huffed before answering, 'Maybe so. But ye'd be a greater help to us, and her, if you'd get,' she now viciously kicked out at Gabby, 'this drunken midden up on his feet and out o' here!'

2

KEEPING RACHEL

'Och, Auntie, why can I no chum ye?' wailed Bella. Anna made no answer. 'Ye ken fine how I've been longing for you to go and fetch wee Rachel so I can have a wee sister.'

'More's the pity that it's her that was left in the hoose for bairns that naebudy wants when it could have been you,' snorted Rab, who was standing close to his brother Jimmy.

'Aye, and what I would like to ken, Auntie, is why you're no taking in her brothers who are more in need o' somebody to be looking after them?' grumbled Jimmy, who was emboldened by the closeness of his brother.

Her face now purple with rage at her nephews' audacity in highlighting her short-comings, Anna made a lunge towards them but the two boys parted like the Red Sea and escaped out of her reach. 'That's enough from the pair of you. Gabby is the father of those laddies,' Anna hotly defended, 'so I couldn't have them even if I was able to take on another two as hapless as you pair!'

Sitting her ample bottom down on the fender stool, which allowed the heat from the fire to relax her spine and shoulders, Anna cast her mind back to six years ago in 1905 when her brother Willie's wife, Elsie, had died and left him with three bairns to look after – Bella, who had been going on seven that year; and the laddies, Rab and Jimmy, who were then eight and seven years old. She hesitated as she confided to herself, 'No decent space between them. An all too short ten months was all that separated the three of them.' Her face was now redder than the fire flames. She wanted to believe Elsie, her sister-in-law, was no better than a wanton woman but she had, after all, been a daughter of the manse and it was so wrong to talk ill of the dead – unless of course, she counter-argued, if that louse Gabby was to do her a favour and die, then telling the truth and saying how useless he had been would be permissible.

Tutting, she conceded that if she couldn't blame Elsie she had no alternative but to blame her seafaring brother Willie who, like herself, had been brought up strict Brethren (and therefore should have prayed ardently for strength to control his urges) for these indecent intervals. Anna seemed unable to make allowances for the fact that Jimmy, a puny four-and-a-half-pound baby, was born two months premature – just as Bella had been. Anna had also to admit that her brother Willie's inability to deny himself the pleasures of the flesh was probably the reason why, within three months of Elsie's going and his dumping the three children on her, he was shacked up with another floosie in Glasgow. That lassie had immediately obliged him by producing another two offspring – which meant he never had so much as a farthing to send on for Bella, Rab and Jimmy's keep.

Checking that her immaculate hair was tightly imprisoned within its grips, she slowly rose to her feet and admitted to herself that all was not lost, for in ten months' time Jimmy would leave school and then he and Rab would apply to be cabin boys on one of the big liners.

Anna's smile was now so broad that it stretched from ear to ear. Andy, her elder brother who was married to an Irish lassie, Rosie, lived just around the corner in Admiralty Street. He, like Willie, was a stoker on the steamboats, but unlike Willie, Andy was strictly teetotal and never ended up legless in the Steamboat pub just outside the Leith docks. Oh yes, Andy might well have married a dim-like lassie from a strange unholy faith – Roman Catholic, angular Rosie was – but he was still a good, upright and honest Christian man, a credit to the Brethren and their strict ways. His being such a good man was the reason he took such an interest in both of his brother's boys and was steering them on the right course – a good life at sea.

'Lads,' he had said wisely to the boys, 'stick in at school and then gang to sea. Oh aye, there's no better life for a man than the one at sea. And you two could get yourselves onto the big liners as cabin boys and work yourselves up.' Andy had nodded sagely before continuing, 'And now that the likes o' me and my mates demanding better conditions for the men at sea, you'll be getting in at the right time and you could even end up captain o' one o' the Cunards.'

This lecture had inspired the boys and nothing else would do until they could both go off together and join a ship. Rab had always looked after Jimmy – a puny wee soul but with a big heart. This meant that when Rab was old enough to go off to sea he had refused to go until Jimmy could accompany him. Not having a lazy bone in his body Rab had marked time by taking on a message boy's job at Binnie the butcher's on Great Junction Street. That job had its compensation: only last night hadn't Rab been given a sheep's bag with a big dollop of ruddican thrown in? True, he had only been given the tripe because it was so filthy that no one would buy it – oh aye, even the poor had their standards – and Anna had stood for hours cleaning the green glaur from it and it had now been simmering slowly for eight hours in some water and onions. And within half an hour potatoes and milk would be added and a feast no king could reject would soon be theirs.

Anna grimaced as she donned her black coat and straw hat. She hoped the odour of the cooking tripe wouldn't linger on her clothes. Chuckling, she muttered to herself, 'So what? It just might be more acceptable than the stink of mouldy mothballs.'

Making her way to the Home for Neglected and Needy Children, Anna accepted that Rachel had been taken in there as she clearly met more than one of the criteria. Poor little Rachel had been labelled motherless with a drunken father and therefore was fully qualified to be in need of care and protection.

The spartan Home was run by strict Christians who opened their arms to those who were too young to be admitted for education at Dr Guthrie's Ragged School. It was situated just off Great Junction Street and lay in close proximity to all the other buildings of importance in Leith.

Before she knew it, Anna was standing outside the imposing locked doors of the stone-built institution and she rang the bell vigorously. While she waited on the steps she remembered to offer up a quick prayer of thanks, recognising her debt to the Very Reverend John Thompson of St John's East Church, who had intervened on her behalf and persuaded the committee, of which he was chairman, that she was a fit and proper person to take on the responsibility of caring for Rachel. Of course, there were conditions attached. First of all, she was required through the law courts to seek a substantial contribution from Gabby towards Rachel's upkeep. Secondly, it would be necessary for her to undertake to bring up the child in the ways of the Lord.

The door finally was opened by the matron of the home – who, to Anna's astonishment, was a dour spitting image of the now deceased but ever mournful Queen Victoria. The woman, who had obviously schooled herself to be able to give a regal look of disdain to anyone who had the temerity to knock at the door, snorted before stating, 'We are just ending our devotions.'

'I was told I could collect Rachel Forbes at four o'clock,' challenged Anna, leaning back to get a clear view of the adjacent church clock and to check that it was just about to strike four.

The woman initially dismissed Anna's reply with a scornful wave of her hands before giving a contemptuous look to the watch that was pinned to the bodice of her dress. 'Punctuality,' she said, giving emphasis to every letter of the word, 'is a virtue, but not when it interrupts the whole household when it's giving thanks to our sweet Saviour, the Lord Jesus Christ, for all he has bestowed upon us.'

Realising that there was no response that would appease the matron, Anna stayed silent and waited patiently to be admitted. She then had to remain seated for half an hour in a large, soulless and very chilly reception room before the matron swept in, followed by a dainty, large-eyed child. Although the hair colouring of the child was chestnut brown, she was quite evidently her mother's daughter. Even though her mother's hair had been blonde with red highlights, Rachel certainly did take after her mother in possessing an innate grace and charm. Anna also observed that she walked with a quiet air of dignity that could not possibly have been instilled in such an austere establishment.

'Rachel,' the matron said, rolling the 'r' for a few seconds before subjecting Anna to a prolonged scrutiny, 'this lady is going to care for you from now on. Not with my blessing, I may add, but with that of those who should know best.' She now clasped her hands and gazed heavenwards in silent prayer.

Incensed by this show of piety Anna had wanted to retaliate but knew she must keep her temper under control until Rachel was safely within her own care so once more she said nothing.

The matron was not finished, however, and continued, 'You will be residing, my child, in a place where there are drunkards and godless women of ill-repute. But you have been schooled in r-r-righteous,' again she lingered on the 'r', 'ways and your duty is to honour your Holy Father, our Lord Jesus Christ, who sent you here for protection.' The matron then turned to Anna. 'You may take her now, but remember to ensure that she acknowledges the goodness of our Saviour.'

Anna grabbed Rachel's hand and swiftly made for a merciful escape. Nonetheless, as she fled from the house she thought that if that matron was an example of devout Christianity, she herself would feel more at home, tolerated and welcomed by the even stricter sect she had been brought up in.

Holding Rachel's small hand firmly in hers, Anna fled along Great Junction Street towards the old Kirkgate. The street was teeming with bustling people and the noise was quite deafening. Rachel, who was still having to race to keep up with Anna, was amazed and her eyes grew larger and larger as she tried to take in the scene around her.

One old man was sharpening knives on a

contraption that had bright red sparks flying from it, while close by he was being watched by a tall, dark woman who was carrying a strange animal on her shoulder.

Realising that Rachel was mystified, Anna stopped and spoke to the woman. 'This here is Rachel, my late friend Norma's lassie. Say hello to Maria, Rachel. Maria comes from Malta – that's a place far away in the Mediterranean Sea. Her monkey comes from there too.'

Maria cackled as she ruffled Rachel's hair. 'Aye, the monkey on my shoulder,' she then put her hand up and began stroking the animal's cheek, 'is from Malta right enough but the drunken baboon that brought me here, with a promise of a better life...' and she now looked about her at the squalor, the filthy streets and broken-down barrows where people were hawking their wares, 'well, he was spawned here.'

Leaving Maria, Anna and Rachel then encountered a huge beast coming towards them and all Rachel could hear was the clip-clop, clip-clop of the animal's hooves as it trotted along the middle of the road, causing everyone to dodge out of its path. As terror engulfed her, Rachel frantically sought to bury her face in the skirt of Anna's long coat while also seeking to calm her terror by grasping for a steadying hand.

Mystified, Anna squeezed the small fingers

that had sought hers and bending down she pulled the child upright. Gently stroking her head she then said, 'Calm yourself, lassie. It's only a horse. Surely you've seen a Clydesdale pulling a cart afore?'

Rachel shook her head. It was then Anna realised that Rachel had never stepped outside the home for destitute children and how terrifying the busy streets of the Kirkgate and Tolbooth Wynd must seem to her. They were now passing Michael's ice cream shop in the Tolbooth Wynd and Anna pulled Rachel inside. 'A farthing cone,' she demanded from Michael Innarelli, the immigrant Italian shopkeeper.

'With or without raspberry?' asked Michael in his cheery Italian accent.

'Well, she'll have it if it comes free,' retorted Anna, who watched as the ice cream cone was smothered in raspberry sauce. Smiling and feeling smug with generosity, she then handed the cone to Rachel.

'Lady, what do I do with this?' Rachel asked as the ice cream began to trickle down the cone and on to her hand.

All Anna could do was mutter, 'Oh, lassie, you have so much to learn.'

Anna and Rachel were about to turn into the stairway of 18 Couper Street when Gabby, from the opposite direction, reeled towards them.

'You're fou' early the day,' remarked Anna in disgust.

'Aye,' lisped Gabby. 'Needed to quench my thirst. That's what a hard-workin' man has the right to dae.'

'So you say. Well, this here is Rachel. You know – your daughter by Norma.'

Gabby eyed Rachel up and down before replying. 'What way is she no in the home run by thon sanctimonious auld cow? Ye ken, that holier-than-thou, administering bloody angel, just like yersel.'

'I petitioned the board and I'm now her legal guardian. Oh aye, she's to bide at home with me. Mind you, I've to take you to court for her upkeep.'

Gabby cackled and fell against the wall.

'What's so funny?' demanded Anna.

'Just that – you're scuppered.'

'How's that?'

Gabby was still sniggering. 'Have you no heard the ship I was working on in Ramage and Ferguson's shipyard is finished now? And I, along with aw the other Leith riveters, are idle again. So just you go to court – because even they law lords,' and he was now helpless with laughter, 'cannae get blood out o' a stane!'

'You're forgetting Lloyd George has just brought in new laws so that means you'll be getting unemployment benefit.'

'Oh aye, the burroo, they're calling it – and

I hear it's to be a whole bloody seven bob a week.'

'That's right. So I'll get a share. And, believe me, even a tanner that you'll no be able to drink will suit me just fine.'

'Look!' Gabby was still euphoric, thinking he had bested Anna. 'Even if it was ten bob a week you wouldnae get a sou because when I tell the court that I have two laddies to provide for and also have to pay a bleeding fortune in rent to that merciless factor, Michie in Charlotte Street—' and he now waved his left hand upwards to indicate the condemned tenement that 18 Couper Street was – 'just to keep this hovel ower our heids, you'll have had it!'

Anna put a restraining hand on Gabby's arm, 'You swine! I'll get my due. You mark my words I *will* get it, one way or another.'

Gabby grabbed at Anna's hand and then pushed her roughly. 'That right?' he snarled. 'Well hear me ... not a penny will your grasping hands *ever* get o' mine.'

Bella, leaning out of the window washing her hands and face in the outside sink, called back to her brothers, 'There's gonnae be a real rammy here. Auntie Anna's raging at Gabby Forbes.'

Jimmy and Rab dragged Bella back from the window and as they leaned out, Rab immediately knew he had to somehow help his aunt. Turning round he grabbed a large cooking pot off the bunker, quickly filled it with water from the tap and sent the contents cascading onto Gabby's head.

'Who the hell did that?' shrieked Gabby as the water drenched him. Looking up, all he could see was the crumbling walls and dark windows – but he did hear the mirthful cackling of the two boys.

When Anna entered the house she was about to remonstrate with the boys but couldn't help laughing. 'Thanks. That dirty pig did need a good dousing.'

Rab never really heard his aunt's words, for instantly he was completely mesmerised by Rachel. He had never seen such a beautiful child before and when she smiled at him he knew he would love her forever. He then grudgingly admitted to himself that he was more than pleased that his auntie hadn't taken in Freddie and Robert instead of Rachel.

3

TRAGEDY

'I don't think, Miss Campbell, that you appreciate how generous I am being,' simpered Mrs Scott-Lyon who was still standing in the middle of the floor, being most unwilling to sit down in Anna's kitchen for fear of catching something one would never get in Trinity.

Anna, who was sitting at her Singer sewing machine, looked disdainfully down at the old herring-bone tweed overcoat that Mrs Scott-Lyon had brought in and was still holding. 'Oh, but I do. All I was saying was that I certainly could unstitch the coat and make you up a skirt but I would need to charge the hourly rate for the time taken.'

'Just a minute,' interrupted Mrs Scott-Lyon. 'I don't think you understand. I only wish a skirt made and all that is left – the majority of this superior Harris tweed material – you may have in payment for your services. Now is that not more than fair?'

Anna's feet set the treadle in motion and she resumed stitching the material she had been working on before Mrs Scott-Lyon had appeared. 'I explained,' she said with a demure smile. 'I have quite enough work now with new material that I no longer need to unstitch old cloth which is so time-consuming and unprofitable.' Anna now looked critically at Mrs Scott-Lyon, deliberately allowing her eyes to linger on the mangy old fox fur draped over Mrs Scott-Lyon's right shoulder before tauntingly asking, 'Besides, wouldn't a lady of your refinement agree that old material never looks anything but tired and second-hand?'

By now, an incensed Mrs Scott-Lyon was about to give Anna a tongue-lashing when the door burst open and a dishevelled five-year-old boy burst into the room. 'Miss Campbell, can ye come quick? My mammy's real no weel.'

Anna immediately stopped working the treadle and without so much as a 'Good day' to Mrs Scott-Lyon, fled from her house, across the landing and into the Pratts' single-end.

The Pratt family had been housed there ever since they exchanged with Gabby four months ago. By then Gabby had become desperate to get away from Anna and her constant complaining – about how he was neglecting his sons, Freddie and Robert, and of course her continual request for Rachel's upkeep – so much so that he felt he simply had to put some distance between

36

them. He was now staying in Coatfield Lane, off the Kirkgate, but that was only a five-minute walk away from Couper Street and at every opportunity Anna pitched up at Gabby's door to harass him.

Anna had already realised that Rye Pratt was about to give birth to yet another child. She sighed, thinking that surely four was quite enough for any woman. 'Right, son,' she said to Jamie who had just turned five, 'you go back over to my house and fetch my bag.' The child looked bewildered and was about to burst into tears when his mother let out another wail.

'It's the big leather nurse's bag that I keep under the bed in the kitchen,' urged Anna, who was pleased to see Jamie nod and dash off.

The bag Anna had sent for was always at the ready because she was known as the Wise Woman for 18 Couper Street. It was she who tended the sick and did both the hatching and despatching, since no other medical help was freely available for the poor and needy. Today it was to be a hatching, and apart from there not being enough natural daylight, there was no gas light either. 'You've not got a penny for the gas, Rye?'

'No-o-o-o,' wailed Rye. 'Aw we had he took for the boozer.'

Anna shook her head just as Jamie returned lugging her bag. 'No matter,' she said, opening the bag. 'I have a torch in here and as I've just put in new Ever-Ready batteries, that will do us just fine.' Anna turned again to Jamie. 'You just go off now, son. This is women's work. But as you go along the lobby tell Mrs Smith I need her to help me.'

Two hours passed, with Anna and Jean Smith doing their best to ease Rye's pain. The kettle was boiling on the fire, which was the only light the women had, Anna having said she would only use the torch when it was absolutely necessary. Suddenly Rye screamed, 'It's comin'. It's comin'. I'm sure the heid's near oot.'

Jean flung back the bedclothes and Anna sprang forward switching on the torch. 'Right enough. You're nearly there, Rye.'

Another five minutes of pushing and pulling and a baby girl slid into the world. 'Och,' exclaimed Anna, switching off her torch. 'With the size you were, Rye, I was expecting a real bruiser – but this wee mite, och, she's no more than five pounds.'

'Oh,' screamed Rye. 'I think something mair's coming down!'

Clicking on her torch again and taking another look, Anna gasped, 'You're right! There's another coming.'

Ten minutes later another small girl arrived but before Anna could switch off the torch Rye exclaimed, 'Oh my God, I think there's another yin coming.'

'Look,' exclaimed Jean, grabbing the torch from Anna and switching it off. 'I think it's that new-fangled light o' yours that's attracting them. So would it no be best to work in the dark?'

Disdainfully Anna wrestled the torch from Jean's hand and, shining it onto the bed again, was relieved to discover that no other baby was on its way. Thankfully the problem was simply the last baby's troublesome afterbirth.

Returning to her own house, Anna found a note from her brother Andy saying he had checked the *Shipping News* in Leith library and found that Rab and Jimmy's ship had docked at Southampton two days ago and it was quite possible the boys might reach home today.

Quickly she grabbed her shawl from the back of the door and ran to Dalgleish's grocery store at the foot of Dock Street. 'Mr Dalgleish,' she breathlessly cajoled, 'you know I never ask for tick. Don't believe in it. But my laddies are on their way home from their first voyage and I need to have a nice tea ready for them. Pay you back tomorrow when I get paid for three of my sewing jobs.' Anna hated to be so grovelling and thought if only that blasted Gabby had pitched up with Rachel's keep she wouldn't have needed to come begging like this.

'Anna, you saying you need some eggs?'

'Aye,' nodded Anna, 'and with five of us sitting down thegither – well, I'll need half a dozen.'

Mr Dalgleish smiled. 'And a half-pound o' best butter? And nae doubt bacon?'

'Most certainly. And make it Wiltshire at that.' Anna winked before adding, 'I'm grateful to you because I know you've been refusing tick to a lot of people.'

'Aye, but now that Ramage and Ferguson have a couple of ships on their books the men will all be back to work in the next few weeks so I'm being a bit more ... let's say ... relaxed.'

Gathering up her messages Anna was about to leave the shop when Mr Daigleish asked, 'Would you also not need some bread and rich tea biscuits?'

Anna shook her head. 'Mrs Smith got me a second-day bread cheap from Scott-Lyons this morning.' She giggled. 'Or, as they would say in Trinity, a cutting loaf, and as for the biscuits – well, since Bella got a start in Crawford's biscuit works, I've got plenty.'

'Aye, but will they no aw be broken an' in bits?'

'Och, Mr Dalgleish, do you no know my mouth's that wee I can only eat broken biscuits!'

'What's the matter with you, Bella?' demanded Anna.

'Just that I've been out slaving all day, taking hot trays out o' ovens, and here it's seven o'clock and I'm still waiting for my tea. Honestly, my belly thinks my throat's cut.'

'Look! Patience is a virtue you don't have.' Anna glanced at the alarm clock on the mantelshelf and sighed, 'Okay. If your brothers are no here in half an hour then I'll give you your tea.'

'Bacon and egg with fried bread?' Bella wheedled.

'Not unless the boys make it home today – otherwise they'll be kept for when Rab and Jimmy get here.'

'So what will I be having?'

'Toast and cheese. What else?'

Bella was about to ask if the cheese was (as per usual) 'Rat trap', when the door sprung open and in bounced her two brothers.

'Rab! Rab!' Rachel called out as she jumped up from the floor, where she had been playing with her aunt's clothes pegs, and raced towards him. 'Did you remember my doll?'

Rab swept Rachel up into his arms. 'Now do you think I would forget that you wanted a doll? And a real doll with a china face, at that.'

Rachel, her face alight with expectation, nodded her head. Rab lowered her to the

41

floor and then fished out a tissue-paper parcel from his kitbag and solemnly handed it to her.

Tearing off the paper, Rachel gasped when she saw the doll. True, it was much smaller than the one in Parker's store window that had always tantalised her, but it had such a beautiful face – so much nicer than the bigger doll. Lovingly, she stroked the small doll's scarlet dress, which was edged with white lace. 'Real silk, that dress is,' pronounced Anna. And to add to Rachel's delight the hair on the doll, which was fastened with a bright scarlet hair-band, bore the same colour as her own – chestnut brown.

'My!' exclaimed Anna. 'Now aren't you the lucky one?' Rachel again nodded and slid her free hand through Rab's.

'And I suppose *I'm* too big for a doll,' moaned Bella.

'Aye, you are,' quipped Jimmy. 'But here,' and he fished in his kitbag until he came out with two parcels, one of which he handed to Anna and the other, a quarter-pound of Cadbury's Milk Tray Chocolates, he passed to Bella who grabbed the box impatiently from him.

'She gets a doll and *me,* yer ain wee sister, only gets the smallest box of chocolates you could buy,' grumbled Bella as she tore open the box and stuffed a chocolate into her mouth.

'Naw,' corrected Rab as he rummaged once more in his bag. 'Here's another box from me because we kent you'd feed your greedy gob with them aw night and never say, "Collie, would ye lick to anyone else?"'

Anna was pleased to find a china cheese dish when she unwrapped her present. Something much more useful than chocolates, she thought, and something she'd always wanted. She hoped, moreover, that she would always be lucky enough to have some cheese to keep in it. However, before she could thank the lads, the door opened and in walked her brother Andy, followed by his son Johnny.

'Well lads,' began Andy, 'and how did you fare?'

Anna by now was preparing the meal and the bacon sizzled and spat in the large frying pan. 'Seems they did okay,' she said, turning to smile at the boys. 'Real proud of them, I am.'

'And so you should be. Now, how long are you home for?'

'Just a week, Uncle Andy,' replied Jimmy. 'We're rejoining our ship at Southampton a week tomorrow. Don't suppose you'll be getting a start on the same ship?'

Anna huffed before chortling, 'A start? Don't you know he's been black-balled for two months now?'

Everybody now looked at Andy, waiting

for an explanation. 'As you will now know,' he confided to the boys, 'some companies don't always treat their crew properly. So me and some others...'

'Mostly him,' Anna declared as she broke an egg into the hissing fat.

'...decided to take on the ship owners and try to get better conditions. They've got to understand that we're no like the darkies – we cannae be treated like slaves.'

'And the result is, he's been up in court and fined for a breach of the peace. Labelled a trouble-maker and so no company will hire him.' Anna sighed before continuing, 'And that's why his wife, your auntie Rosie, has had to take on a job slaving in the Roperie – just to let him keep his principles and supply him with baccy.'

Andy sniffed, took out his clay pipe and began to fill it with Irish Roll tobacco. Lighting it with a Swan Vestas match and allowing the strong aroma to drift around the room, Andy smirked. 'But you lads will have had it easier on the liners.'

'Aye, we liked it fine. Right guid it was being at sea – except when you were seasick going round Cape Wrath,' replied Rab, who was wondering why Johnny was standing there gawping at Rachel.

'Loves her, so he does,' mumbled Bella as she secreted yet another chocolate in her mouth. 'Just stands all the time staring at her. He's cuckoo.'

No one responded to Bella's remarks since Anna had now dished up the tea. To the amusement of the whole company, as soon as Bella took her seat, Anna grabbed one of the boxes of chocolates from her and opened it up. 'Right, Johnny, I've just a bit o' fried bread to offer you and your dad, but Bella here wants to give you the pick of her chocolates.'

Bella's mouth was now full of egg, bacon and bread but that couldn't deter her from trying to retrieve the precious box. To her annoyance, this led to her aunt smartly smacking her across the wrist.

'So,' remarked Andy, who was desperate to be like the boys and join a ship again, 'it's Southampton you'll be sailing from. Pity you couldnae have got a start on that big new White Star liner. They say she's taking her maiden voyage out o' Southampton next month.'

'Aye, she's a real beauty. Built in Belfast, she was. And they say she's unsinkable,' mumbled Rab as he gobbled up his food, but before he could continue Jimmy butted in with a dreamy look in his eyes.

'Aye, we saw her. And do you know this? She has no three but four funnels. Rab did ask if we could get a start on her...' Jimmy went on wistfully, 'but they said we didnae have enough experience for the toffs that'll be sailing on her.'

All too soon the boys' leave was over and as they strode up Couper Street on their way to catch the tram on Great Junction Street that would take them to the Waverley Train Station, they stopped and waved to Anna – whom they considered mother, as she was the only person who really had cared for them.

Rab nudged Jimmy and smiled when he saw their aunt had climbed up onto the coal bunker and was now hanging out of the top of the kitchen window frantically waving a dish towel at them. 'Haste ye back!' she called out earnestly but they never heard her greeting, the words being completely drowned out by the howling of the wind.

'Wonder what Rab will bring me back next time?' pondered Rachel, pulling on Anna's skirt.

'Och, probably a pram to put that doll in,' replied Anna, thinking that Rachel was never going to stop stroking the doll.

Three weeks later Anna was again sitting at her sewing machine and Rachel was busy picking up the pins that had dropped from her aunt's hand when the door was flung wide open and in burst Andy.

'Have you heard?' he shouted.

'Heard what?'

'That the *Titanic*...'

Anna interrupted with a sigh. 'I know. She was hit by an iceberg but she's being towed somewhere. Favourable outcome is what's expected.'

'Naw,' exclaimed Andy. 'The newspapers – they have it aw wrong. She sank. They're now saying the blasted iceberg hit on the fourteenth of April just afore midnight and that she sank to the bottom of the Atlantic two or three hours later on the fifteenth.'

'What!' Anna was flabbergasted and, being a good Christian woman, was deeply moved by the plight of the passengers and crew of the stricken vessel. 'But seeing they had time, the folk must surely have been able to get into the lifeboats,' she managed to mumble while saying a silent prayer.

'You never listen to me, do ye?' Andy challenged. Anna shrugged. 'That's one of the things I rant on about.'

'Aye, and what one o' your rants would that be exactly?' asked his sister.

'The conditions at sea. Don't you realise that there's never enough lifeboats? People get left to drown.'

'Are you saying the folk on that ship h–have all drowned?' stuttered Anna. Then she added bitterly, 'But not the first-class passengers, I bet.'

'Them an all – the men anyway,' nodded Andy. 'Because, and rightly at that, it was women and children first.'

'You're joking?'

'Naw. They're now saying o'er fifteen hundred have perished – drowned in the icy waters. They're also saying some bodies will never be recovered.'

'How many saved?' muttered Anna, wondering what would have happened to the crew, especially the lowly stokers like her brothers.

'Just over seven hundred,' replied Andy.

'Oh.' Anna said nothing further as the postman chapped on the door and handed her a postcard. Looking at the handwriting, she gave a deep sigh of relief. 'It's from Rab. Posted in Ireland.'

'What's he saying?'

Sinking down on a chair, Anna handed the card to Andy.

His voice cracked with sobs as he read out aloud: 'Great news, Auntie. When we got to Southampton I was told to go and join the *Titanic* as they were a cabin boy short. But I said I wouldnae go unless Jimmy went with me. And know what? I wangled him on too. Have to look out for him, don't I? Hope to post this card when we stop at Ireland to take on more passengers.'

'Oh, my laddies! They were just bits o' bairns,' sobbed Anna. 'Aye Andy, along with your braw Johnny and Norma's two, the only laddies I'll ever have.'

Andy mused before conceding to himself that was only a half-truth, as the two wee lassies she had fostered before taking on Bella, Rab and Jimmy were hers and hers alone as from the day they were born, nobody but Anna had had anything to do with them. But that time was long ago and best left in the past.

Shaking her head and going over to look out from the window, Anna continued, 'Just my Johnny, Freddie and Robert left now.'

'But Rab and Jimmy might be among the survivors. We cannae give up hope. Well, no for both of them,' pleaded Andy.

'Naw. If there was any hope, then why is our brother Willie, their father, who would be listed as their next of kin, coming now towards our stair?' was Anna's bitter reply.

4

WINNING AND LOSING

Although the day was grey and dismal and the dreich weather made you shiver when it appeared to eat into your bones, it had not deterred nine-year-old Johnny Campbell from playing chuckies – a game involving the throwing and catching of pebbles – on the cold flagstones with his best friend, Eddie Cappatelli. In an effort to get some shelter the boys were huddled halfway into the entry mouth of 35 Admiralty Street, the tenement where they both lived. They were so engrossed in the game that neither appeared to be aware that, like Couper Street which was situated just round the corner, their homes had also been condemned as unfit for human habitation.

'Here,' exclaimed Eddie, throwing up the stones and trying to catch all five of them on the back of his right hand. 'On the other side o' the street there – is that no your cousin, Rachel?'

'Aye,' replied Johnny.

'But why's she walking funny and clinging onto the wall?'

Johnny didn't answer as he was now standing in front of Rachel. 'Why have you no got yer shoes on?'

Rachel, trying to hug even further into the tall stone-built wall that bounded the railway yard, spoke through gritted teeth, 'Auntie took them off me.'

'But she bought them just last week. Real braw they were. And they looked just dandy on you,' said Johnny, looking down at her unshod feet.

Rachel didn't reply. She just shivered – not so much from not having a coat on and only being clad in a thin old cardigan which had no hope of keeping the cold out – but from humiliation.

'And where's the coat Auntie Anna made for you?'

'Och, Johnny. You think your auntie Anna just does nice things but she's...' Rachel stopped to think what word she could use to describe Anna and what she had told her she must do. 'She's...' again she stopped. 'She's a ... *witch* ... that should be burnt at the stake.'

'What?' Johnny exclaimed. 'My auntie Anna's everybody's friend and I think she's just great. So what do you mean by calling her a witch?'

Rachel hunched her shoulders. 'Don't know. But my dad says she's a witch and should be burnt.'

'Well, that doesnae sound nice. I mean, why would you want to set her on fire? It could kill her, you know. And maybe *you* wouldn't miss her – but *I would*.'

'Oh, Johnny, I liked her too, until she...' Rachel hesitated and looked sorrowfully down before sniffling, until she took the shoes and socks off me and told me to go down to the shipyard gates and wait for my dad.'

'Why?'

'Because it's payday and I'm to tell him it's getting cold now – real cold – and my feet are blue and frozen so I need shoes and he's

51

to give me money to buy them – even though they're already bought.'

Johnny looked down at his own heavy boots. 'Could you no ask the Leith Polis Board for a pair o' boots like mine?'

Rachel shook her head.

'Look!' Johnny continued. 'They run yon clothing scheme for poor bairns like us. And I ken they would be sure to give you some shoes ... and when they do Auntie wouldnae need for you to beg from your dad.'

Rachel looked down at Johnny's police-aided clothing boots that had the regulated five holes punched in them so that his mother couldn't pawn them, and shook her head again. 'But Johnny, I just cannae get boots from them...'

'Why no?'

''Cause I have a working daddy.'

'Right enough. I got ma boots afore my daddy went back to sea,' replied Johnny, admiring his own solid boots.

'Besides,' Rachel went on, sucking in her cheeks. 'You know fine Auntie doesnae like charity. And if I get what she's due from my dad, she says I'll get to put my fine new shoes back on.'

'Huh!' snorted Johnny. 'Could she no have let you wear them down the street and then you could have taken them off at the shipyard gate and hid them?' Rachel shrugged again in resignation. 'Look,' continued Johnny, bend-

52

ing down and wiping Rachel's feet with a piece of rag, 'yer feet are aw bloody and bruised and you're no even halfway to the yaird.'

Rachel was about to reply that Auntie had said lots of bairns had no shoes to wear *all the time* – but she jumped with fright at the screeching of an unseen train thundering into the goods yard behind the wall. As it clanked to a stop Johnny put his arms round her and whispered, 'Don't be feart. It's only a train. Now, would ye like me to chum ye down to the docks? I mean, *I'm* no scared o' yer dad.'

Rachel sank back against the wall again before shaking her head. Then, wriggling out of Johnny's arms, she began to pick her way gingerly through the broken glass, gravel and stones that littered the road she had to travel on.

It seemed to Rachel that she had been waiting at the shipyard gates for a long, long time. In fact it had only been half an hour. During that time she had begun to day-dream. As always, she dreamt that her mother was alive. Rachel was always so sure that if her mother had lived she would have made a good home, not only for her but her two brothers as well. She knew that they would have had a two-roomed house in 18 Couper Street with linoleum on the floor, real blankets on the beds and furniture you could polish. She never thought of living anywhere else but Couper Street, regarding it as a village where everyone knew everybody and looked out for one another. She also dreamed that if her mother had lived her father would, like Mr Skivington who worked as a welder in the shipyards, have worked hard to support his family. He even might have come home with fish suppers and a big bottle of Vimto instead of going down to the pub.

Rachel was now so engrossed in her make-believe world that she was quite unaware that the men were now racing out of the gates. As they pushed past, she flung herself hard against the wall. All she could now see were legs racing past, until one set of legs stopped and asked, 'Rachel, what on earth are ye doing here, lassie? Dangerous, so it is, for bairns to get in the way o' men running hame with their pay packets.'

Before answering, Rachel gulped. 'Oh, Mr Skivington, Auntie sent me to get money off my dad.'

Mr Skivington looked down at Rachel's bare and battered feet. 'Well, lassie,' he said, scanning the crowds, 'he's always one of the first oot o' the yard so I think ye've missed him.'

'Oh, no!' wailed Rachel. 'What can I do? I just have to see him.'

'Well in that case you'd better make your way ower the road to the Steamboat Tavern. For sure that's where he'll be.'

Rachel's eyes widened with horror. 'G-go into a pub?' she stammered.

Mr Skivington nodded. 'Here, take my hand and I'll take ye to the door. Then I'm afraid you're on your own. I dinnae frequent such dens o' iniquity.'

When Mr Skivington left her at the door of the pub, the sudden realisation that the Steamboat Tavern was a dangerous place, especially for a wee frightened lassie, engulfed her. She took a deep breath and was just about to go into the pub when the door flew open and two drunken men looking for a fight staggered out and tumbled down at her feet. Grabbing wildly at one another, they tried to rise but without warning the smaller of the two retched violently and threw up the several pints of beer that it had taken him all afternoon to down.

Rachel was now in great alarm and, deciding that flight was her best option, turned around but was stopped dead in her tracks. Advancing towards her were two women who appeared, because of their long flowing black robes, to be menacingly floating towards her. Looking into their ghostlike faces, Rachel couldn't understand why their hair and foreheads were almost hidden by carefully folded wimples. Without a word, both women raised their skirts very slightly before savagely kicking the fallen men.

'Oh, please stop, Sisters,' pleaded the smaller man as he cowered into a ball to protect himself. 'Stop it. I promise, so I dae, that I'll no drink any mair. Besides, kicking a man when he's down isnae fair.'

This plea, to Rachel's surprise, was answered with another vicious gleeful assault – this time into the man's raised buttocks. The nuns then turned their attention to Rachel. 'Why are you here, child?' asked the senior of the two. Being still quite dumbstruck, Rachel could only shake her head.

The nun now looked down at Rachel's feet and this immediately caused Rachel to think she might be taken away into care because she had no shoes, so she quickly stammered, 'My auntie who looks after me sent me to ask my dad for the money to buy me shoes. She said my feet need to be shod.'

The second nun smiled and her face lit up. 'Do you go to St Mary's School, child?'

Rachel shook her head. 'Naw, miss. I'm a Proddie.'

Both sisters looked at each other and shrugged to indicate that Rachel's plight was accordingly none of their business. They only concerned themselves if the child, who might be in moral danger and therefore in need of care and protection, was one of their faith. So, without a further word to Rachel, they each hid their hands in their habits, cocked their heads firmly to one side and silently glided off towards the swing bridge.

Nothing else for it now, thought Rachel to herself as she pushed on the heavy door and entered the melee.

The Steamboat pub was a popular watering hole for workers, immigrants and refugees from all over the world. Seeing her father holding court at the bar, Rachel immediately went over and pulled at his jacket.

'What the hell d'you want?' growled Gabby, grabbing Rachel by the shoulder and pushing her towards the front door.

Rachel squirmed out of his grasp. 'I'm here – and I'm no leaving until you give me money for shoes. Look!' she said, holding up her right leg and exposing the cruel weals on her cold foot.

'Och, Gabby,' urged one of his cronies, 'surely ye're no that skint that ye cannae buy your ain bairn some decent shoes? Walking on her bare feet, so the bairn is.'

Incensed and embarrassed, Gabby slapped Rachel so hard on the side of her face that she reeled across the room and landed at the feet of the man who had had the temerity to challenge Gabby.

Helping her to her feet and wiping her tears with a filthy red polka-dot handkerchief, the man then fished in his pocket and took out a florin, which he pressed into

Rachel's hand. 'Here, hen. You take this. Sure if I had a bonny lassie like ye, I would dress her in silk and she wouldnae ever need to walk barefoot.'

Rachel cried all the way home. 'Why,' she asked herself, 'did my stupid mother have to let herself die and leave me with her stinking friend who doesn't really want me or she wouldn't have sent me out to beg?' Sniffing and wiping her nose on the back of her cardigan sleeve, she wondered, *Why doesn't my dad love me? Suppose Freddie's right when he says, 'My mammy was fine till she had you.' Killed her, he says I did.*

Bella was seated at the table having her tea and her mouth dropped open in horror when she saw Rachel's battered and bleeding face. 'Good grief! What on earth happened to you?' she gasped, rising to comfort Rachel.

On hearing Bella's cry, Anna, who was making the tea, set down the green enamel tea-pot with such force that some of the boiling liquid splashed out of the spout and onto her hand. 'Oh no! Who did that to you?' she asked, putting her injured hand under her oxter.

'My dad. Who else?'

Going over and dragging out her nurse's bag from under the bed, Anna choked back her tears. 'The unfeeling pig! I'll get even with him for sure, so I will. Oh aye, for what he's done to you this day, I'll make him pay,' she muttered, bathing Rachel's swollen eye. 'And I don't suppose you got my money out of him either?'

Pushing Anna's hands away and choking back her sobs, Rachel screamed and flung the two-shilling piece towards her aunt. 'No from him. I got it from a stranger who was so upset about my bleeding cold feet.' Rachel hesitated, ran her hands over her swollen and bruised face, before continuing sardonically, 'No to mention the battering my poor face got all for asking for your blasted money!'

A tearful Bella stepped forward and began rocking Rachel in her arms, 'Rachel,' she sobbed, 'believe me when I say, from this day on you'll never be sent out to beg again.' She paused to give Anna an unmistakable warning glower before adding, 'Even if it means me working more overtime than I already do!'

Bella's rebuke had hit home and Anna was now visibly upset. She did try to voice an apology but no words seemed appropriate. All she could do was nod her head to acknowledge that Rachel would never again be used as a battering ram against Gabby.

Sensing the reason for Anna's discomfort Bella moderated her tone before saying,

'Look Auntie, why don't you give up trying to get even with Gabby? He's no worth it.' With that Bella led Rachel into the bedroom and, as the door closed, Anna knew the girls, who were now bonded like sisters ever since Rab and Jimmy had been killed, would sleep all night long in each other's arms.

The church clock was striking three and Anna was still tossing and turning in her bed. She had sat up until midnight trying to figure out how she could master Gabby. She had at one point even lifted up the large carving knife from the table and imagined how good it would feel to plunge it into his cold black heart. Letting slip the knife from her grasp, she remembered only last week saying to Rye Pratt that she would like to murder Gabby. Rye had sarcastically replied, 'Aye, that would be a real clever thing to dae. And dinnae worry your head about the nightmares Bella and Rachel will have when they can do nothing else but wonder if you suffered very much when they strung you up on the gallows.'
Anna already knew Rye was right. Gabby wasn't worth swinging for but as she clenched her hands into fists she also knew that somehow she had to get him. Turning yet again in her bed she suddenly remembered the words of the matron when she had handed Rachel into her care: 'Remem-

ber, you *must* take her father to court and get an order against him for her upkeep.'

Sitting bolt upright in the bed she called aloud, 'That's it. He's back working now. So I can ask the bailie to hear my case against him in court!'

The day for the court hearing was now set. Gabby had been served the papers and Anna knew she would now get satisfaction when told by the court what his duty was towards Rachel and that failure to carry out the court's demands would result in him being imprisoned.

Days before it was necessary, Anna had vigorously brushed her coat and hat. She knew how important it was that she should make a good impression on the bailie. She also knew that when he looked at her and then at the now debauched Gabby they would find in her favour. She could see no way that she could possibly lose.

At five o'clock Anna arose. Since midnight she'd tossed and turned as her stomach did somersaults with nerves. After cleaning out the grate and laying the fire, she again started attacking her coat with a clothes brush. Only a loud insistent banging at the outside door stopped her.

Unlocking the door and opening it she was surprised to be faced by a distressed young

Jamie Pratt. 'Quick, Miss Campbell. Ma's needing you – real bad,' the boy blurted out as he tried to grab Anna's arm and drag her over to his house. 'Ye see, there's only you can help her. Dad's no come hame. Listen!' Jamie paused so that Anna could hear Rye's insistent loud shrieks.

'Don't tell me she's in labour? The baby's no due for another four weeks.'

'Well, naebudy telt it that. So it thinks it can come right now,' replied Jamie.

Anna turned swiftly and fished her nurse's bag out from under the bed. 'Just as well I always keep it ready. Oh, by the way, I hope ye have the money for the gaslight this time?'

Jamie shook his head and so did Anna, before turning to snatch some coppers off her mantelshelf.

Without even giving Rye a cursory examination, Anna knew that this was not a normal birth. There was something far wrong. She knew she should be sending Rye to the specialists up in Edinburgh's Royal Infirmary which was situated in Lauriston Place but not only did she not possess the twelve shillings and sixpence which was the charge imposed by the hospital doctor to deliver a baby – she didn't even have the tram fare to get there. For three hours Anna struggled with Rye but the baby was a double-breech presentation and not only did she lack the experience to deal with such a problem but neither did she have the necessary instruments.

By nine-thirty Anna knew that Rye and the baby would both die if she didn't get help quickly.

Bolting out of the house, she ran down the stairs and into the street. She couldn't believe her luck because there, sauntering along the middle of the road, was PC Jack McIntyre – a bachelor man who happened to be one of Anna's admirers.

'What's up?' asked Jack, approaching Anna and noting that her arms, right to the elbows, were covered in blood.

'Oh, Jack, you've got to help me. Rye Pratt's real bad. Believe me, she and the baby will both die if she's not admitted to the Royal Infirmary! Please. Please call an ambulance.'

Jack wanted to help but he knew he was not allowed to send for an ambulance for a woman in labour unless she had the necessary twelve and sixpence. 'Could you no, like you usually do, have a whip-round to get the money?' he asked, stroking his chin.

'Jack! Payday's the morn! Nobody has a brass bean.' Anna suddenly grabbed Jack's arm and pleaded, 'Please ... somebody has got to do something to help us.' Continuing to stroke his chin, Jack pondered.

'Look Jack,' Anna urged, 'it's a quick

solution we need.'

'Here's what we'll do. Now as ye know, I'm allowed to summon an ambulance provided the sick person,' he looked about to make sure he wasn't being overhead, 'has fell down in the street. So, I have to go round the corner to the box and ring into the station now. And,' he stopped with a wink at Anna, 'if on my way back I was to find your patient lying in the gutter here I could summons an ambulance and get her the help she needs – and free at that.'

Anna flung her arms around Jack and kissed him on the cheek before racing back into the stair and organising a team to assist in carting Rye down the stairs and placing her in the gutter.

They had just laid Rye on the pavement and covered her with a shawl when the ambulance screeched into view. Anna was mystified because when the ambulance appeared so also did Jack, who obviously had telephoned for the ambulance as soon as he'd reached the police box.

Eleven o'clock was chiming when Anna raced into the courthouse on the corner of Constitution Street and Charlotte Street. 'I'm late,' she panted. 'Should have been here at ten – but I had an emergency to attend to.'

'Maybe so,' the sheriff clerk replied. 'But the court waits for no one.'

'But,' Anna protested. 'I'm here because I'm a witness in the Gabriel Forbes case.'

Solemnly shaking his head, the clerk advised her, 'That case has already been heard and the decisions made.'

'What do you mean the decisions are made?'

'Just what I say. Decisions have been made and you must ask Mr Forbes what these are.'

She had run like a demented hen, hopping on and off the pavements as she made the short way to Gabby's house in Coatfield Lane. She was so sure he would be holed up there licking his wounds. Reaching Gabby's tenement, she made no attempt to go inside. Instead, she hollered up at the window. 'Come right down here, Gabby Forbes.'

The window remained firmly closed. 'Freddie! Robert! Do you hear me? Open up the window and speak to me.'

Again Gabby's window remained closed but the window of the next flat up was flung open wide and Peter Crone, a man whom she admired because he had done well, rising from locomotive cleaner to engine driver, hollered, 'He's no in, Anna. And I've been on the nightshift and would like some peace.'

'And the boys?'

'They never came back from the court.'

65

Anna realised she would now have to run all the way to the Steamboat pub, opposite Bond Nine in Commercial Street, where she was sure she would get hold of Gabby as he drowned his sorrows. 'Surely,' she kept arguing with herself as she sped along the worn streets, 'he didnae get away with it because I couldn't get my part of the story heard. After all, the boys would tell the truth – I mean, why wouldn't they?'

On her arrival at the pub door, Anna paused to get her breath. 'No use going in for a fight when you're out of puff,' she reasoned to herself.

Once she had calmed down, and with her hair and hat patted back into place, she forcefully opened the door and went straight over to Gabby. 'Think I wouldn't turn up, did you?'

Gabby took another swig of his beer and wiped his chin with the back of his hand before starting to snigger. 'Oh, darling Anna, ye missed yourself, so you did.'

'Are you saying you talked them into agreeing I'm entitled to nothing for Rachel's upkeep?'

Rubbing his hand over his nose, Gabby nodded and then shook his head.

'And what does that mean?' demanded Anna.

'Just that I won and ... I lost.'

'What did you lose?'

Gabby fished in his pocket and brought out three one-shilling pieces, which he flung at Anna. As they bounced and spun on the floor, Anna gazed at them in wonder. 'So you'll have to pay me my due every week?' she said gleefully, stooping to pick up the coins. 'I really knew that somehow I'd get even with you in the end.' Unable to hide her delight, she looked upwards before remembering she hadn't asked Gabby what he'd won. 'And now,' she simpered, 'what else was it you wanted to tell me?'

Gabby drank long and hard from his pint and again wiped his mouth with the back of his hand before replying with a satisfied smile, 'Just wanted to say thank you.'

Growing wary, Anna tentatively asked, 'What for?'

'Getting the laddies taken aff my hands.'

'What do you mean? Where are they?'

'They now have to bide at the Industrial School in Lochend Road.'

Anna let the three shilling pieces fall from her hand. 'Why? They're good laddies,' she protested. 'Yon's a home for bad laddies – thieves, rascals and vagabonds!'

'The court didnae think they were guid laddies when I explained that every week, without fail, I'd given them the money for Rachel's keep and I'd also made sure they knew they were to take it straight to you. Now, how was I to ken they used it to play pitch and toss? Frowned on by the bailie, that was. Then I had to be truthful and also tell about them buying sweeties,' he now smirked gleefully at Anna before spitting, 'wi *your* due.'

Anna's breath was coming in spasms. What *had* she done?

Relishing her distress, Gabby went on. 'Then when the bailie asked if they were out of control I could only nod my head in agreement before wiping the tears from my eyes. The whole court was sorry for me. The bailie even said that I was a poor industrious widower trying to do my best and that Freddie and Robert should be ashamed of themselves for the disgrace they'd brought down on my honourable heid.'

Realising that the bailie would have had no other option but to place the boys into corrective care because of Gabby's lies, Anna was dumbstruck. I mean, she thought to herself, would anyone believe a man could tell such lies about his sons? She pictured the two boys standing huddled in the dock with no one to speak up for them. She knew Freddie would have put a protective arm around Robert as they were led away – branded thieves and felons by the very man who should have protected them against the world.

Without another word Anna turned to leave.

'No gonnae pick up your due?' sniggered Gabby as he kicked the three shilling pieces towards her.

5

THE HEADMASTER

Leith Industrial School had been opened in 1892 and was supported by donations willingly gifted by friends and subscribers who were mostly the owners or directors of Leith's many businesses, together with the wealthy folk associated with the port.

The house itself was a substantial, well-constructed two-storey building with carefully tended gardens, bounded by a low wall surrounded by railings. Being situated at 57 Lochend Road, it was no more than a fifteen-minute walk from Couper Street but Anna had travelled the distance in only ten minutes.

Only when she reached the gates of the Industrial School did Anna stop running. Closing her eyes, she tried to compose herself by taking several deep breaths. Once calmed, she slowly raised her right hand to ensure that her hat and hair were in place, only to discover that her hat was no longer there and her hair was now sadly awry. Generally the loss of her only hat would have vexed her but all she did was shake her head and fish in her handbag for a comb. Once satisfied that she'd tidied herself up as much as possible, she opened the gate and advanced hesitantly towards the main entrance.

As she walked up the path she thought that in contrast to the Leith Poorhouse at Seafield, this building had a welcoming and non-threatening appearance. Ringing the bell, she was surprised to find the door was being opened by one of the boys. 'How can I help you?' the young man enquired.

'I must speak to your headmaster.'

Indicating with a nod of his head that she should enter, he then led her along the first corridor until stopping at a well-polished door. After knocking gently he turned and bowed his head to Anna before saying, 'The headmaster will call you in when he's ready to see you.'

Anna was about to thank the boy when the headmaster did indeed call, 'Come in.'

The man was seated behind a large desk and as Anna entered he looked puzzled. 'I'm Mr Guthrie. Is there something I can do for you?'

Swallowing hard, Anna looked directly at the man. She judged he was in his early fifties. It was difficult, however, to be certain

70

because his immaculate shirt, tie and suit were complemented by a clean-shaven face and well-groomed hair, indicating to her that he was a man who had never performed manual labour and so would not age prematurely. 'I, er...'

Mr Guthrie put out his right hand to indicate that Anna should sit opposite him. Once seated, Anna again attempted to speak. 'I ... no ... what I am trying to say is...' She then blurted out, 'You got two boys from the court today – Frederick and Robert Forbes – they're only ten and eleven.'

Mr Guthrie nodded.

'Well, it's all a mistake,' Anna continued breathlessly. 'The guilty party is not either of the children but their father. They're less sinned than sinned against. By sending them here they're paying for the crimes of their father and–' she hesitated before going on in a cracked voice, 'and the neglect of me!'

Having decided it would be best to allow Anna to get her anger out Mr Guthrie sat passively, only nodding when he thought it appropriate to do so.

'Sure,' Anna went on, 'they boys are good honest laddies. Even if they'd been bad like the court said – which they are *not* – who could blame them for living with a degenerate father who is nothing but an irresponsible drunken waster? Do you know he lied in court today to get rid of the boys? And the only time he puts his hand in his pocket is to buy booze, pay the bookie or send one and sixpence for Jenny Greenhill to come and iron a shirt.' Anna was sobbing uncontrollably now. 'And they poor wee innocent laddies, who were in need of a good feed, knew well that neither Gabby nor Jenny Greenhill owned an iron.'

Allowing Anna to compose herself, Mr Guthrie, who did not quite understand about Jenny Greenhill and her ability or inability to iron shirts, thought, *Now what is the best course of action here?* He deliberated for a while before saying, 'Look, if what you say about the boys' father is true...'

'True?' screeched Anna. 'Look, I don't lie. I'm a Christian. Albeit a lapsed from the Brethren but I attend the Salvation Army down in Bangor Road every week – and I can tell they're not into fabricating either.'

'Okay, I accept that the boys were wrongly accused by their father but you agree that they require care and protection so the removal from their father's control was necessary.' Anna pursed her lips and nodded. 'Now, what exactly do you know about this Home?'

'Just that it's for bad boys who need correction – which they do *not!*'

'Believe me,' continued Mr Guthrie, 'the aim of this school is to educate, feed, clothe and house. And what would you say if I told you that not all of the one hundred and forty boys housed at this school were brought here by the detention orders from the court?'

'Were they not?' exclaimed Anna.

'No. Over half are here because a parent has died and the other parent is unable to control or support the child and wishes him to be admitted here into our care. We also take in destitute children – those found wandering and not having a home or visible means of support. Child beggars. All they require is to be under the age of fourteen, in need of care and protection or brought under discipline.'

Anna hung her head but was listening intently to Mr Guthrie, who then handed her a sheet listing the names of all who were members of the General Committee.

'Not only do we guide the boys up to the age of sixteen and ensure they lead happy, useful lives, but they are also instructed in industrial skills, trained in community work, honour and responsibility. First of all, however, and most importantly, we wash, feed and nourish them when they arrive. And since this is not a large school we have what I consider to be a manageable number of children.' Mr Guthrie now pushed over a dietary table, pointing out that the boys were fed three times a day.

'So,' observed Anna as she scanned the

page, 'they will have porridge every morning and cocoa and bread each night but at lunchtime they will have soup and on Sundays Irish stew, always accompanied by bread.' Better feeding than the boys had ever known!

'We also,' continued Mr Guthrie, 'have a constructive timetable for each day. Oh yes, every day the boys spend part of their time in school while also being trained in the industrial workshops.' Anna nodded. 'They are also encouraged to play a musical instrument and attend band practice. Two doctors and a dentist visit the school on a weekly basis to ensure the boys' health and well-being.' Mr Guthrie paused before adding, 'And I make it a personal commitment of mine to ensure that twice-daily prayers and Bible studies are undertaken.'

Pursing her lips Anna acknowledged that Norma's beloved boys would be far better off here under the guardianship of this upright Christian, Mr Guthrie. They would, she knew, resent what had happened to them but in time they too would realise that it was for the best. Especially when they left the school, suitably trained and so able to work and thrive in the cruel world into which they had been born. *And, of course,* she confided to herself, *an added bonus is that the boys will be encouraged, unlike their father, to be good Christians. What else would you expect when* (and she now scanned the papers again) *there are the names of not one, but at least eighteen, ordained reverend ministers on the General Committee list?*

6

RESENTMENT

The malevolent glares from Bella and Rachel that greeted Anna when she eventually arrived home made her imagine that they already knew the fate that had befallen Freddie and Robert. And they were laying the blame squarely at her door.

Lately she had become aware that encouraging the girls to stand up and speak out for themselves, no matter the consequences, had resulted in their continual questioning of her actions. A wry smile crossed her face when she remembered her sister-in-law, Rosie, remarking that Rachel was so advanced in her speech it appeared that she'd been trained by Anna's friend, Eugenie – one of the most vociferous members of the Edinburgh suffragette movement.

In an effort to delay the eruption of the argument that Anna was sure was about to occur, she adopted a belligerent stance before saying emphatically, 'I've had one blooming day of it. So before either of you start – one of you had better make me a cup of tea.'

Surprised at the tone of their aunt's voice, both girls exchanged bewildered looks before Bella stood up and went towards the fire to mask the tea. As she poured the boiling water into the teapot she retaliated, 'We've no exactly had a picnic the day either. That's the reason I hope you're no expecting your usual three teaspoonfuls of sugar in your tea ... as we have none left.'

Anna glanced into the empty sugar bowl. 'But it was half-full when I left.'

Bella shrugged. 'Aye, but didn't wee Jock Preston and Iris Simpson come to have their soap and sugar poultices changed. And as you weren't here I had to put on new dressings.'

'Are you saying it took half a bowl of sugar to make *two* soap and sugar poultices?'

'Naw! Three. You see, Jock's other knee's has gone aw scabby and filthy too,' countered Bella, pouring out her aunt's tea. 'So I thought it best to treat it right away as he aye takes that long to heal.'

'Aye,' retorted Anna, taking the cup from Bella, 'but a poultice just needs one teaspoonful of sugar to be effective, not half a pound!' Slowly sipping the hot tea, Anna decided it was time to put her side of the story concerning the boys. 'Look,' she tentatively began, 'Mrs Pratt went into premature labour...'

'Aye, we ken,' Bella informed her as she lifted up a ham hock. 'Yon policeman, Jack McIntyre, came up to tell you she's got another wee lassie and they're both doin' well. And he left you this.' Bella now pushed the hock towards her aunt. 'No doubt something else that got lost in the docks.'

'He'll have got it out o' the Danish Bacon Company and paid for it. An honest man he is,' retorted Anna, taking hold of the ham.

Bella sniggered.

'Anyway, because I was tending to Mrs Pratt, I was late getting to the court and the case...'

'What case?' Rachel asked.

'The one where the bailie was to order your father to pay me for your keep.'

Rachel's face fired. She was just so fed up being reminded she was a charity case!

'And?' asked Bella, who was fully aware of the effect that Anna's constant rowing with Gabby was having on Rachel.

'The case was over. And...' Anna hesitated as she realised Rachel didn't know what fate had befallen her two brothers. She also accepted that no matter how well she put her case, it was still going to prove a shock for Rachel. Swallowing hard to control her panic she eventually stammered, 'Gabby lied and blamed the boys!'

'Oh no!' gasped Bella.

'Yes,' Anna replied defiantly. 'And he also said they were out of control and he wanted them to be taken into the Industrial School for ... correction!'

Overtaken by fear, neither of the girls could speak but Bella went over and put her arms around Rachel.

'Now, before you get upset,' continued Anna in a more conciliatory voice before being abruptly interrupted by Rachel shouting angrily.

'Hold on a minute. Are you saying, Auntie, that my brothers, who are good laddies, are now in a home for bad boys?'

'But listen. Next week you'll be able to see for yourself how well-run these places are.'

'Don't tell me you're thinking of sending Rachel there too,' exclaimed Bella.

'Don't be ridiculous. It's a boys' home,' Anna angrily protested. 'The girls' home is in Restalrig Road.' She now looked over to Rachel, whose eyes were wide with fear, and in desperation Anna waved her hand towards her before whispering, 'But I would never send you there. You're mine.'

'So my brothers belong to nobody? Nobody cares about them. Nobody wants them – but me!'

'Look. Mr Guthrie will do well by them. Teach them a trade. How to look after themselves.' Anna could see Rachel was not impressed, so she quickly added, 'And he will even teach them how to play a trumpet.'

Bella and Rachel, shaking their heads, stared at one another. There was a short pause before Bella said with deep irony, 'Now, isn't that what we've always needed – someone to blow a trumpet!' Without another word to Anna, Bella guided Rachel towards the bedroom door and both sisters disappeared inside.

The girls had scarcely fallen asleep when Anna was surprised by her sister-in-law Rosie coming into the house. Swathed in her black woollen shawl Rosie was still caked in the dirty hemp dust from the Roperie.

'Where's Paul?' asked Anna, unable to keep the alarm from her voice. 'Don't tell me,' she urged Rosie, 'you didn't collect him from the nursery!'

Rosie nodded. 'Oh, Anna, I did go straight to the Tolbooth Nursery and...' she now opened up her shawl and there against her breast lay eleven-month-old Paul.

'Oh no,' cried Anna. 'He's not...'

Tears cascaded down Rosie's face. 'Aye. The unfeeling buggers that they are didnae even come and tell me he'd passed away this morning. "Sudden" was all they said.'

Weeping sorely, Anna went over and lifted Paul into her arms. Kissing him tenderly on the forehead, she then went on to wash and dress him to get him ready for a pauper's funeral. 'You know? Some day,' said Anna wistfully, 'we just might get some justice into this blasted world of ours.' She then cradled the dead baby in her arms and promised, 'And ... some day I just might stop hurting Rachel in an effort to get even with Gabby.'

Rosie nodded. Tears for her baby still ran down her cheeks as she thought, *Aye, Anna, but you and I both know you'll never give up trying to get retribution for Norma.*

Feeling she had nothing else to lose, Rosie decided to warn Anna against persisting in her vendetta against Gabby. However, as morbid exhaustion overtook her all she did was sigh.

A short week later Rosie was prematurely gripped with the labour pains of the child she was carrying and three hours later the bairn struggled, without dissent, into the world. Unfortunately, despite Anna's valiant efforts, the bonnie wee lassie was immediately laid out as her brother had been. Oh aye, wee Bessie never drew a breath, but at Rosie's insistence, Anna did christen her with some drops of tap water.

7

CHANGING TIMES

'Auntie, know how I...?' wheedled Rachel as she toyed lazily with her porridge.

'Well, as I'm no clairvoyant, not until you spit it out,' replied Anna.

'It's just that ... remember Rosa Liston's mother invited me over to their house for tea?'

'Aye.'

'And I told you how we got fried fish and mashed tatties to eat and ... the cover on the table was real linen. No wax-cloth like this one,' mused Rachel, who dreamily continued to stir her breakfast with her right hand whilst running her left hand over the cracked oilcloth, 'and they drink their tea out of china cups. Royal Albert at that.'

Anna sniggered. 'Aye, but then they're bow-tows and they earn their money through fish. The father trawling out o' Newhaven, the mother going round the doors up in posh Edinburgh town selling from a creel – even the auld granny has to sit aw day, hail, rain or shine, gutting and selling fish on the broad pavement in Leith.'

'So, why can't you sell fish? I mean, you sew all day but we haven't...'

Anna just huffed and vigorously started to work the treadle.

'And while I remember, do you know if I have a granny?'

The treadle stopped abruptly. 'Rachel, I'm all that stands between you and the lassies' Industrial School in Restalrig Road. Now, if fishcakes made from a cod's head that's been flung away by Rosa's folk and drinking from a cup without a handle is no good enough for you – how about when we go up to see your brothers this afternoon, I ask Mr Guthrie about taking you in too!'

'Auntie, you know fine I don't want to live with anyone but you. It's just that I have to ask Rosa back here for tea and what I'm wondering is...'

'How she's gonnae cope with a jam piece and her tea dished up in a jam jar?'

'No. What I didn't tell you was when I had tea at the Listons and when I said my brothers were musicians, Mrs Liston was pleased, very pleased. However, when I explained that Freddie and Robert were being taught the trumpet at the Industrial School, her face fell. Jumped up, she did. Emptied the tea in our cups into tinnies, she did, and then washed and dried all the china before putting it back in the glass cabinet.'

'See what I mean? When dirt rises it blinds

you. But there's something's no ringing true here. Like … why did she ask you to her braw new house round the corner from the Leith Provident Store in King Street?'

Rachel's face fired. 'Um-m. I suppose,' she stammered, 'that with me getting pally with Rosa when she came to Couper Street School last year and me…'

'I'm waiting.'

'Well it wasn't a lie. Just letting out a secret.'

'What secret,' Anna demanded.

'Just the one about my granddad, my dad's dad, having been a master mariner and when he was too old to go to sea how he taught navigation by the stars in the Nautical College in Tolbooth Wynd.'

'Well, you've got that off pat, have you no? And did you also mention your other secret?'

'Which one?'

'The most important one, how most nights your granddad's son, your dad, cannae navigate himself out of the Steamboat Tavern.'

'No,' shouted Rachel. 'I just said the family had come from South Queensferry and my two great aunts were schoolteachers and that makes me middle class.'

'That right?' chuckled Anna. 'And did you also say you were lucky that I, who came from…'

'Right enough, Auntie. Where do you come from?'

Anna turned to gaze out of the window and the clock ticked slowly by before she said, 'Smithton. A wee huddle of houses half a day's walk away from Inverness and a stone's throw from the Culloden battlefield. Lovely wee place it is.'

'What do you remember best about it?'

'Just that on a clear day you can stand in our garden and look out over the Moray Firth and beyond to the Black Isle,' was Anna's emotional reply. 'Mind you, the Black Isle isn't really an isle. Och,' she continued, turning her attention back to her sewing. 'That was all yesterday. And in life, Rachel, believe me, you can go forward but you cannae go back.'

'But if you loved it that much, why did you and your brothers leave?'

'My mother died when I was twelve, Andy and Willie were two and three years older than me. My father, who was a pillar of the church – strict Brethren, he is – decided that every night he should knock obedience and the fear of God into my brothers – and in no way were they to interfere in his life. As for me, well, I was just a lassie so I had to leave school to become the housekeeper.' Anna was now talking more to herself. 'Could have lived with that but men are always hankering to have their shirts ironed. Luckily, before any...' Pursing her lips, Anna stopped, brushed her hands over her chest and shook

84

her head before continuing, 'Enough to say, that I was taken in every night to sleep with my auntie, who lived in the next cottage with my granny. Then one day they decided it would be best for my brothers and me to leave. So they packed our bags and sent us off to Leith. The boys decided to go to sea. My auntie then paid for me to go to that posh college in Edinburgh's Atholl Crescent – but she couldn't afford more than a year. That was where I was taught to sew and keep house. That was good because when the boys came home on leave I kept house for them until they got married.'

'But if Smithton was so nice, why didn't you go back?'

'Don't be silly, Rachel. The reason my auntie and granny sent us off was that my father got his eye on a half-wit of a lassie, just a year older than me, I might add. Took her up the aisle, he did, when he discovered she was more than happy to oblige and iron for him as often as he wanted. From the day they married my brothers and I were no longer welcome at Smithton, my mother's folks' house. Mind you, from time to time my auntie, who said his getting married again was really a blessing in disguise, sent me a wee bob or two to help out. And know something? I couldn't tell you often enough how that wee handout was our lifeline. Sure miss it since she died last year – but I know sweet Jesus, who has never let me down, will somehow throw me another lifeline.'

Rachel was all for further probing into her aunt's background but Anna was aware she'd already said too much to eight-year-old Rachel, who had inherited her mother's innate abilities and was therefore more able than fifteen-year-old Bella to hold an intelligent conversation. Slowly lifting the bowl away from Rachel, Anna then announced, 'Time for you to get ready. The boys will be expecting us. And I like to get a front seat.'

'But Auntie, what are we going to do about Rosa?'

'Tell her to come on Monday afternoon after school and also say to your other pal, Jenny Steele, that she's welcome to a jam piece too.'

Rachel and Anna should have made good time to Lochend Road but a young, lugubrious-looking lad, Sandy, who was obliging Anna by carrying away the dead on the back of his father's horse-drawn coal cart, appeared to be anxious to engage her in conversation.

Cocking his head he quickly began, 'Anna, admit it now. You and I are making a name for ourselves. We're the talk of the place.'

Anna, who had at first decided to quickly walk on past Sandy, drew up sharply. 'Look here,' she shouted then continued in a rasping whisper, 'I hope you've not been reading anything into my falling on top of you and grabbing your leg when both of us missed our footing and fell into the Poorhouse Mortuary last Saturday night.' Sniffing indignantly, Anna drew herself up before adding, 'Knocked poor Frank Skinner off his trolley, so we did. Honestly, if he hadn't been dead already he'd have died of fright – I nearly did! Should have that place lit at night, so they should.'

Sandy cackled. 'Not that kind of name. After aw, you're auld enough to be my granny.'

Anna's mouth dropped open as she thought, *His mother maybe – granny never.*

'I mean,' continued Sandy, quite unaware of the effect his statement had on Anna, 'that folk are now saying you and I make a great pair of undertakers.' Anna's mouth gawped further and her eyes rolled. Still undeterred by her reaction, Sandy sallied on regardless, 'And not only do they say we're good at it but they're also saying we both look the part. Natural we are.' Sandy preened himself as he admired his reflection in Binnie the butcher's window. Anna also looked at the reflection and admitted that in his case people were probably right because the corpses they attended to very rarely looked quite as dead as him.

She was about to question his reasoning

when he went on, 'And we are so guid now that half o' our customers pay and get lowered into bought plots.' He paused briefly and looked at Anna's stoical expression, becoming aware she would still require some more convincing. 'Look,' he cajoled, nudging her with his shoulder, 'at what we made last month. And I can tell ye – it was far more than I ever make from lugging bags o' coal up three and four flights of stairs.'

Anna knew that what Sandy was saying was true. Most people now paid for her services. Okay it might only be a wee something or it might take them a few months to square up, but so what? Aye, Sandy and she were making an honest bob. Certainly not by much, but she could now pay her way without wondering where the wherewithal was coming from. And who knows? If she and Sandy did make a go of it one day, she might even be able to buy some china cups and a linen table-cover to sweeten up Rachel.

Still pondering, she mumbled, 'But what will your dad say? After all, he's no going to be happy that you're not going to be helping him with his coal deliveries any more.'

'You're right, he's no happy. He says it's just like me to want to take on a dead-end job.' Sandy adopted a far-away, dreamy look before adding, 'But I have ambitions. Gonnae get a proper hearse, so I am. Oh aye. Folk now want to go on their last journey in style – no, if they can help it, slung on the back of a coal cart whether it's been washed or no. So I'll cut the prices o' the posh undertakers and oor ain folk will be able to go on their last journey in style – in a glass-sided black hearse, no less.'

This statement jolted Anna and she quickly declared, 'Look, I'll help you start a business but understand this – them that cannae afford to pay still have to be accommodated.'

'Done!' chortled Sandy. 'We can still do that. And to show good will, I'll even have them carted away to Seafield cemetery in my hearse – mind you, out o' normal business hours of course.'

'But where's all the money coming from for this hearse?'

'A wee borrow here and wee borrow there.' He stopped, cocked his head and winked knowingly at Anna. 'Believe me, some clever Leith business folk see that no matter what happens people always support their local undertaker and keep dying! Remember last year when there was a seven and a half week dock strike, there was no money – no nothing. Only thing that increased was folk giving up the ghost and passing away.'

'Look, I'm in a hurry right now. But tell you what, I'll think about it, but if I do come in with you it would only be as your teacher.

I'm no wanting folk to think that I'm now money-grabbing and they cannae come to me for help.'

'Please yersel'. And, again to show goodwill I'll even take on your own lassie, Bella. Oh aye, with her face always tripping her she'll be a real asset!'

By the time Anna arrived the only seat left for the Industrial School Brass Band Concert was at the back where Rachel had kept a place for her.

'This is your fault, Auntie,' hissed Rachel standing up so she could see over the sea of heads.

'What do ye mean?'

'Just that you're spending so much time talking to that guy that looks like Frankenstein.'

'And who's Frankenstein?'

'Oh Auntie, you know fine he's the monster in that Mary Shelley book. I told you about it last week after Jenny Steele, whose father lets her read any kind of book, told me about it. So scared I was I couldnae sleep. And remember, Auntie, you asked me if that was the same Mary Shelley – as the feminist you admire – and I said it was.'

Before Anna could reply, the conductor called for silence by tapping his baton. Soon the hall was filled with the sound of the boys' brass band playing popular tunes of the day. Anna was so delighted to see Freddie and Robert both included in the ensemble but she wasn't prepared for Robert being called forward to give a solo performance of 'Land of Hope and Glory'

As the notes faded, a rapturous standing ovation filled the hall. Anna, who was first to have leapt to her feet, was obviously overcome with emotion. Partly because Robert quite evidently had the natural ability to become a competent musician but more worryingly because she wondered if the piece had been chosen because of all the talk of a war being in the offing!

Immediately after the concert, Freddie and Robert joined Anna and Rachel at the back of the hall. 'That was a very fine performance, Robert,' Anna declared, patting him on the shoulder. 'Your mammy would have been so proud.'

'Aye, but no my dad,' he replied bitterly. 'And there's nothing to stop him from being here.'

Anna could have launched into a tirade about Gabby's failings but decided that would only add to the boys' resentment, so she asked, 'In here, do you hear much talk of a war coming?'

Freddie nodded. 'Aye, five of our laddies joined the army and six the navy last year, and there's talk that another dozen will go this year.'

'As many as that?' queried Anna.

'Aye. But that's because most of the boys here haven't got homes to go back to and the army and navy are good options for them.'

'But that won't happen to you two. When the time comes you'll both make your home with us – that is with the girls and me.'

Rachel beamed with delight until Freddie started to snigger.

'Oh, I see,' he said taking care over each word. 'When we're auld enough to be working and no longer a burden, both you and our erstwhile faither are willing to have us. No bad, Robert, eh? Oh aye, son, what's being said is that when you're fifteen and I'm sixteen and we're having to leave here, awbody wants to find us a bed.'

Anna was still mulling over the events of the day. Sandy's idea of starting an undertaking business she put to the back of her mind. It was the realisation that Gabby had already intimated that he would take the boys back when they were released that was vexing her. After the upright-start they had been having in the Industrial School, going back to live with Gabby and his debauchery would be so utterly wrong. The only hope she had, and it was the one that was keeping her going, was that there was more than a distinct possibility that Gabby would drink himself to death in the near future.

So engrossed was she in her thoughts that she was quite unaware that the outside door had opened until her brother Andy spoke, 'Did I no tell ye when I was home on leave in June that the assassination of yon Archduke Ferdinand would lead us all into war? And here we are just two months later, and we've declared war on Germany! Now if that's no putting the cat among the pigeons, I dinnae ken what is.'

'Declared war on Germany, have they?' Anna replied absently, as her thoughts were still on what might happen to Norma's boys when they were released. Rising, she continued with bitter irony, 'Now, is that no a clever thing to do.'

'Anna, I know you're all against war. Don't know why – because you'll no be, like us men, fighting in it.'

'Naw. But when all you stupid men and boys go off to play warriors, I'll be here holding all the families together. And talking of holding the fort, remember to take the legs for your alarm clock back.'

Andy puffed as he reached up and took a small paper bag off the mantelpiece. 'Had to take the legs off the clock or she would have pawned it for drink. And how was she when I was away?'

'If you mean, was your Rosie sober every day then...'

Andy gasped. 'How the devil she got herself into such a mess I simply dinnae ken.'

'Suppose it's too much to ask that you might concede that Rosie having eight bairns in eight years and only two surviving might have something to do with it.' Andy's only reply was to click his tongue. 'I think you know, brother, that if I had been Rosie, not only would I have found refuge in Red Biddy, I'd also have jumped into the docks.'

'Aye, but thank God she's Catholic, so jumping in the docks is no an option.'

'Talking about Rosie being a Catholic, your Johnny came over to me just about four month ago. Breaking his heart, he was.'

'About what?'

'Och, nothing really. Just didn't like that his mother was lying in the gutter blind drunk and that two ministering angels, masquerading as nuns from the convent – the ones that come and take two loaves of bread from her every week to feed the orphans – were kicking her all black and blue. Mind you, that priest, Father what's his name?' Anna stopped till she recalled, 'Father Kelly. Aye, well him. He came on the scene and told the holier-than-thou sisters to get back to their convent. Picked Rosie up out of the gutter. Took her to the chapel house and talked things over with her. Supported her, he did, while she kicked the drink habit. And, good for her, she's been on the wagon ever since. So, brother, you can go off to war or back to sea with no worries – because both me and Father Kelly will be here to look after your responsibilities.'

Andy's face was purple with rage. 'What's got into you, Anna? You've turned into a right shrew. Finding fault with awbody, so you do. And it's blooming true, what folks say, that you're worse than any of these suffragettes ever were. You know if you hadnae been so brittle someone might have taken you off the shelf. But naw, you have to give every man you meet a tongue-lashing.'

'That right? Well, let me tell you. Get used to it because ... I'm just starting.'

The door opening, which had been preceded by a loud knock, halted Anna and Andy's argument.

'Oh, it's yourself, Jack,' Anna said sweetly as the police officer came into the middle of the room and laid down a sack on the table.

'Just a wee boiling of my garden tatties for you and your lassies, Anna.'

Andy chortled, but before leaving he managed to whisper to Anna. 'Now any man who'd come a-courting a feminine lassie would bring her flowers from his garden... It says it all, Anna ... you get wooed with a big bag o' garden tatties!'

8

A STRANGER COMES ASHORE

The late bright October sun streamed into the room and Anna had flung the window wide open to welcome it and the cool accompanying breeze. Eyes closed, she now sat on the bunker nursing the newborn baby. How grateful she was for the cool air that blew relief on her perspiring face.

It hadn't been a long labour, only two hours, and Rye Pratt had been such a help to Anna by assisting in the safe delivery. A sly smile spread over Anna's face as she thought, *If anyone should be expert at births it should be Rye – after all, hadn't she delivered all eight of Rye's bonny babies who were all still alive and vigorously kicking unlike–*

'Anna.' Rosie's tired voice interrupted Anna's thoughts. 'Did the bairn make it?'

Swinging her legs down on to the floor Anna then made her way towards the bed. 'Sure. Now how could you doubt it? Surely you knew I wouldn't let you down.'

Before answering Rosie struggled up in the bed and Anna laid the baby in her arms. Pulling down the shawl Rosie gazed at the child. 'Well at this size it has to be a dainty lassie.'

'Naw. It's a laddie. And, okay, he's no a heavyweight but sometimes the wee ones surprise you and flourish the best.'

Rosie nodded but Anna could see she wasn't convinced. After all, before today Rosie had had eight births. Only Johnny and Ella had survived and the death of Paul had been the cruellest blow. 'Know what?' murmured Rosie, cradling her new son close to her breast. 'I don't think this wee mite will ever be a Samson but I'm so grateful to God for giving him to me that I'm going to call him ... David.'

Anna smiled, 'A wee Davy in our family – is that not just dandy?'

Davy was four weeks old before his father came home on leave. Before Andy left on his last voyage, six months earlier, Rosie had known she was four months pregnant but she'd decided that, with the war raging at sea as well as on land, there was no use in giving her own Andy any further worries – so she hadn't told him.

'Well I never,' exclaimed Andy when confronted with his new son. He then pointed backwards with his thumb. 'And this here is Gus Cochrane who comes from the far-flung Hebrides. We've been told we're not home for long so it's no use him trying to get back to Stornoway.'

'Stornoway. Where's that?' queried Rosie.

'Capital of Lewis – one o' the biggest of the islands in the far-flung Hebrides but Gus comes from a tiny wee island nobody's ever heard of. But o' that's bye the bye, didn't I say to him he could bunk in with us but...'

Rosie eyes rolled before she suggested, 'Would he not be more comfortable at Anna's? She doesnae have a bairn greeting four and five times in the night wanting fed.' Rosie chuckled, 'Och, Andy, our wee Davy here likes to be sooksooking aw night long, so he does.'

Stroking Davy's wee face Andy nodded his approval.

When Andy arrived with Gus in tow, Anna was more than a little surprised. On learning that Andy was asking her to put him up (just for a few days, he had emphasised) she was even more disconcerted.

'Suppose I could,' said Anna hesitantly. 'But that means the girls will have to sleep with me in the living room. What's your name, by the way? I didn't quite catch it.'

'Gus Cochrane,' came the answer accompanied by a warm, engaging smile.

Anna took her time to study the young man. He was so very tall, dark and handsome. She could see by his tanned skin that there was some truth in the rumour that a hundred or so years ago a Spanish galleon had floundered in the ever turbulent sound of Barra. The story also said that some of the young seamen had reached the shore on numerous Hebridean islands. Chuckling, Anna mused to herself that the survivors must have looked so much like Gus that it was no wonder the women on the islands had been more than happy to mate with them. Hence the reason that most men who came from the Outer Hebrides and the north of Scotland had that intriguing, seductive and mesmerising Mediterranean look about them.

'So it's settled then. Gus will be with you until he gets word to board his ship.'

Still unable to take her eyes off the Adonis-like young man and wondering why she felt quite so apprehensive, Anna nodded her agreement.

'And I'll pay whatever you ask,' Gus hurriedly assured in his enchanting lilt.

Far from calming Anna, she found her misgivings were growing out of control again.

By the time Rachel came back in from school, Anna had rearranged the house to accommodate the lodger.

'What's going on? Are you getting us ready to do a moonlight?' Rachel asked, picking up her Wellingtons that had been thrown out of the bedroom and into the living room.

'A friend of your uncle Andy's is going to be lodging with us for a few days.'

'Thank goodness for that. I thought you hadn't the money to pay the rent.'

'Don't be ridiculous, Rachel,' huffed Anna, who prided herself in being a good manager of money.

Rachel looked absently about before asking, 'But why can't she share your bed? After all, you have the big bed all to yourself and Bella and I have to share the wee one.'

'She's a he. So you, Bella and I will all have to bunk in together.'

Kicking her Wellingtons under the bed, Rachel grumbled, 'And here was me running all the way home to tell you.'

'Tell me what?'

Rachel drew herself up and looked haughtily about. 'Just that I have come first – in the whole school's composition competition!'

'Oh,' gasped Anna. 'You have? Is that not just wonderful! Mind you, I would rather you hadn't taken after your father.'

'What on earth do you mean?' exclaimed Rachel, who felt that Auntie was again casting scorn on her achievements.

'Just that he's the biggest storyteller in the whole of Leith and now your story has come

100

first in the school folks will be saying you take your creative flair off him.'

'Och, Auntie, he tells fairy stories that nobody believes. My story, says the teacher, is a work of genius. And tomorrow I'll have to be very smart when I go to school because I have to go into each classroom and read my wonderful fable.'

Anna was rather at a loss to know the difference between a fairy story and a fable so reluctantly she asked, 'Rachel, have you got the story in your schoolbag?' Rachel nodded and fished the precious pages out. 'Okay. Now read the story to me.'

Imitating a professional she cleared her throat before beginning. 'Once upon a time, a little girl's mother died and therefore she'd never known her. As time went slowly by she longed to see her mother. One day, she met a crooked old man on the stairs and, as she stood aside to let him past, he slipped and tumbled down the steps. Quickly the little girl ran down to help the old man up and as she stroked him he said, "You have a great longing in you. But tonight when you go to sleep you will have a most wonderful dream. In that dream you will come face to face with your real mother." How, wondered the girl, could this man know her innermost thoughts?'

Rachel continued her story until the end. During the whole time Anna sat silent, wondering if Rachel knew she'd written a fairy story but based on facts that shook Anna. Facts that told her how Rachel had resented always being reminded she was a 'charity' child.

Fortunately before Anna could comment, Bella arrived home with the customary bag of broken biscuits. 'Chocolate ones this time,' said Bella, opening up the bag so that Anna could see inside. 'And look – some good milk ones that aren't too smashed. And there's even enough to give Auntie Rosie some.'

Rachel vigorously shook her head and fished in the bag and brought out a biscuit to nibble. 'Sorry, Bella, but there will be no biscuits for Auntie Rosie or Johnny. You see, we'll need all of the biscuits here to feed our lodger.'

'Lodger?' exclaimed Bella.

'Aye,' interrupted Anna. 'A sailor pal of your Uncle Andy's. And that means you and Rachel will be sleeping in here with me.'

'Oh, no!' cried Bella loudly. 'He can go and take a run and...'

The door opened and Gus Cochrane advanced into the room. Bella's jaw dropped. Gus, being dressed in an Eriskay hand-knitted sweater and seaman's coat, looked so utterly fetching. Anna swallowed hard as she experienced the return of the same apprehension that she'd felt on being introduced to Gus. Bella at nearly sixteen had no real experience of men and still was quite immature. *Oh God,* she thought. *What if Bella goes and makes a fool of herself?*

'Gus, these here are my girls. Bella's my brother's lassie and Rachel I got...' Anna was about to say from the destitute children's orphanage until she remembered Rachel's winning story and so continued, 'Just because I wanted her.'

Gus nodded to Rachel and winked at Bella, sending her face bright red while Anna's apprehension grew until she looked again at Gus and gratefully conceded that a good-looking, worldly man like him would be looking for a more sophisticated mate than sweet but callow Bella. She also knew that in the Hebrides, as in the Highlands where she had been raised, it was unthinkable to abuse your hostess's hospitality.

9

TWO MONTHS GONE AND STILL NO SIGN OF HIM

The living room come kitchen of Anna's house was filled with the acrid aroma of onions. 'Great that your pal Jack McIntyre spent his day off trapping rabbits,' commented Rye, whose eyes were streaming. 'Mind you, I didnae mind the skinning and chopping them up, but see thae onions? Och, my eyes are fair stinging.'

'Aye, with food now as scarce as money because of this blooming war, five rabbits is a Godsend,' chuckled Anna. 'And with your Jamie getting the tossed-out onions, carrots and tatties out o' Rankin's market, what a feed the whole o' 18 Couper Street will have the night.'

Going over and lifting the kettle, Rye advanced to fill it at the sink. 'Aye, and it must have taken Jack the whole day to get all the trapping done.' A sly smile crossed her face before she continued, 'Mind you, I think it was you trapping him with a flash o' your ankles now that you've lifted your skirts a good four inches that got him in the mood.'

'Don't talk rubbish, Rye,' Anna retorted. 'The reason my skirts are no longer sweeping the floor is so I don't get muck and bugs on them. Besides, shorter skirts don't get worn out so quickly.'

Rye flopped down on a handy chair. 'Have it your own way, Anna, but I ken fine Jack has an eye for you.'

'That's where you're wrong. And even if he had, it would do him no good. I'd never saddle myself with any man.'

'Wish I hadnae. Here, Anna, did I tell you?'

'You're no away again?'

'Naw. But wait till you hear this – that man o' mine, who cannae get by unless he has his oats *every* night, has joined the 7th Battalion Royal Scots Territorial and they're getting sent to the front.'

Not wishing to know anything about anyone's sex life – least of all Rye's – Anna pretended she was clearing her throat by giving a few grunts before remarking, 'That right?'

'Aye. Mind you I think he'll find it a lot different from being a flour miller in John Wilson's. And he'll no be able to get hame every night like he does from the mill in Bonnington Road.'

'But on the bright side,' Anna predicted, 'you'll no be having any more bairns.'

'You're right there – eight bairns are enough for any woman and by the time he gets back I'll be right through the change. Funny me going into the change early. Anyway, they say thirty-four is early – mind you, if I'd known the work eight bairns were I'd have started the change before I left the primary school.'

Anna and Rye looked questioningly at each other when the sound of heavy footsteps in the passageway stopped at the door, followed by a loud thud of something being dumped down. 'Oh, no,' gasped Anna, 'don't tell me that Gus is back again?'

'Right enough. Him asking you to put him up just for a few days and then it turning into eight weeks was a bit of a cheek.'

'Bit of a cheek? That was nothing to the worry I had, keeping Bella from getting smitten by him.'

'Don't tell me she fancied him?'

Anna's face reddened. 'No. She thought she did, until I told her she didn't. Honestly, what a job I had convincing her that a handsome lad like him usually has a lassie as daft as herself in every port.'

'Then what kind o' smit was it she was getting off him?'

'A big doze o' that malaria thing he got in the tropics. That's what kept him here all these weeks.'

'That so?'

'Aye, continually shivering and delirious and calling out for his mammy, he was.'

Sucking in her cheeks Rye lazily responded. 'And all the poor soul got was Bella, whose face has been longer than Leith Walk ever since you got rid of him three weeks ago.'

The insistent knocking on the door finally caused Anna to open it. 'Oh my goodness,' she exclaimed when she saw a coal man standing there.

'Are you Anna Campbell?'

'Aye,' replied Anna nodding. 'But I didn't order any coal for the simple reason I'm skint.'

'Then let's just say it's your lucky day because a Good Samaritan paid me to bring a bag up for you.'

Once the man had dumped the coal into Anna's bunker, Rye asked, 'You've really nae idea who your hearth-warming fairy godmother is?'

'No. But seeing it's Christmas next week I suppose it could well be Santa Claus,' replied Anna, who had no desire to enter into any explanation with Rye.

'Now,' Rye continued, 'it could only be from one or two people. I think the best bet would be Jack McIntyre who is desperate to get you into his custody.'

Anna sighed. 'Look. Giving me rabbits he trapped for nothing is one thing but him parting with siller for a bag of coal would take some doing.'

'Well, in that case, maybe that Gus lad sent it on as a thank you for keeping him warm when he was shivering.'

'Oh look,' cried Anna, going over and vigorously stirring the pot. 'That's the rabbit stew simmering and isn't it just great that when my auntie up north died I inherited her cauldron? You know, that pot is so big that when it's on the fire I can get nothing else on.' Turning to Rye she sweetly sighed. 'So that means, as much as I would like to ask you to bide for a wee cup of tea, I can't.'

'No offence taken, Anna, especially as neither o' us has any tea, never mind there no being enough room on your fire to boil the kettle.' Rye inhaled long and deep before noisily exhaling. 'And they say the men at the front are suffering. I mean, what about us women who try to keep the home fires burning with nae coal and having to feed awbody out o' nothing?'

Quickly Anna retaliated in a heated voice, 'Aye, but we're no going over the top of they blinking trenches and getting slaughtered in our thousands.' Anna then moderated her tone when she saw the look of embarrassment on Rye's face. 'Look, Rye,' she continued in a conciliatory voice. 'You're a real pal so why don't you go and get your pail and fill it with enough of my coal to give you a wee heat the night.'

'Auntie,' Rachel began wistfully, 'I'm to write the Christmas pantomime. So listen. Does this sound right?'

'What pantomime is it?'

'Dick Whittington.' Rachel inhaled deeply before going into the drama, 'Two months gone and no sign of Dick.' She now stretched out her arms but before she could dramatise further Bella walked in unsteadily.

'No feeling any better?' asked Anna, squinting at Bella. 'That potion I made you should have worked by now. Maybe I'm wrong and you can pick up that malaria thing from someone and no need to be bitten by a fly. Never mind, we've got rabbit stew for tea. Now that's sure to put a lining on your belly.'

Bella belched before sitting down at the table. 'Auntie,' she began in a tearful whisper, 'the lassies at work are being horrible to me.'

'In what way?' asked Anna, as she pulled out a chair and sat down.

'They say that my puking every morning means I'm like what Rachel just said…'

'Remind me what she said,' demanded Anna, impatience ringing in her voice.

'Just that somebody was two months gone and there was no sign of somebody else.'

An uneasy silence broken only by the ticking of the pendulum clock and the bubbling of the stew pot enfolded the room. Bella and Anna didn't see each other even though they were staring right into each other's eyes. Meanwhile, Rachel was surreptitiously making for a quick getaway.

Rising, Anna walked over to the outside door and without a word turned the key in the lock and then placed it securely in her pocket. She then turned and smiled directly at Rachel who accepted her aunt had securely barred her escape route.

Resuming her seat, she indicated that Rachel should also take a seat. 'Now,' she began, eyeing both girls whilst she thumped the table, 'who has something to tell me?'

Both girls looked down before Rachel finally said, 'I know you said that when you went to your Salvation Army meetings both Bella and I were to stay in together. And never were we to be in the house alone with Gus and we never were. Well, not ever alone with him.'

'So how's Bella in the mess she's in?' bellowed Anna. 'Not to mention the disgrace that's been brought down on *my* head!'

'It was,' continued Rachel quickly, 'because of the man who came to the door and said that he was on the run and starving. He asked us to give him some food and a few coppers. And, Auntie, whenever he said coppers I told him to wait and then banged the door shut, didn't I, Bella?' Bella nodded.

'And I then spoke to Bella and we decided that she would stay at home and give the man a jelly piece and I would run and get the copper – your friend Jack McIntyre.'

'Is this another of your prize-winning essays, Rachel?' asked Anna, emphasising every word.

'No.'

'So what happened then?'

'Well, Jack wasn't on duty and I couldn't find another cop but I did bump into my pals Rosa and Jenny.' By now Rachel was quite breathless but she blundered on. 'And they were on their way to the Band of Hope meeting. And since I'd not been able to go for weeks because I was watching Gus and I knew that the man on the run was in the house so nothing could happen that you didn't want to happen, Auntie, I went with them.'

Anna now turned her attention to Bella. 'And what happened then?' she asked, sharply.

'The man finished his piece and as I had no money to give him he wouldn't stay. I did ask him to – but he wouldn't.'

'And?'

'Nothing, Auntie, except Gus was shivering and he asked me *politely* to warm him up.' Bella swallowed hard. 'And because there was hardly any coal for the fire ... well.' Her voice tailed off.

'And that was the start of it?' fumed Anna.

Bella nodded. 'Whenever he was cold, and that was nearly every day after that, I had to cuddle him in.'

'Let me get this straight. You're saying that under my roof you had the audacity to fornicate?'

'No. I never forni ... whatever it is,' protested Bella. 'We were just kind to each other. And it wasn't like what you have always told us that forbidden thing would be – horrible, painful and we wouldn't like.' Bella hesitated. Anna panted whilst she ran her hands through her hair. 'Well,' continued Bella, 'the first time it was a bit sore but after that it was nice. Really nice and I liked it.'

Anna, now beside herself with worry, could only ask herself, *Why is this lassie so naïve? Doesn't she realise that men only want one thing and that it's a woman's Christian duty to deny him any, or no, satisfaction – or at least that is what my granny up north told me.* Sighing, she continued to ask herself what she could do. Wringing her hands she eventually spoke out vehemently to the wall, 'This is all the fault of my brother Andy, and he's at sea so I'm left to sort it out.'

'He's not at sea,' chirped Rachel. 'I met Johnny at school today and he said that his dad had come home unexpectedly last night. His ship was damaged in a battle – or maybe it was a storm?' Rachel paused briefly before adding, 'But it really doesn't matter because he's all right.'

At that Anna leapt up from the table, unlocked the door and fled off in the direction of Admiralty Street.

The cold of that December day ate into Anna's feet but being in such a hurry she'd quite forgotten to put her shoes on and all too soon her stockings were sopping wet.

Taking the worn wooden stairs two at a time, Anna was soon at Andy's door, which she flung open with such force that it noisily bounced back towards her. As she entered the house she caught a full picture of herself in the mirror of the wardrobe that faced the door. Had she not been in such a hurry to confront her brother, she would have been horrified at the image she presented – a madwoman, hair standing on end and giving every appearance of being wholly out of control.

'What the devil's wrong with you?' enquired Andy, staring in bewilderment at his distraught sister.

Racing across the room she slapped him hard across the face, but before she could inflict another blow he managed to grab her by the arms and restrain her. 'Now,' he demanded, still holding her firm, 'have you lost your mind?'

Sinking against Andy's chest Anna started to sob. 'You – you – you brought that child molester into my home and now...'

'Are you really saying,' sceptical Andy asked, 'that Gus abused your hospitality and assaulted your Rachel?'

'No. But he has taken advantage of my glaikit Bella and now she's nearly three months gone and where is *he?*'

'On his way to India on board a tramp steamer,' Andy muttered, letting go of Anna. 'Oh bloody hell. What's our Willie going to say? Here's me and you supposed to be looking after Bella for him and now we've let her...'

'Don't you dare say *I* let her get... And the worry is, yes I can keep her indoors and out of sight until she's better but then when the bairn's born I, a *virgin spinster,* can hardly claim it's mine.'

'Right enough. In a case like this,' agreed Rosie, 'that's what usually happens – saves the family from disgrace. Och aye, the granny says she's the mother and she brings the bairn up and all's well.'

'And,' said Andy, looking fixedly at Anna, 'we cannae says it's Rosie's and mine because I've been at sea for ten weeks.'

'Aye. Well, if we cannae come up with an answer, we'll sure all be at sea,' muttered Anna sardonically.

'Could she no get a back-street abortion?'

Andy suggested.

'What?' Anna exclaimed.

'You know,' Andy continued blatantly. 'Send her down to Button-hook Nell.'

'Oh no,' screamed Rosie. 'That's a sin. You'd never be forgiven. And that Nell will roast in hell's fire for eternity for what she does.'

'I don't care if I'd be forgiven or not ... but my Bella's just a bairn and she's not going to be forced to have an abortion. Could kill her, that could.' Anna sniffled as the tears spilled over. 'And bad as things are, I still want my stupid Bella – disgraced or not.'

Time slowly ticked by until Andy laid his hand on his sister's shoulder. 'Greet no mair, lass. There's a ship leaving Leith to-morrow for India. I'll try to get a start on her and with a bit of luck I'll meet up with Gus in Calcutta and see ... well... just see what can be worked out.'

After Anna had left, Andy asked Rosie if Father Kelly could be trusted. 'Of course,' she replied indignantly. 'He's a good man – an ordained priest of the only true faith.' Andy was so engrossed in his own concerns he ignored Rosie's remarks about the only true faith so she continued, 'But why would you, a staunch Protestant, want to see him?'

'Rosie, I know something about Gus that's so serious that I could make him marry Bella by threatening to expose what he's

115

guilty of.'

'But wouldn't that be dangerous, Andy? Please, don't be a hero. We need you. Look here at wee Davy. Does he not come first?'

Andy went over to the dresser and took out writing paper, pen and ink. Then he sat down.

'You see, Rosie,' he said as he wrote, 'when I catch up with Gus – and believe me I will – I'll leave him in no doubt that Father Kelly has a letter written by me outlining his crimes and that if anything happens to me the good Father will give you the letter and you'll take it immediately to the police. So, my dear Rosie, it will be in Gus's best interests to marry our Bella in order to keep my mouth shut!'

10

GUS

Anna, being a slave to cleanliness and addicted to fresh air, had flung the kitchen window open wide and the glow of the May sun shone into the room.

'Auntie,' a cowed Bella asked, 'why can't I sit up on the sink bunker and just look out into the street? It's been years since you've allowed me to go out.'

'Bella, since I found out about your,' Anna coughed to signal disapproval before continuing, 'condition I had you leave Crawford's to save you getting a red face. Then I begged Sandy to give you a job at night looking after the dead.'

'Yeah, and why did you do that?'

'Because the dead wouldn't be able to notice that you were piling on the beef in areas that you should not be piling it on!' Bella looked nonplussed. Anna sighed. 'And therefore, being dead, they couldn't inform the world at large what you and that,' Anna stopped again, this time to allow a long remonstrating pause, 'seducing, Mr – blooming – Cochrane had been up to!'

'But did you not say that Uncle Andy might catch up with him in India, because he's working on a tramp steamer there, and send him home to marry me?' Anna just looked at the wall. 'And I would like being married now. And I could be. Lots of lassies get married when they turn sixteen.'

'That right?'

Bella nodded, 'And they also get to keep themselves and not have to hand over their pay-packets unopened to their...'

'Look, Bella, while you're under my roof you'll not be keeping yourself. And might I remind you that since you started to look like a stranded whale and I could no longer safely let you out you haven't earned a penny.'

Before Bella could retaliate Rye flung the door open. 'Anna, it's a disaster.' Rye stopped abruptly as she stared at Bella.

'It's not a disaster – it's curable,' Anna quickly responded. 'Didn't my poor Bella no go and get a wee, very wee doze of that ... that ... elephantiasis ... when she was in Glasgow last month.'

Rye went over and grabbed Anna's hand. 'Not Bella's disaster – the troop train!'

'What are you talking about?'

'Just that, och ... you mind how we waved them off at the Central Station on Leith Walk. Proud they were to have volunteered to serve King and Country.'

'Aye, but what's the panic? They were only going to take part in training exercises at Larbert, so they must have got there by now.'

'Their orders were changed and they were being sent out to reinforce the troops at Gallipoli. Oh God, I wish my James hadn't listened to his boss and joined up.'

'But, Rye, you're no making sense. What's happened?'

'The train they were travelling on to Liverpool – it crashed at Gretna!'

'What?' exclaimed Anna, who felt her spine chill as terror gripped her.

'Aye, hit a stationary train and then ... oh

... they say they hadn't got over the shock of what had happened when the London to Glasgow Express, going like a bat oot o' hell, ploughed into the scattered carriages. Burst into flames, they did. Oh Anna, they say us relatives have to go up to the Royal Scots Drill Hall in Dalmeny Street where they left from,' Rye was now sobbing loudly, 'and wait for more news. But Anna, my bairns are too wee to go with me so I've naebody to support me – unless you chum me?'

Anna, who was thinking of all of Leith's young men who might have lost their lives, nodded sombrely. Instantly she lifted her coat off the door hook but remembered to mumble to Bella, 'And you, my lady, get back into the bedroom and don't move out of it for one minute until I get back.'

Hundreds of people had gathered at the drill hall in Dalmeny Street. Everyone in Leith knew someone who was in the Royal Scots 7th Battalion Volunteer Brigade so it was only natural that so many would congregate there.

Rye was relieved when she was taken aside by an officer and advised that she would probably be taken by train to the hospital in Carlisle where the injured were being treated.

Unfortunately, three hours later when the

list of the dead was posted on the outside notice board, James Pratt was among the names. He would be returned to Leith in one of the one hundred and twenty coffins that arrived back at the drill hall in Dalmeny Street over the following days.

It was difficult for Anna to persuade Rye to leave Dalmeny Street where an uneasy echoing silence had engulfed the crowds. Holding onto her as they travelled down Leith Walk, Rye insisted they stop at the Central Station and then again at the Foot of the Walk where they joined the traumatised groups that huddled together for comfort.

Three and four days later, 25 and 26 May, these same people stood silently to attention as the full military funerals for the men's coffins that had been returned to Dalmeny Street made their way up Leith Walk and then down Pilrig before arriving at Rosebank Cemetery for a mass burial.

Standing beside Rye, who was surrounded by four of her eight children, Anna's tears brimmed over as she witnessed the devastating grief of the whole community of Leith. Men, women and children were all weeping sorely and Anna realised it would take a long, long time for the wounds of this cruel accident to heal, conceding in Rye's case that they might never do so.

Returning from the funeral, Anna glanced

up at the windows of the Couper Street tenements and noted that most windows still had their blinds drawn in a mark of respect for the dead. Tears brimmed in her eyes again as she acknowledged that this war where young men in their thousands were being maimed or killed seemed (to her) not to have a real purpose and was therefore senseless – unlike the fight for women's suffrage where she had been at the forefront of the battle.

Slowly climbing the stairs to her home her thoughts had turned to Rye and how she would cope in the coming years. *Surely,* she thought, *the government will provide her with a pension or some means of financial support so that she can provide for her bairns. That would be the very least a grateful country could do.*

Opening the door, Anna sensed a presence in the room but because her curtains were still drawn she wasn't quite sure. Advancing to the window she drew back the curtains to let the daylight flood into the room. On turning round she gasped, for looming in front of her stood the figure of Gus Cochrane!

'How the devil did you get here?' she demanded.

'Well, thanks to your – let's say persuasive – brother who unfortunately caught up with me in India, I was left with no other option than to jump the tramp ship and join the first steamer coming back here.'

Anna knew she should have asked him what he meant about her brother being 'persuasive' because it could not have been in a physical sense. After all, Andy was only five foot seven and of a slim build, whereas Gus was very tall and muscular.

Removing her coat Anna found it difficult to keep her contempt for Gus in check. She was a woman who abhorred physical violence and had to be sorely tried before she would so demean herself as to lash out. However as she looked at Gus Cochrane's sullen face she not only wanted to attack him verbally for the dishonour (as she saw it) he'd brought to her door but she also had a mounting desire to clench her fists and soundly punch his handsome face.

Deciding to put into practice her own advice to control both pain and anger she took four deep breaths and focused her eyes towards a spot on the wall before finally asking, 'And have you spoken to Bella?'

'No. I only just beat you getting up the stairs and there was nobody at home. So I took it Bella was at work.'

'At work! Haven't you the savvy to work out she'll be due in the next four weeks,' exclaimed Anna, who snorted angrily before going on, 'and I've got to keep her hidden in case anybody discovers that you're ... no better than ... a philandering child rapist!'

Gus lifted his hands defensively and held them out. 'Look, I admit I was ill and got quite carried away the first time, but after that she was keener than me!'

Anna, who had no wish to hear what she already suspected – that Bella could be easily 'persuaded' to be a bit shameless at times – brushed brusquely past Gus. On opening the bedroom door she sharply called out, 'Bella! Come here!'

Emerging from the bedroom Bella gently stroked her swollen breasts. 'Auntie,' she emphasised, 'I did hear someone come into the house but I did as you said. Honestly, I've stayed in the room since you went away.'

It was then that Bella saw Gus. Without warning, her knees buckled and weeping bitterly she dropped to the floor.

Gus, bristling with malevolence due to his resentment at being pushed into a shotgun wedding – especially to Bella, who he considered inferior to him – surprised Anna when, without saying a word, he bent down and lifted Bella's pitiful form up and into his arms.

Immediately Bella raised her eyes towards Gus and as the tears ran down her wan face you could see a different kind of rage growing within him. *Why,* he thought, *had such a helpless creature, whose only crime was to want love and affection, been imprisoned within this dreary hovel? Denied daylight by a woman, a professed practising Christian, who insisted she just wanted the very best for Bella? Did she really believe that what she'd inflicted on poor Bella was in any way charitable?* Awash with pity Gus stroked Bella's thick black hair before whispering, 'Never mind,' but he had to hesitate, swallow a large gulp, before grudgingly adding, *'my dear,* I'm here now.'

Bella wiped her nose with the back of her hand before spluttering, 'Do you mean you've come home to marry me? Make an honest, respectable woman of me?'

Anna knew Gus was tempted to say 'Not really' because she could read in his demeanour that being tied to Bella would only be done under duress so all he could do was nod.

Before anything further was said the door opened and Rosie, carrying Davy in her arms and with Johnny and Ella in tow, came in and sat down on the fender stool. 'Aye, it's a sad, sad business,' lamented Rosie. 'Breaks your heart, so it does.' She then squinted at Gus. 'Here. How did *you* get home on leave and my Andy hasn't?'

'Jumped ship, he did,' crooned Bella, who couldn't hide the delight she was now experiencing. 'And just,' she sighed, 'so he could ask me to marry him.'

Rosie looked at Bella's bulging form and then at Anna. 'And by the look o' things my Andy has just got him back in time.'

124

'Aye, you're right, Rosie,' confirmed Anna, before looking directly at Gus and Bella. 'And quite enough time's been wasted so you pair get away to the registry office, right now.' Gus, however, seemed reluctant, or was it maybe that he didn't know where the registry office was, so she quickly asked, 'You do know where it is – in Fire Brigade Street.'

'He's no from Leith,' Rosie, quickly pointed out, 'so he'll no ken Fire Brigade Street is just what Leith people caw Junction Place 'cause the fire brigade work out o' there.'

A contemptuous look from Anna withered Rosie before she added, 'And see about getting a special licence.'

'Oh, Auntie,' wailed Bella. 'Are you saying you want me to go out in broad daylight?'

'Aye, they close at three o'clock which means they're only open in the daylight – so you'd better get a move on.'

'B–but, b–but what will people think ... when they see this?' Bella now gave her stomach a slow massage with both hands.

Rosie and Anna looked at each other and Ella gave a sly snigger, as they silently agreed it was far too late to bother about what people thought and that the matter had to be sorted without delay.

By the time Gus and Bella returned from the registry office, Rosie and her bairns had gone home. Anna had been pleased, though not to see Rosie go. Ella, her niece, on the other hand ... well, she was always glad to see the back of her. She had tried not to have reservations about Ella, but she was a spoiled, envious child who always had been her mother's favourite. Anna, on the other hand, had always favoured Johnny and, as for Davy the latecomer, who could help but love him – poor wee mite?

'We can get married in a week's time,' Bella blurted out as soon as she came in the door.

'In the registry office?' asked Anna, trying to keep the disapproval she felt for that kind of wedding from her voice.

'Naw. We've also been up to see the minister in St Thomas Parish Church and he says that since I'm one of his flock he'll marry us in his manse.'

Anna felt her shoulders sink with relief until she looked at Gus's set face. Gone was the compassion he had shown for Bella – to be replaced by a thunderous expression.

Bella however seemed not to notice. 'All this excitement has been too much for me so I'm going to have a lie down,' she said, smiling coyly at Gus so that Anna knew she was hoping he would join her – but he didn't!

'So, you're going to stand by her?' Anna asked as soon as Bella was out of earshot.

Gus looked directly into Anna's eyes before replying, 'And I suppose you want me to believe that you don't know that your brother gave me an ultimatum that leaves me with no other choice?'

Anna was bewildered. 'What are you talking about?' she spluttered.

Bringing his face up to hers, Gus hoarsely whispered, 'Just because your brother always does what you want and since you demand a ring on Bella's finger and thus saving your bloody torn face – I have further to incriminate myself and make a show of marrying your wanton niece – or suffer the unpalatable consequences.'

Swallowing hard, Anna realised for the first time that her brother, her Andy, knew something about Gus and he had *black-mailed* him into coming back. *But what was it? And should, or should not, this marriage go ahead?* she wondered.

'And for why?' Gus went on. 'Just to make sure that your Bella's child won't appear to be the bastard it is! And even if the truth about me does eventually come out sympathy will be with Bella and she won't be shunned.'

Anna was now panting with fear. The only reason she could think of as to why Gus was saying such things was that somewhere on his travels he'd got married, and Andy – and only Andy – knew about it. Reluctantly she thought her poor Bella would unknowingly be tied to a conniving bigamist! But why was it that she, a devout Christian, thought that would be better for Bella than being an outcast when people found out she was the unwed mother of an illegitimate child?

Gus however wasn't really aware of Anna's dilemma and went on, 'Well, Miss Campbell, I might have to go through with this marriage sham but, believe me, the world is a big, big place and people go missing in it!'

Unable to take in what she was hearing, Anna stammered, 'Are you saying you won't be setting up home with Bella?'

'What I'm saying,' cackled Gus, 'is that I could possibly get swallowed up in India, Australia or wherever – I know plenty folk who have! Oh yes, Miss Sanctimonious, the ink won't be dry on the certificate before I'm sailing away into the deep blue yonder.'

'But what will I tell Bella when you go?'

'That, like you, I've been well and truly sunk in more ways than one.'

The day of the wedding, Bella was at fever pitch. She had wanted to be married in white but Anna had to remind her that white was only for virgins and that she, being eight months gone, was hardly that. To soften the blow Anna had stitched Bella up a lovely roomy, very pale, nearly white, lilac taffeta dress. She felt no guilt about this because,

128

she argued with herself, to be truthful Bella was really still a virgin in so many other ways. She had also had to make up a frock for Bella's best maid, Jane Gibson, a long-time pal from schooldays.

Gus, on the other hand, who was meeting them up at the manse, had managed to pay a dollar to persuade a seafaring stranger to act as his best man.

Walking along Couper Street and on to Coburg Street, Anna prayed that Gus would not jilt Bella. The poor soul had begged, from the first day he'd arrived back, to let him share her bed. This request was hastily denied with Anna pointing out that she was in no position now to prevent the happenings of eight months ago. However, no way would she allow fornication she knew about to take place in her house. Bella had protested that there would be no fornication, just a wee kiss and cuddle, as she was too cumbersome for anything else. Anna didn't reply but the look of contempt on her face clearly said, 'No. Most certainly not!' Nonetheless she did manage to mutter, 'Look, as he's a sailor he can bunk in the Sailors' Home on the Shore.'

Anna need not have worried. Whatever it was that Andy had threatened Gus with was still working and he and his best man were already in attendance even though Gus's demeanour was truly hostile.

129

The minister immediately began the wedding service and had just got to the part where he asked Bella if she took Gus as her lawfully wedded husband, to have and to hold ... when it was evident she could hold out no longer. So instead of saying, 'I do,' she let out a gasp as her breaking waters turned her lovely pale lilac dress to purple.

Racing from the back of the room Anna grabbed Bella by the arm and shaking it she commanded, 'Don't you dare give birth right now.'

'But, Auntie,' wailed Bella, 'what else can I do?'

'Cross you legs and say a quick, "I do", and I'll attend to the rest.'

Gus, who couldn't believe his luck in finding a way out of his predicament, smiled triumphantly. 'Look,' he said, 'let her give birth right now and we can marry some other time.'

'Not on your life, boy,' was Anna's sharp retort. 'The only thing that's going to wait for another time is the egg sandwiches.'

Turning to the minister, who she knew, she abruptly said, 'Right, Reverend King, get a move on and cut out the bits you don't really need to make it legal.'

Surprisingly, three hours went by – too quickly for Anna's liking, but on the other hand too slowly for Bella, who was eager to get it all over and done with. Notwithstanding the rush, Anna's house witnessed a newly married woman giving birth to a legitimate son – a sturdy, black-haired boy that Bella called Nathaniel, knowing full well it would be shortened to Nat.

Gus should have been nearby but having been trapped (as he saw it) into a spurious marriage, he had adjourned to the Black Swan pub for a few consoling pints.

When he did eventually decide to show his face with the intention of saying that he had signed up on a merchant ship that was leaving immediately. Bella, who was tucked in bed with her precious bundle, protested, 'Look, Gus. You cannae deny him. He's your spitting image. See how his front hair curls round on his brow, same as yours.'

Looking down at the child Gus could see he actually did resemble himself and Anna was surprised to find that the harsh scowl that had been present since he arrived in the house seemed to thaw. It was now replaced by a gentle expression that Anna thought him incapable of – and she also had to admit reluctantly that it further enhanced his handsome features.

'What did you say about getting a start?' Bella tentatively asked, as she cradled the baby close to her breast.

Gus sucked in his cheeks. 'Just ... och, Bella, I have a start on a ship that leaves tomorrow on the morning tide.'

An uneasy silence only relieved by the ticking of the clock filled the room until Gus continued, 'And now that I've seen my son I know I have to get back to work right away to get money to rent and furnish a house of our own.' Gus lifted his head to look directly at Anna, although he was still speaking to Bella. 'A place of our own where we won't be obliged to any interfering, holier-than-thou, old biddy!'

Anna was at a loss to know whether Gus, on looking at his defenceless son, had changed his mind and he would come back or if he was just using words to console Bella whose face now was awash with tears.

Silence fell again in the room until Bella pleaded, 'But, Auntie, now we're married surely Gus can share my bed tonight. Please!'

11

A YEAR LATER

Lifting the teapot Anna was pleased to inform Rye, who had just come in, that not only was there enough in the pot for her but it was also still warm.

'Oh, Anna, after last night, how can you think that a cup of lukewarm sugarless tea will calm my blasted nerves?'

'Aye, so many guid folk killed. But then it was a bright moonlit night so they two Zeppelins had the poor sods in the docks and round about all lit up for them.'

'And here, Anna,' a breathless Rye went on, 'did you ken they dropped twenty-seven big bombs by hand frae they airships and it's been said they were aw the size o' a sack o' flour?'

'Wish to hang they *had* been bags of flour. There being hardly any food to be got is driving me mad.'

Rye went on as if Anna hadn't replied. 'They say they were aiming for Rosyth and the ships at anchor in the Forth and it was when our ships started to fight back that they turned in on us – seems we were easy targets.'

'Aye, it was just a pity that one of their first hits was the bonded warehouse.' Anna shook her head. 'It going up lit up no only our poor Leith but Edinburgh as well. Oh aye, the louping flames showed them airships their way right up to the castle.' She paused. 'And the bond is still alight. Hope to hang they get it put out before dark descends the day.'

Bella, who was also seated at the table nursing one-year-old Nat, wistfully said,

'And d'you know? One o' the bombs hit old St Thomas's manse where a year ago,' and she paused, 'Gus and me were ... married.'

Anna and Rye both looked at each other and shrugged. 'Well all I can say,' began Anna, ignoring Bella's remarks, 'is that if last night's attack was our first taste of getting bombed I'm going to pray that it's also our last.'

'Or that we're ready for them next time,' countered Rye.

'Right enough, we all had our lights on. And seeing we'd no blackouts they seemed to think we were inviting them to blow us to smithereens.'

Bella, whose thoughts were obviously still harkening back to her wedding day, sighed before saying, 'Wonder if that was what happened to my Gus?'

'So you think the reason you havnae heard from him for a year is because he's a casualty?' asked Rye.

'What other reason could there be?'

Anna sat tight-lipped. She did so want to tell Bella to forget Gus, who was in her opinion a casualty in more ways than one, and get on with her life but the last time she'd said that Bella had sulked for a whole week. So how could she really say to naïve Bella that he'd done a runner? That he had never any intention of coming back to her and wee Nat.

'Here, talking of people coming back, has there been any sign of your brother Andy? I mean he's been gone a lot longer than Gus.'

'He certainly has. But the good news is that there's been no news. No telegram boy rapping on Rosie's door,' was Anna's philosophical reply.

Six months later Anna was vigorously working the treadle of her sewing machine while she pushed through the linen sheet that she was repairing. As the hum of the machine heartened her she thought how lucky she was that Rachel had become so involved with Nat. Every day now she would take the toddler down the stairs and let him explore around the street. So when the door was pushed open, Anna thought it was Rachel returning with Nat, but she was surprised when Jamie Pratt slunk in. 'Miss Campbell,' he cheerily said looking about the room. 'I met your guid sister, Mrs Campbell, and she said that you were to go over to her hoose this afternoon and have yer tea.'

'Are you sure?'

'Aye, because didn't her man came hame last night.'

Anna jumped up and clapped her hands. 'My brother Andy's come home?'

'Seems like it. Oh, and one other thing – ye've to go to Mrs Stoddard on the ground floor and she'll give ye some ham.'

'Some ham? But there's a war on. So where on earth will she find some ham?'

'Her man, the rat catcher, was working in the Danish Bacon Company this week so – need I say mair?'

Jamie had just turned for the door when Anna called after him, 'Would you like a piece, son? I've got some bread and treacle.'

'Treacle? Oh aye, I would really like that,' replied Jamie, licking his lips before seating himself on the fender stool.

As Anna busied herself spreading the two-day-old bread lavishly with the treacle, she took time to study young Jamie. He was a lanky lad and today he looked cold and she wished she'd lit the fire to thaw out his bones but coal was scarce and pricey so fires didn't get lit until nightfall.

'Jamie,' she said eventually, 'haven't you got a jumper with long sleeves? Sure that slipover will never keep your arms warm.'

Jamie just wriggled on his bottom. 'Sure, Miss Campbell, it would be nice to have a jumper but Mammy says we'll have to wait till it's really cauld.' Anna shook her head in disbelief. 'Miss Campbell,' Jamie went on. 'Do you think, like your Rachel says, that the dead come back every night to see you?'

Anna was caught unawares and had to think before replying, 'Well, they might. Were you thinking your dad comes back to see you?'

136

'Aye,' replied Jamie, thoughtfully. 'You see, Miss Campbell, I miss him – terribly.'

'I'm sure you do, laddie. And know something? I bet he does look in on you all at night just to make sure you're all right. And, believe me, he knows all that's going on with you.'

Licking the treacle that had run onto his fingers, Jamie seemed a bit hesitant before asking, 'All that's going on?'

Something in his tone made Anna wary of saying, 'yes' so all she answered was, 'Most certainly the important things.'

This was not what Jamie wanted to hear and he immediately blurted out, 'Like Nicol's coal man saying he could give Mammy something of the price of a bag o' best coal if she was willing to give him a wee heat?'

Not bothering to hide her contempt, Anna screamed, 'That brazened brute said what?'

'Just what I said. And Mammy giggled. I was worried in case it meant Mammy would get married again.'

'She may well do some day but not to Iain Crosby – he has a wife.'

'I wouldn't like that,' Jamie absently replied. 'Look at you, my mammy says that yon policeman, Jack McIntyre, is crackers about you and brings you all sorts of things – like that deer meat last week and half a dozen huddies he got from the Newhaven trawler-men the week afore.'

Anna shook her head. She didn't want simple Jamie to see that she was annoyed – actually angry – that people speculated about her and Jack so she decided to tell him the truth. 'Jamie,' she began 'can you keep a secret?'

'Aye.'

'Well you see, it's really difficult to explain about Jack and me,' her voice drifted off a bit before she picked up from where she'd left off, 'but you see the real reason Jack and I never get near to being married is – he has a mother!'

'So has everybody,' Jamie replied, with incredulity ringing in his voice.

'Yes, they do. But on their fortieth birthday they hardly send for them to come to live with them, do they?' retorted Anna through clenched teeth.

Jamie knew he'd upset Anna, so hanging his head, he got up and made for the door. 'Sorry, Miss Campbell. And see, if I was Jack McIntyre, I would rather stay with you than with my mammy! Honest, I would. And oh, dinnae forget the ham.'

Two hours passed before Anna could get everything done and over to Admiralty Street. She had sent Rachel and Nat on ahead, leaving a note for Bella to say that when she got in from work to come over to

Rosie's house.

She was now at the bottom of her stair and about to go into Mona Stoddard's house when the door was flung open and Mona dashed into the passageway screaming, 'Bloody thieving pigs. Thieving pigs!'

'Calm yourself, Mona,' advised Anna. 'What's the matter?'

'I'll tell you what's the matter,' she screeched. 'My poor honest Eck risked getting nicked for stealing a whole leg of ham when he was working yesterday.' Anna looked perplexed. 'Do you ken how hard it was for him to hide a ham that size in his breeks?' Anna shook her head. 'No. Then I'll explain. Him being a rat-catcher, he has to wear wide trousers but they have to be tied securely – very tight at the bottom in case a rat runs up his leg.' Mona could see Anna was still finding it difficult to follow her story so she digressed. 'You see if a rat did run up his leg it would bite – well he wouldn't have a man's voice any more, would he?'

Anna nodded and was about to speak when Mona went on, 'But that's bye the bye. Yesterday he got the chance to snaffle a whole ham and he then, guid soul that he is, had to limp all the way hame with it hidden in his right trouser leg.' Mona's eyes widened before she went on. 'See! When I saw the size of it I decided to cook it and divide it up amongst us aw – like we always dae when manna from heaven drops doon on us.'

'So what's the problem?'

'Well, didn't I cook it beautifully and when it was ready I opened the window and put it on the sill to cool so I could cut it up.' Mona started to cry before adding, 'And some bugger passing by stole it! Didnae even leave enough for a sandwich for Eck!'

Scratching her head Anna said, 'Look, how about I ask Jack McIntyre to investigate the theft for you?'

Suddenly Mona stopped crying and in a voice ringing with incredulity she hissed, 'Are you bloody mad, Anna? You just cannae report the loss of a leg of ham, that my Eck stole in the first place, to that Jack McIntyre. Don't you realise he's a Leith Docks' polisman?'

'So?'

'That means it's mair than likely it was him who nicked it! And the thieving blighter didn't even say thank you for cooking it.'

While wearily trudging over to Rosie's house Anna wondered what Rosie would give them to eat now that the ham had been purloined. Mounting the stairs she was pleased to smell the aroma of frying onions, which grew stronger the nearer she came to Rosie's house.

She had just opened the door when Andy

rose to greet her. 'My, but you're a sight for sore eyes. Been gone too long, so I have.' He then squinted at Anna. 'The bairns have all thrived. I just couldn't believe how my wee Davy has grown and Nat walking – but you and Rosie are just skin and bone.'

Rosie chortled, 'That's because there's never enough food for us all, so Anna and I go without most nights.' Exposing her remaining three front teeth she grinned broadly before announcing, 'But tonight, thanks to wee Eck Stoddard, nobody's dead and yet we're going to have a boiled ham tea!'

'Rosie.' Anna grimaced. 'The ham was stolen.'

'I know that but this war has made thieves of us all, so I'll enjoy the ham and confess everything on Friday.' Rosie laughed and patted Andy on the back. 'And I'll have you know Father Kelly is a very forgiving man.'

'You don't understand. The ham was stolen from Mona. The poor soul put it on the window sill to cool and...'

Without asking anything further, Rosie looked down at the frying pan where three slices of liver shared the space with some onions. 'I wonder how the guid Lord managed to feed the multitude with five loaves and three fishes? Because I dinnae think I can feed anyone but my Andy with this,' she said, giving the pan a hearty shoogle.

Two hours later Andy had devoured the liver and onions while the rest of the family, thanks to Andy having come home with a good pay-off, had been fed with a carryout from Angelo's chip shop.

Wanting to speak with Andy on his own, Anna had dispatched Bella, Rachel and Nat off home. She could hardly hide her impatience when Rosie decided to wash up the tea things before bedding Davy down.

Once the bairn was in bed and Johnny and Ella had left because Andy had given them some pocket money to spend, Rosie lifted her shawl from the hook behind the door.

'Don't tell me,' exclaimed Andy, 'that I've been gone for nearly two years and you're going to chapel?'

'Oh, Andy, you know how I like to go to church every night and speak to Jesus. And tonight I have a lot to thank Him for.'

'Like some scallywag stealing Eck Stoddart's ham?'

'No. Like bringing you home safe. Do you know how many laddies we both ken that will never come home? Besides, Anna and you have things to discuss.'

The door had just closed on Rosie when Anna pointed to a seat at the table for Andy to take. Sitting opposite him, she felt the rising panic that thinking of Gus always gave her. She thought she knew the truth but she really needed it confirmed. 'Andy,' she began in a faltering voice. 'On your travels did you come across that Gus Cochrane?'

Andy shook his head before replying, 'Never clapped eyes on him – well not since India.'

'It's about that we need to talk. I'm grateful you sent him back to marry Bella, but – oh, Andy – how do you think she'll cope if it ever comes out that her wee Nat is a – well he will be labelled "bastard" when folk find out that that dirty swine Gus bigamously married our Bella?'

Andy huffed and snorted. 'And who says he's a bigamist? What proof have they?'

'But I thought that was what you blackmailed him with?'

Taking out his pipe, Andy filled it with Irish Roll tobacco and as he struck a match, he looked hard at Anna before saying, 'Bigamy? Huh, if only that was it all. Naw, naw, Anna, you've got it all wrong – he's no bigamist.'

Anna was silent as Andy lit his pipe and began to puff it leisurely. Her mind was in turmoil as she argued with herself. *If he's not a bigamist, then what hold is it that Andy has over him?* When she could bear the agony no more she leaned forward and took Andy's hand in hers, 'Brother, what did he do that was so heinous that you were able to frighten him into marrying Bella?' she pleaded.

Puffing away at his pipe and blowing a wreath of smoke into the air, Andy withdrew his hand from hers and spat into the fire. 'All I can tell you is that what he did will never reflect on Bella.'

'But why can't you tell me?'

'Because part of the bargain was that would I tell no one – especially you.'

'And do you think he'll come back and honour his responsibilities?'

Andy shrugged, spat in the fire again so that it sizzled before he replied, 'Only God knows.'

12

TURNING POINT

All over Europe the people were weary with the war and in Scotland almost every family had known the heartbreak of losing a loved one or having him injured.

Even the warmth of the strong May sunshine was unable to thaw Bella's mood. 'You look as if you've lost a sixpence and found a penny,' mocked Anna.

'Wish it was just that,' Bella sulkily replied. 'But, Auntie, my Nat will be three next week and he's never yet seen his dad.'

'Aye. But on the bright side, you've never been told he's been killed.'

'Auntie, don't you realise that I know he's not coming back and as I've now turned nineteen I'm too old to get another man?'

'What? Look at Rye next door. She's knocking forty-two and still gets offers.'

'That's because she's got eight bairns to take with her.'

'Look, Bella, eight bairns are a fair drawback. Rye gets offers because she's always smiling. You should try it.'

'I do smile when I'm at work. But as they're all dead, they don't appreciate it.'

Anna impatiently drummed her fingers on the table before emphasising, 'And I don't think you appreciate how lucky you are having Rachel helping you to rear Nat. Second mother to him, she is.'

Bella huffed but she knew there was no use in arguing with Anna. Her only retaliation was, 'And where is Rachel? She knows I'm working tonight and she's not home from school yet.'

Squinting up at the clock, Anna said, 'Aye, where is she? She's never this late. I'll go and look for her.'

Emerging from the dingy bottom passageway of 18 Couper Street, Anna was surprised to be confronted by her sister-in-law Rosie. Anna looked down and was not surprised that Rosie, as usual, was accompanied by four-year-old Davy, who smiled warmly at his aunt.

'Oh, Anna,' exclaimed Rosie, letting go of Davy's hand. 'See. When Johnny telt me that you'd lost Rachel, I just couldnae believe it. Just couldnae.'

'Och, Rosie. She's just late getting back from school. Sure she'll be away skiving with that Rosa Liston or Jenny Steele.'

'Anna, don't you know Gabby was waiting for Rachel at the school gates and she went off with him!'

'But why? Is there something amiss with Freddie or Robert?'

Rosie shook her head. 'Anna, he's been to the court and got Rachel away from school so she can keep house for him now the two laddies have been released from the Industrial School.'

'The boys have been released?'

'But you must have kent that now they've turned fifteen and sixteen, they couldn't stay there any longer.'

'I did know that. But I visited them last week and nobody said a word about them leaving. But just a minute ... what's them coming home to do with Rachel?'

'Gabby told the court he's her father and he wants her to keep hoose for him and the boys and the silly beggars – said okay to that.'

'But they can't!' You could almost see

146

Anna's mind ticking over before she eventually said, 'Look, Bella's got to get to work, so Rosie, could you look after Nat until I get back?'

'From where?'

'Coatfield Lane. The court might think they can decide but Rachel's mine. Who is it that has provided for her these last seven years?'

'There's no disputing you did that. But as you know, Anna, as far as the courts are concerned, women are second-class. Remember what they did to Freddie and Robert. They believed lying Gabby, they did. So what chance have you got of getting justice?' Rosie pointed out as Anna began to race away.

Anna was out of breath when she reached Coatfield Lane. Quickly she made her way to Gabby's door. Then without knocking she flung the door open. 'Rachel,' she called out, 'Are you in there?'

'Of course I am, Auntie,' Rachel replied lightly.

'Then get your coat. You're coming home with me where you belong.'

'But Auntie, I belong here. Don't I, Robert?'

Robert, who was seated on a rickety kitchen chair, nodded.

'No Rachel, you belong with me,' Anna

shouted. 'And where is your ne're-do-weel father?'

'He's at the Steamboat Tavern. But Auntie, do try and understand. My brothers want me to be with them. They really do want me. I've left school now and we're going to become a family.'

'You'll be just a skivvy,' scorned Anna. Rachel just hunched her shoulders while Anna continued, 'And you're actually going to keep home for the man who was responsible for bringing your mother down to his gutter level? And what will you do when he sends you to get some whore to come and iron his shirt?'

'He's changed,' Rachel protested. 'He even went to the court and got an order that says I'm to bide with him and my brothers now.' She paused. 'Auntie, can you not be happy for me? I'm part of my real family now. A family that really wants me.'

Anna felt her legs tremble as she realised she'd lost Rachel. Before turning to go, she said quietly, 'Remember, I'll always be here for you. Promise you'll run to me if anything goes wrong?'

Rachel nodded. 'Auntie, every day I'll come and see you, Bella and Nat.'

May soon gave way to June. At first Rachel did come often to see Anna, though not on a daily basis. Four weeks later, three days had passed and she hadn't visited. However, on the afternoon of the June solstice the door opened and Anna called out, 'Come away in, Rachel.'

'I'll gladly come in,' a male voice answered. 'But I'm no Rachel.'

Anna squinted at the tall stranger who advanced into the house, wondering who he was. It was a shock to realise that he was the overdue Gus. 'Are you real or a ghost?'

Slipping his kit bag off his shoulder he replied, 'I'm real. And where's my son?'

'Over the road at Rosie's. Ella's always home sharp now that she has a job in Leith Hospital – which means she looks after Nat to let me get on.'

'Where's his mother?'

'I suppose you mean Bella, your pining wife. Well, as you've been missing, presumed dead...'

'Which you hoped and prayed I was.'

'She's had to work for Sandy at the funeral parlour to keep Nat.'

'Going up in the world, so we have. A funeral parlour and no longer just slinging the happy dead on the back of the coal cart.'

Ignoring Gus's sarcasm, Anna continued, 'If you're desperate to see Nat we could go over to Rosie's.'

'I'd like that, provided your obnoxious brother's not at home.'

Choking back her anger Anna hissed, 'But

a better man by far than you'll ever be.'

When Anna and Gus, who was now carrying Nat on his shoulders, returned to 18 Couper Street, Bella was already home.

'Honestly,' Bella called out as the door opened, 'here am I out working aw day and I came in and the house was like the Mary Celeste.'

'Well if you were expecting your tea on the table then I have to tell you we've all had a bad day,' retorted Anna.

Bella now looked beyond Anna and let out a scream that hadn't died before she raced over and flung herself at Gus. 'Careful,' he said, taking Nat down off his shoulders.

'Oh, Gus, they aw said you'd left me in the lurch but I knew some day you'd come back. Where have you been?'

'All over the world. You see I re-joined the tramp steamer and we just took whatever jobs we could get but none of them ever touched a British port. And see three days ago when we docked in Belfast, I said, "No more. I'm away to see my boy."'

'And me,' Bella reminded.

'Aye, aye of course,' replied Gus, sitting down and lifting Nat onto his knee.

Bella's attention now turned to Anna and she asked in a defiant tone, 'Isn't it just as well Rachel's now with her dad because Gus will be sleeping with Nat and me.'

Anna did not respond.

Rachel was really enjoying keeping house at Coatfield Lane but then having been taught by Anna, she was good at it.

Payday was the day that was really great. After they'd had their tea Robert and Rachel would go over to the Gaiety Theatre in the Kirkgate. It didn't matter what the show was – Rachel just enjoyed being entertained.

On the fateful Saturday that no one in the family would ever forget, Rachel, Freddie and Robert were seated around the table enjoying their treat of fish and chips. Robert had been regaling Rachel on what a great show they were going to see at the Gaiety.

'Honestly,' he said. 'Drew at work says that the Great Armundo actually swallows fire and his assistant stands upright with a big board behind her whilst Armundo, blindfolded, throws knives at her.'

Rachel's mouth gaped. 'You mean he actually throws real knives and he never hits her?'

Before Robert could answer, the door flew open and in staggered an inebriated Gabby.

'What's going on in here?' Gabby roared, tossing himself heavily down to where his armchair should have been. Regretfully Rachel had scoured the house and trying to make it more homely she'd reallocated his chair two feet to the left. Trying to get himself up from the floor, Gabby grabbed the tablecloth, which resulted in the contents of the table crashing down on him.

Freddie, Robert and Rachel could do nothing else but laugh when they took in the spectacle made by their father, who now was wearing a half-eaten fish supper on his head.

Gabby however did not find the situation at all funny and began to curse and swear while rolling over the floor towards a chair, which he used to assist himself to get upright. Once he was on his feet he undid the broad leather belt that held his trousers in place and began a frenzied attack on his helpless children.

Freddie managed to duck and dive out of his reach but Robert, trying to protect Rachel, took the full force of the flaying belt across his face. Looking at the blood gushing from her brother's face Rachel screamed, 'Why did you do that, you sadistic swine? It's you who's the hopeless drunkard – not Robert.'

Gabby's attention now turned to Rachel. 'Talk back to me, you guttersnipe that you are?' He now lunged at her but she easily evaded him. 'And another thing,' he shrieked, 'what do you mean by telling Jenny Greenhill that she won't be needed to iron any more shirts for me?'

'Because she won't,' Rachel retaliated defiantly as she dodged around him again. 'I do all the work in here and that includes ironing the rags you call shirts and I don't get a farthing from you, never mind two bob a time.'

'That right,' lisped Gabby. 'Well, now you've got folk thinking I get you to iron my shirts, maybe I should just do that.'

Still swinging the belt in Rachel's direction, Gabby made a grab at her but both Freddie and Robert managed to pull her free. Nonetheless, Freddie could see that Robert was hampered by the blood streaming from his forehead and running into his eyes.

'Robert,' he hissed, 'you're nae use in this fight now. We need reinforcements. So run and get Auntie Anna. She'll settle his hash.' As Robert fled, Gabby lifted a chair and sent it hurling after him.

Having despatched his brother, Freddie took the opportunity to jump on Gabby's back and curl his hands around his father's throat. Letting go the belt Gabby reached up and tore at Freddie's grip. Recognising the chance that this gave her, Rachel dived for the belt and hastily flung it into the fire. By now Gabby had managed to free himself from Freddie's grasp and realising the belt was no longer available, his eyes darted about the room until he saw the sweeping brush. Once he had the brush in his control he began to beat Freddie mercilessly with it. Being athletic and agile, however, Freddie was able to grab one end of the brush handle. Gabby and Freddie then began to dance around the room until they reached the open door where Gabby seized the chance to lunge at Freddie who then toppled over the doorstep and into the passageway.

Unfortunately before Freddie could regain his balance and resume his attack on Gabby, the door had banged shut and Freddie panicked when he heard the lock being securely turned. Thumping furiously on the door and screaming to be let back in, Freddie conceded he could only blame himself for letting Gabby get the better of him.

Gabby now turned his attention to Rachel who, realising that she no longer had her brothers to protect her, was cowering behind the easy chair. Leaning over Gabby seized Rachel's hair and dragged her screaming from her refuge.

When Robert arrived at 18 Couper Street, he bounded up the stairs two at a time. On entering Anna's house he was breathless but managed to splutter, 'Auntie, you've got to get over to Coatfield Lane. Gabby's gone mad – he's gonnae kill Rachel and Freddie. Murder them.'

Unshod as usual, Anna immediately raced from the house. 'Dear God,' she prayed as her thick stocking-clad feet sped over the cobbles. 'Be with my Rachel. Please, please, God, save my Rachel!'

A crowd of voyeurs had gathered at the foot of the stair in Coatfield Lane. Without uttering a word, Anna pushed past them and ignored the old crone who shouted, 'Been some racket.' The hag cackled merrily before adding, 'But she's no screaming noo so I think ye'll no save her this time. Lay her out is about aw ye'll able to do.'

Arriving at Gabby's door Anna caught hold of Freddie who was still banging furiously on it and shouting, 'Let me in. Let me in. Leave my sister alone! Rotten sodding pig that you are.' Overcome by exhaustion Freddie then sank to the floor and wept bitterly.

Anna would have comforted Freddie but she had to get inside the house. Looking around, she was relieved to see the kitchen chair, which Gabby had hurled at the departing Robert. Picking it up she used it as a battering ram against the aged door which reluctantly broke open.

On gaining entry to the house Anna gasped. There lying in a huddle on the floor was the barely conscious Rachel.

Her outer clothes had been ripped from her and bright red blood was streaming from her nose, lips, arms and legs. 'Auntie,' she whimpered, 'please, please come – I need you…'

Taking Rachel into her arms Anna rocked her to and fro. 'I'm here, bairn. And I'm no only taking you home but I'm also taking your brothers as well. Oh aye, back we'll all go to the safety of Couper Street.'

'Auntie, you're here? You're really here,' wept Rachel. 'I didnae let him – Auntie, I did fight him off as best I could. Tried to do what you said I must – and I did.' Rachel was now so distraught that Anna was hardly able to make out what she was saying.

She did, however, hear Gabby's drunken roars and at the sound of his voice, Anna lost all control. All her eyes could see was red-hot anger and her need for vengeance rose so strongly in her chest that it began to choke her.

Gently laying Rachel down, she picked up the bread knife that was lying under the table and raced into the bedroom. Pulling back the blanket that was covering the semi-conscious Gabby she raised the knife. No longer was she able to distinguish right from wrong and she was overwhelmed by all the years of hatred and frustration. She became engulfed in a thrilling sensation of realising that she was now in a position to put an end to him – an end to him being able to torture and humiliate all those she loved and valued.

Making a downward plunge of the knife

she cackled insanely but the laugh died in her throat when two strong arms encircled her and a hoarse, strong voice breathed in her ear, 'Don't be a bloody fool. Do you think he's worth dangling at the end of a rope for?'

With great effort Anna managed to turn her head. She gulped when she found herself looking up into the face of Gus Cochrane, who had snatched the knife from her hand and had tossed it across the bed. 'Yes, I do,' she sobbed.

'Believe me,' replied Gus, dragging her back into the living room. 'The last thing you should ever do is tie an albatross around your neck. Tired you would be of never being...' Gus abruptly stopped and Anna could see he was now reflecting.

'Look at her,' screeched Anna. 'And also poor Freddie there in the lobby weeping and cuddling his knees as he rocks himself backwards and forwards. Surely that fiend can't get away with all he has done to these defenceless bairns?'

'Look. He will pay. I promise you that. But right now we need a barrow. So where will we get one?'

'A barrow!' she hollered. 'What on earth for?'

'Well, it's true I'm strong – very strong. But I can only carry one of them. And as we need to get both Rachel and Freddie out of here I need something to carry them on.'

'You're right,' Anna conceded. 'Now you go back over to the Broad Pavement and asked Mary Croan, who will be sitting there selling fish, if she'll lend us her fish cart.'

'No,' replied Gus, shaking his head. 'I'm not sure what you'll do if I leave you here – so you go and get the barrow and I'll fix things here.'

Gus was surprised when Anna returned within fifteen minutes with the stinking fish barrow. Even so, there had been time enough for him to do what he had to.

After Anna had wrapped Rachel in a sheet, Gus lifted her up and as he was leaving the house Anna asked, 'What about Gabby? He'll come after us and take them back and the law will give them to him.'

Shaking his head, Gus said, 'No he won't. He'll never bother you again.'

'He won't?'

'No. Just as long as he remembers what I'm capable of.'

'What have you done to him?' Anna stuttered as fear overwhelmed her.

'Not that much,' smirked Gus, thinking, *Oh, Anna, there's more than your brother who can make a man so terrified that he'll do what he's told.*

Once everyone was safely in the house at Couper Street, Anna said, 'Right, Bella, get

158

the kettle on. I need hot water to wash Rachel. She's had a right good doing but...' she couldn't continue for the extent of Rachel's injuries were now more evident and were more than she could bear.

'I'm going to put her on the bed in the back room,' said Gus, who was still holding Rachel and had taken control of the situation. 'There she'll have some peace and privacy.'

Rolling up her sleeves and putting on an apron, Anna nodded. 'Aye, I'll sleep with her there tonight. You, Bella and Nat can have the big bed in the kitchen.'

'And what about Robert and Freddie? They need a place for the night or have they to go back to Gabby?' asked Bella tentatively, worried in case she would not be able to be alone with Gus.

Anna mused. 'Tell you what, Bella. You go and ask...'

'Rye Pratt if they can bunk with her,' Bella interrupted hastily.

'No. Sure, nine folk in two rooms is enough, is it no? Mind you, good soul that she is, she would make space for them and I know she would be the soul of discretion.' Anna paused before quietly admitting, 'But what I urgently need is some time to get things sorted out – so Bella, off you go and ask Mona Stoddard.'

'Mona Stoddard?'

'Aye, there's only her and her rat-catcher man living in that house so they've got room to spare.'

13

EUGENIE FRASER

Three weeks later the physical scars of Rachel's ordeal had vanished. In that time Anna had reached the reluctant decision that she must put Rachel somewhere safe. Gus did continually assure her that he'd put Gabby's gas well and truly at a peep but she was never completely sure that when he had a good drink in him he might not get gallus and pitch up at her door. No doubt accompanied by at least two misguided law officers.

She further argued with herself that the boys were of an age to decide whether to remain with her and there was nothing their father could do about that – but in Rachel's case he could demand that she be returned to his custody. Sighing, she knew there was nothing else for it but to put Rachel beyond his reach. Parting with her, she knew, would be unbearable but she must endure it. Tearfully she acknowledged that what was best for Rachel was paramount. Inhaling deeply she wondered who could help her? Within a minute she smiled. 'Eugenie!' she called out loudly. 'Now who else could be more suitable to help with my dilemma than her?'

Having decided to enlist the help of Eugenie she wiped both hands over her wet eyes, sighed and looked towards the front door as Bella, Nat and Gus came in.

'Auntie,' crooned Bella, who was so besotted with Gus that Rachel's plight hardly registered with her. 'Wait till I tell you. We've...' and she now slipped her arm through Gus's, '...we've got a house.'

'You have? Oh, that's just wonderful. And here was me thinking that Michie didn't have any empty houses.'

'We didn't go to your factor to rent a condemned one,' Bella smirked. 'You see, we're buying a main-door flat in Lochend Road. And not only does it have an indoor lavvy but also a bath with running water and a wee front garden.'

'Are you saying you're going to buy one of these posh new red sandstone houses that are still under construction in Lochend Road?' Anna stuttered with a voice ringing with incredulity.

'Aye,' Bella chortled. 'And our one will be ready in a year. And by that time Gus will have done another long trip and we'll have all the money they want for it. You see, Auntie, my dear husband doesnae like debt.'

Looking at Gus, Anna wondered where he could have found the money for the deposit, which she knew was more than fifty per cent. Suddenly she recalled what he'd said to her in Gabby's house on the day Bella had dragged him out of the Black Swan pub and begged him to help herself and Rachel. The words about him being capable of doing what was required without thinking of the consequences caused a fear to grow in her. She knew she should question him and try to find out exactly what he meant that day but she found she could only mumble, 'A house in Lochend Road. That's just great.'

Sighing cockily Bella enthused, 'It's just so grand. A world away from what I'm used to but Gus says it's what he wants for Nat and ... well, he hasn't said it in so many words, but I know he means me too.' Bella stopped babbling and took time to look at Anna whose face was solemnly set. 'And yet, Auntie,' she continued, 'it's not Couper Street where I was brought up and where, no matter what, there was always someone to hold out a helping hand to you.'

Gus had been gone a fortnight and Anna had rearranged the house, giving Freddie and Robert the bedroom while Bella, Nat, Rachel and herself squeezed up in the more commodious sleeping accommodation in the kitchen. Nonetheless, Bella, who was counting the days until she moved into her main-door flat in Lochend Road, continually complained about not having enough room to turn in the bed. 'Funny that,' remarked Anna, 'you didn't seem to be crushed when Gus, who's three times the size of Rachel, was hemming you in.'

Bella snorted. 'Talking of which, Auntie – I think I'm away again.'

'Don't think it. Know it,' retorted Anna.

'How do you know? I'm not showing yet.'

'No. But when you throw up at the mention of a plate of buckies there has to be a reason. Anyway, this time you're married – so there's no shame attached to it.'

Lifting up her coat Anna brushed it well again. It was the coat she kept for all-important occasions and as she donned it she said, 'Bella, I'm going out on business. Important business. Now Rachel's away for a wee paddle in the water down on Annfield beach with Jenny and Rosa – do her the world of good, that will – so when she gets back mask her a cup of tea.'

Travelling on the tramcar from Leith to Pilrig and changing for another to take her to Edinburgh's West End was a real treat for Anna.

As she enjoyed the luxury of being driven along Great Junction Street she was able to see the new Leith Provident Building from a new perspective. Glancing firstly to the new Taylor Gardens part of the store she shivered at the thought that it had been built on the site of the now demolished old South Leith Poorhouse.

Looking upwards as she passed King Street, she had to admit that the new housing above the shops was a welcome improvement. She had smiled proudly when she'd been faced with the main shop itself. It had been opened in 1911 and the people in Leith, occasionally including herself for threads and cloth, flocked to shop in the magnificent emporium. She sniffed, thinking how she'd have loved to have been a shareholder in the successful co-operative that had built it all. Biting her lip she vowed that someday she was going to have a spare pound to do just that.

So engrossed in her thoughts she was that she nearly missed her connection at Pilrig. As the tramcar trundled along prestigious Princes Street she admired the elegant shops. There on her right was Mackie's Tea Rooms. She smiled thinking the first, and only, time she'd visited the shop was at the invitation of her friend, Eugenie.

Turning her head to admire the beautiful gardens her thoughts returned to Gus's intended purchase of the main-door house in Lochend Road. Naturally she again pondered the mystery of how he had gathered enough cash to be able to purchase the house for Bella, or to be truthful Nat, in such a modern and stylish street.

The more she thought of it the more she agreed with Rye Pratt, who would have loved to have been a detective, that he hadn't been to India on his last trip but that he'd sailed out of Leith on a Christian Salvesen whaling vessel ... but was too proud to say so. This would explain his long absence – because the whalers, before sailing, had to sign up to do a minimum of two years down in Antarctica's South Georgia whaling station. Most who had decided to go thought life would be hard but they had not reckoned they would have to endure the back-breaking work in such an unrelenting, bitterly cold, hostile climate. Anna had been told, naturally by Rye, that life was so difficult there most returning whalers claimed that even God had forsaken the Antarctic and was forced to admit He'd got it wrong and it was, and never would be, fit for humans to live and work in.

Alighting from the tram at the West End she wistfully looked over to Robert Maule's corner where his upper-class department store dominated. One day, she thought, she would be able to go into that shop and buy instead of just looking as she had done once before.

Thinking about the future her thoughts

returned to Gus and his obsession to get the money, and enough of it, for the house. She also wondered if there was another pressing reason. Did he think that by going to South Georgia he'd be doing self-punishment and that this would cut his imaginary weighty albatross from his neck? Anna was so engrossed in her perceived notion that Gus had a great yearning for forgiveness – and why the answer to exactly what he was guilty of kept evading her – that she had to sternly tell herself these were problems for another day – today was the day she had to sort out Rachel.

Now walking purposely down Queensferry Street to her destination – the everelegant Edinburgh Georgian New Town's Moray Place – Rachel and what she had to do for her was all that concerned her.

After pulling the newly cleaned brass bell she gave herself a quick dust over. Waiting for the door to open she wondered if she should flee. What if her friend of years ago, when they were both active suffragettes, didn't wish to know her now? More importantly, what if she couldn't or wouldn't help?

So engrossed again in her thoughts was Anna that she wasn't aware that a middle-aged, suitably uniformed female servant was now standing with the door ajar waiting to admit her.

'You are Miss Campbell,' the woman

stated as they proceeded up the elegant stairway. Anna nodded. 'Miss Fraser has asked me to take you straight to her. She's in the drawing room.'

The room was so spacious that the four large portraits of past ancestors hanging on the walls seemed necessary to emphasise the upper middle-class position of the family who had and still did reside here. However, Anna felt dwarfed by them and the unease she, now a lowly working-class woman, had experienced on the doorstep rose within her again.

The maid had just closed the door when Eugenie arose and advanced over the room, extending both hands to Anna, 'I'm so pleased to see you again – it's been too long.'

Anna smiled but not sure of the exact etiquette she only offered her gloved right hand in greeting to Eugenie.

Sensing her unease, Eugenie indicated with her right hand that they should sit on the two plush chairs that faced each other and were separated on the side by an occasional mahogany table.

Once seated, Anna removed her gloves but she clasped her hands so Eugenie would not see how work-worn and rough her palms were.

'And how has life treated you since we marched together?' Eugenie asked lightly, lifting a small brass bell and ringing it.

'You see it all,' Anna answered. 'I've brought up four children.'

'I didn't know you married?' replied Eugenie, turning to the maid who had just come in with a tea tray. 'Thank you, Mary. We will manage to serve ourselves.'

Nothing more was said until the curtseying maid left. 'Where were we?' continued Eugenie. 'Ah yes, you were saying you married.'

Anna shook her head. 'No. My brother's wife died and I took in his three children – two boys and a girl.' Anna's lips trembled. 'The laddies, I mean boys, were lost on the *Titanic* but, Bella, their sister, although married, is still with me – for a while anyway.'

'And the fourth child?'

A long pause hung between the two women before Anna said, 'Rachel. Her name's Rachel. She's the only daughter of my dead friend Norma. And...'

'And what?' Eugenie asked, pouring up the tea and passing a cup to Anna.

'Her father, a drunken brute that has fallen so far that nothing – and I mean nothing – gets in the way of him satisfying his addictions.'

Eugenie's eyes widened. Anna, unaware of the venomous tone she had adopted, seemed surprised.

'So what is it you think I can do about this degenerate?'

'No. I don't want anything done about him. You see the sheriff had recently given him power over Rachel's future but – Oh! Eugenie, can you understand how much Norma meant to me?'

Eugenie nodded. 'As Clara meant to me.'

Anna stopped and looked about the room. 'Oh no, did Clara die?'

'In a manner of speaking – yes. Three years ago she married a widower with six children and has played the good step-mother ever since, which leaves her no time for anyone else.'

'Oh, but I thought...'

'Best not to think, Anna. After the Drumsheugh Gardens School Scandal...'

'But that was back in 1810.'

'Yes. But try and understand, the working class women you associate with can have very special relationships with each other and there is never a whiff of it being unseemly – they are judged just to be helping one another to survive the poverty.' Eugenie chuckled, 'But since 1810 in my walk of life – it is a must for men to have long-standing close relationships with other men.' She paused. 'However, women dare not appear to be too close to any other unmarried female. Or people end up adding two and two and making let's say – anything but four.'

'As happened to poor Marianne Woods

and Jane Pirie at Drumsheugh Gardens?'

'Precisely. Now we have digressed enough, pray proceed,' said Eugenie, raising her hand in permission.

'Well, when Norma was dying I promised her I'd look out for Rachel and I did but as I said, recently the court,' Anna stopped and leant over and took Eugenie's hand in hers, 'agreed he should have custody of her.' Anna was beginning to get emotional. 'So you see I need to hide her. Have her safe and I was thinking – you wouldn't need to pay her – could you not take her as a scullery maid or something? She's a clever girl, with her mother's grace and charm, but I don't care if she has to scrub,' Anna was now sobbing, 'just as long as she's protected!'

'What makes you think she would be in any danger?'

'He's already beat her senseless and I know he wants her back to keep house for him – Eugenie, have you ever known me to beg – but the court favours men.'

Eugenie nodded before rising to pace about the room. Eventually she laid a hand on Anna's shoulder. 'Calm yourself,' she began. 'For your sake I'll take her but she will have to start as a teenie in the kitchen. Unlike my father, who doesn't seem to realise that with war raging we all have to make sacrifices, I only have four servants to look after me now.

170

Therefore no one will consider it unreasonable for me to take Rachel on. And I will pay her what she's worth.'

Anna had thought approaching Eugenie and begging her for help would be the hardest part of her plan, however, sitting down with Rachel and explaining to her that arrangements had been made for her to be given employment in Eugenie's home was quite traumatic.

'But I have done nothing wrong,' screamed Rachel, thumping the table. 'So why am I being sent away?'

Anna tried to get hold of Rachel who was now shying away from her. 'No. No. Look, I promised your mother I'd look after you. She'd want you safe and you will be at Moray Place.'

'Look,' Rachel retorted vehemently. 'If my stupid mother wanted me safe then why did she die?'

Running her hands through her now white hair Anna conceded that somehow she was going to have a difficult time convincing Rachel of the benefits of her going to Eugenie's. 'Rachel,' she began with a gulp, 'don't worry – you will still be able to see Bella, Nat, your brothers and of course myself...'

'And when will that be?'

'Every week – because you'll be given a

few hours off and Miss Fraser is going to arrange with Mackie's Tea Shop on Princes Street that we will all meet there...'

Rachel's hysterical laughter echoed through the house. 'Oh, I see I'm not being sent away from where I thought I belonged, with my family and my pals, Jenny and Rosa. Oh no, once in a blue moon we'll all sit down and sip tea together. Tea in china cups that no doubt has been paid for by a woman who wishes to please *you* by getting me out of your sight!'

Standing at the back door of Moray Place Anna wished that Rachel would speak to her. Not a word to anyone had Rachel said since Anna told her about going into service. She knew Rachel was extremely disappointed, as she'd hoped she would have started in a better job other than one of *skivvy*. Nonetheless, no matter the atmosphere Anna never once considered changing the plan. She firmly believed that, hard as it was to part with Rachel, it was in her best interest.

When the door opened Rachel hauled her small bag from Anna's hand, and without a backward glance or a word of goodbye, she entered the house. Head held high she knew that her new life, without the support of the only family she'd ever known, had begun.

14

SPANISH FLU

The church bells were ringing out to proclaim the end of the war. The Great War, as it was now being called, was thankfully over. When the peals rang out the weary people were told that the sacrifice of the nation's youth had been worthwhile because it had resulted in it being the war that had ended all wars.

With the peals of the bells echoing around them Anna and Rye sat pensively. They knew that everybody who had survived, as they had, would remember the eleventh hour of the eleventh month of 1918. How could they ever forget with ten million lives lost and twenty million either maimed or injured?

Slowly Anna allowed her gaze to wander over to Rye who was staring silently into space. Anna accepted that today would be difficult for Rye. This was a day for her to remember her beloved husband, James, who'd never made it to the front line because he'd been killed in the Gretna rail disaster. That tragic happening was for Rye every bit as shattering as it would have been if he had been killed at Gallipoli. Both women had been told it would have been kinder if the one thousand plus officers and men who survived that crash and went on to reinforce Gallipoli had died quickly at Gretna. Regrettably by July mothers, wives and bairns had been notified that fierce fighting in appalling conditions meant that only one hundred and seventy four of those gallant men would ever return to tell the tale.

'Would you like to go to Rosebank Cemetery the day, Rye?' Anna asked, before covering Rye's hand with her own.

Rye shook her head. 'Naw. No feeling myself. Aw shivery and sore, I am.'

'Hope you're no coming down with that blasted Spanish flu. And it wouldn't be surprising if you did. After all, you've been helping me nurse them that have gone down with it, not just in our stair, but the whole of Couper Street.' Rye nodded and Anna went on, 'Not to mention doing a few shifts help-ing Sandy and Bella who cannae cope with all them that have died.'

Rye chuckled. 'Face reality, Anna. We're far too auld in the tooth and gnarled in our bones for the flu to get its grip on us. It's just...' Rye sighed and it seemed to come from the very soles of her boots. 'Well, you ken yourself. Never a day goes by – och. This armistice is just opening up auld raw wounds again.'

Refreshing their teacups, Anna nodded.

'And I ken tae that you think every day,' Rye continued wistfully, 'about your Jimmy and Rab – just like me with my James. Funny ... how the three of them aw died in accidents ... if you could call the sinking of the *Titanic* an accident.'

Puffing out her lips before inhaling deeply was all the response Anna was capable of.

'Here,' said Rye, through a spasm of coughing and spluttering. 'Is it Wednesday coming that you're meeting up with Rachel again for a posh afternoon tea?' Anna still made no answer so Rye nudged her before lifting her own cup and sticking out her pinkie finger while taking a dainty wee sip of tea.

The trick worked. Soon Anna's laughter was echoing round the room.

There was no denying that she was so pleased that after having months of no contact with Rachel three weeks ago she'd received a letter. Turned out Rachel was writing to ask if they could meet the following Wednesday at two o'clock in Mackie's Tea Rooms on Princes Street.

It had been a long overdue reunion. Anna had wanted to force Rachel into meeting with her but Eugenie had said to let some time go by and all would be well.

On the designated day for the meeting Rachel was already at the teashop when

Anna arrived. Rachel was so changed that Anna just couldn't conceal her surprise. The gawky, truculent young lassie she'd left on the doorstep of Moray Place had been transformed into the confident, well-groomed young lady who seemed pleased to greet her.

'My! If scrubbing floors and pans makes you look like you do, I must try it,' remarked Anna, sitting down opposite Rachel.

Before Rachel could reply, the waitress arrived with her notepad. Anna was about to say that they hadn't yet made up their minds when Rachel smiled sweetly before confidently giving the order.

The waitress had just left when Rachel giggled before saying, 'But you see, Auntie, I look good because I'm *not* a skivvy.'

'You're not?'

'No. The cook asked for me to be *dismissed*.'

'Sacked?' shrieked Anna, consumed by rage.

This unladylike outburst was clearly overheard by all the genteel customers nearby and all eyes were now focused disapprovingly on Anna and Rachel. To defuse the situation Rachel smiled and signalled discreetly for Anna to calm down.

'You see,' she whispered, leaning forward so that only Anna could hear, 'when I started at Moray Place I was in charge of sorting and preparing the vegetables for dinner and

I also had to wash up all the pots. But after a few months I was so, so tired. Honestly, Auntie, that cook was never off my back.' Rachel paused, hoping that some sympathy would come from Anna but since none was forthcoming she continued, 'Well, one night about a month ago, I had to prepare cabbage and after the meal I had to clean the pot I'd been using to cook it in. It looked clean to me so I just put it back on the shelf. Next morning, Cook used it to make Miss Fraser's porridge.' Rachel giggled again. 'Miss Fraser had just taken one spoonful when she spluttered, "This porridge tastes frightful!" I was then summoned and forced to sample it and yes, it certainly was disgusting.'

Rachel was now laughing so hard that she stopped to wipe the tears from her eyes. 'And,' she went on while chuckling and wiggling her shoulders, 'that was when our cook, dear Jessie, demanded that I should be sent packing.'

'But why wasn't I told? And I can't help thinking...' Anna stammered.

'Then don't think and let me finish,' suggested Rachel. 'When Miss Fraser looked me over she agreed that, unlike Jessie, I didn't have the necessary attributes to be a kitchen maid. Jessie just couldn't conceal her delight.' Rachel again had to signal with her hand to silence Anna before mischievously adding, 'But the smirk died on her face when Miss Fraser said, "I think Rachel would be more suited to being my personal maid"!'

'You're Eugenie's personal maid!' Anna expounded loudly, drawing all eyes towards her again.

'Yes,' replied a delighted and proud Rachel. 'And when we're alone she teaches me how to speak, dress and conduct myself.'

'Thank you God,' said Anna, clasping her hands together and looking heavenwards.

'Mind you, she can be – well–. Just listen, Auntie, to what she said to me yesterday,' whispered Rachel, leaning closer to Anna. 'Combing her hair, I was.' To Rachel's annoyance Anna feigned nonchalance by resting her elbows on the table and cupping her face in her hands. Anna's action perturbed Rachel who realised her aunt was indicating that she didn't wish any criticism of her friend Eugenie. Nonetheless, Rachel, now mimicking Eugenie, pressed on with her story.

'When she said, "Rachel, my dear child,"' she began, taking care to roll the 'r' of Rachel as Eugenie always did. '"How on earth did an intelligent girl like you choose such inadequate parents?"'

A further fit of coughing from Rye suddenly brought Anna's thoughts back to the present. 'Look,' she observed, picking up her glasses and polishing them on her apron before putting them on to get a better look at Rye, 'you do look peaky. So I think, to be on the safe side, you should go home and have a lie down.'

Rye was about to speak when Eck Stoddard, the local rat-catcher known to all as Ratty, burst into the room. 'Anna,' he shouted, but as she had her back to the door she had to twist around to face him. 'You've got to come! Mona's caught this blasted flu and, in no time at all, she's got it real bad. She's raving and you could fry an egg on her face – like hell's fire it is.'

Before Ratty could plead further, Anna had lifted her ever-ready nurses' bag from the table. Even more speedily she followed Ratty from the house. 'Rye,' she called back over her shoulder, 'will you please ask Rosie to keep wee Nat with her? Just tell her it looks as if Bella and me will be busy, very busy, well into the night.'

That week it became evident that the flu in its wake would take more lives in Leith than had the front line of the war coupled with the Gretna disaster. The situation was so critical that doctors had ordered Boots the Chemist shops to stay open so they could be kept supplied with drugs – not that any of the potions were really effective against the virulent influenza virus. The result was that Sandy and the other undertakers struggled to cope, while gravediggers worked around the clock.

For two days Anna fruitlessly battled to save Mona. After doing all she could to comfort Ratty she climbed the stairs to Rye's house. There she found not only Rye seriously ill but also six of her children. Shivering from the extreme cold that had engulfed the house, and even although exhaustion was overtaking her, Anna firstly set about cleaning out and rekindling the fire. Then it was on to sponging down her patients, dosing them with cough syrup and keeping them hydrated.

Three days later, having done all she could for the Pratts, Anna wearily crossed over to her own house. On entering she saw Robert seated at the table with an envelope in his hand. 'A message boy brought this for you,' he said, handing over the letter. 'Hope it's not more bad news.'

'Hope not,' agreed Anna tearing open the envelope and removing its contents. Seeking for a chair she sat down to read. After a while she wearily murmured, 'Suppose it's all for the best.'

Taking the letter from her Robert began to read it aloud. 'Dear Anna, by the hour the situation being caused by the influenza outbreak is getting worse in the towns and cities. Therefore I have decided that I, along with my personal staff, should travel to my father's estate in the Borders and stay there until things improve. I know you will have been looking forward to meeting up with Rachel again but I also realise how busy you will be doing what you can for those about you who have been afflicted. Finally I do hope you do not succumb and please be aware I will take as good care of Rachel as you would yourself. Kind regards, Eugenie.'

Placing the letter back on the table Robert said, 'Never mind, Auntie. At least you know Rachel's safe. How about a cup of tea? That usually perks you up.'

By the New Year the epidemic still raged. Rye had lost two of her children but thankfully she herself had survived and Bella had been on hand to make the necessary funeral arrangements for Rye's children.

Reluctantly Anna conceded it was a highly unusual type of flu virus since it mostly attacked healthy teenagers. That being so, Anna was surprised that no one in Rosie's family had fallen victim. Rosie, of course, explained this miraculous happening by pointing out that she'd gone to chapel every night and prayed. So like the Passover, her God had taken care of His own! In addition to that wonder it was not until January that Freddie, Robert and Anna succumbed.

Anna had been delirious for three days. Her memory of that time could not be relied upon. She did, however, vividly recall that her thirst had been raging and that she was begging for somebody to help her – if only to give her a drink. Fortunately someone did answer her call. Her saviour held a cup of ice cold, quenching water to her parched mouth before going on to mop her hands, face, neck and brow. Valiantly they struggled to remove her sweat-sodden nightdress before laying her head back gently on the pillows. After that an overcoat was carefully laid on top of the threadbare blankets that covered her. Anna, shivering uncontrollably, realised she felt both hot and cold by turn and as the coat landed on top of her she felt a comforting surge of love and warmth radiate about her.

Realising that the person saving her life was putting themselves in mortal danger, Anna forced open her weary eyes and bravely tried to mouth a 'thank you.' But as the face of her Good Samaritan loomed above her she begged God to sink her back into merciful oblivion again. Before losing complete consciousness she heard the man's wavering voice implore, 'You've got to hold on, Anna. It's true, at times that you're a pain in the arse – but folks need you. So forget about drawing your last breath and just pull through.' His voice was hardly audible now but before it drifted completely away she was sure he mumbled something like, 'Besides look how upset Ra-a-a-achel…'

Regaining her senses, Anna warily opened her leaden eyes. Praying earnestly she begged that the demon she thought had saved her life was just a figment of her delirium and would no longer be within her house. Focusing her eyes on the room she was grateful to find that she was all alone. Running her tongue over her lips she tried to convince herself that it had all had to have been some sort of nightmare. Surely it had never, ever happened! The very thought of Gabby Forbes touching her, bathing her, covering her with his filthy coat, had her squirming with disgust.

Reaching down to pull the blankets about her a scream died in her throat as her hands curled around an unfamiliar object! Struggling to a sitting position, she discovered it was a coat – but try as she might, she did not recognise it. It was a working man's coat but whose? Ratty's? Now that would make more sense, she thought, as every day since Mona passed over he'd called in just to talk with Anna. Always he was on his best behaviour – very rarely swearing and never leaving without pleading with her to be less rigid in her views.

Relief was seeping into her when she concluded, *I'm right. I know that I am. It was dear, considerate Ratty who tended me – so*

*there's no need to worry about anything –
especially the coat – after all it would be clean
dirt that surrounded Ratty's things.*

Summoning up the little strength she had
left, Anna threw the coat away and pushed
back the blankets. 'Legs like jelly,' she told
herself, swinging them onto the floor. She
was still swaying backwards and forwards
when Rye and Rosie came in.

Chuckling and offering Anna a supportive
arm, Rosie said, 'Good to see you back in
the land of the living. See, when I was sent
for two days ago I thought you were a
goner.'

'*You* thought?' echoed Rye. 'I was just
about to send for Bella and a shroud.'

Sitting on the fender stool with her back to
the fire had always been one of life's little
luxuries for Anna – precious times when she
could relax and reflect. Today, as the crack-
ing flames warmed her back, she thought,
*Weak I may be but how lucky I am to be still
alive.* Waving her hand to attract her two
friends' attention, Anna heaved a contented
sigh before saying, 'Oh, ladies, the nightmares I had. You just wouldn't believe them.'
She stopped to have a little laugh. 'Do you
know? I actually thought that useless,
degenerate Gabby...'

'Oh here, afore you go on,' Rosie interrupted, 'I met him in the Kirkgate the day.
Still cold and shivering, he is. Like he was

184

that day he came over to ask you to nurse him! But he says to tell you, without your help, he's recovering just fine. And he also said, to say to you, "There's nae hurry but as soon as you're able to be without his auld coat could he hae it back…"'

Shaking with laughter, Rosie grabbed the back of a chair before spluttering, 'With or without the half-bottle o' Johnny Walker whisky he left in the pocket!'

15

AWAY HOME

By April the brightness of the mornings and the warmth of the returning sun had the people of Leith begin to hope again. True, there were still some cases of flu being reported every day but gradually they became less and less. The worry now was the lack of food and resources.

Rachel, who'd settled well in the Borders, had no such worries. She was fed from the fat of the land and had a bedroom to herself, yet recently she yearned to be back with her ain folk.

Each morning after breakfast she would attend to Eugenie's wishes. Sometimes it was just seeing to the laundering of her clothes, welcoming ladies who had come to call, or they were driven by the young and handsome chauffeur from the country estate into the town of Melrose. No matter why they journeyed into the town, they would always end up in a first-class teashop.

Lazily stirring her tea that had just been served up by a waitress, Rachel appeared calm and collected and yet she was in turmoil. How, she wondered, could she summon the courage to ask Miss Fraser when they might be returning to Edinburgh?

She should not have worried because Eugenie, who was sensitive to her moods, realised something was amiss and looking directly at Rachel she kindly asked, 'Is something troubling you, Rachel? You seem so far away today.'

Screwing her eyes shut, Rachel replied. 'It's nothing really. I'm very happy here but it's such a long time since I've seen Auntie and...'

'You're longing, as they would say in Leith, to see your ain folk.'

Rachel nodded. 'I know most people regard Couper Street as a slum – but I grew up there – was accepted there. Yes it's true, I do like the much better life I have here but I still have a need to see Auntie, my brothers and all the others.'

Eugenie smiled. 'You've seen my father.

He's old now and the time has come for me to reside with him for the short time he has left. But I think it's also important that...'

'No. I don't want to leave here.'

Eugenie leant over and patted Rachel's hand. 'I understand that completely. But I do think, every month, you should have a weekend back home with Anna.'

Bella and Anna had, for months now, taken turns working shifts at Sandy's undertaking business. Today Anna had been on early duty and after doing some sewing jobs she'd stopped to make a meal for herself and Bella, who should have been home some half an hour ago.

Lifting the soup pot off the fire and resting it at the side Anna was pleased to hear Bella come in. 'What kept you?' she enquired.

'At the last minute another two needing boxed. And do you ken? I'm so bleeding tired I wouldnae mind being boxed myself and as if...' Bella firstly rubbed her swollen cheek and then her even further extended belly, '...this blooming throbbing toothache isnae enough I've – you know, well, I could be starting my labour.'

'Don't be ridiculous. You're not in labour.'

Taken aback, Bella parked herself down before pointedly saying. 'And how would you, a woman who's never given birth, know better than me?' Gripped by another spasm

187

of acute pain she then sought for her aunt's hand before gasping, 'Oh. Oh. What *am* I going to do?'

'Make up your mind, that's what. Now, which has it to be – a visit to sadistic Miss Cowie to get your tooth out or a lie-up on the bed whilst I help you evict the bairn?'

'Oh, Auntie, I've no choice.' To emphasise her point Bella let out a further agonising screech before crying, 'It's up on the bed – and double quick at that.'

Without replying, Anna opened the door and proceeded over to Rye's house. Young Jamie looked up expectantly when she entered. 'If you're looking for my maw, she's doon at Ratty's.'

'Oh blast,' Anna spluttered. 'Look, son, this is important: go and tell her that I need her and she's to come right away to my house.'

By the time Rye arrived Bella was in bed and everybody at home in 18 Couper Street knew by the never-ending shrieks that she was in labour. Immediately assessing the situation Rye turned to Anna and shrugged her shoulders before saying, 'But I thought she was refusing to give birth until Gus puts in an appearance?'

'Aye well, she might look like an elephant but she's no one, so nine months is all she carries a bairn for,' was Anna's sarcastic reply. 'And, here,' she continued, 'what's going on? I mean, every time I see you in the lobby you're taking food down to Ratty.'

'Och, it was just that when you were laid up I felt sorry for him. Went down and had a wee blether with him and then – you know how it is. Oh aye, afore I kent it every night I was taking a hot dinner down for him and then redding up.'

'Hope he's paying you?'

'Well, just a couple of bob in hard siller but I get everything else I need in kind.'

'Oh, I see,' responded Anna with a smile. 'Like that four pound of purloined shoulder steak last week?'

Rye winked. Bella shrieked and the two women knew it was time to stop the chit-chat and get on with the delivery.

The birth of the baby girl, in Anna's opinion, was easy and straightforward. Nonetheless, Bella thought otherwise and was now lying in bed with her back against raised pillows, eyes closed and either loudly sniffing or whimpering.

'Pity,' observed Anna, 'you didn't think it was such a chore making her.'

'Why can't you see that the agony of giving birth is all too much for me?' whimpered Bella. 'And Gus not being here to see what a great job I've made of his daughter is unbearable.'

With a smile that brightened up her whole

face, Anna cuddled the baby into herself and asked, 'And what are you going to call her?'

'Bluebell?' replied Bella, gesturing to Anna to give her the baby.

'Bluebell,' gasped Anna. 'That's no half some label for the wee mite to go through life with. I mean, when she's young it might be okay. But what if she turns out to be built like a floribunda?'

'Bluebell it is.'

'Why?'

'Oh Auntie, do try and understand that now we're moving to Lochend Road we'll no longer be working-class.' Anna gasped as Bella went on, 'Can't you see that names like Jessie, Meg, Nettie, Effie and the like wouldn't fit in there.'

Astounded by Bella's unfounded delusions of grandeur Anna allowed several minutes to pass before saying, 'And talking of Lochend Road, when will the house be ready?'

It was now Bella's turn to let time go by. 'That's another problem,' she eventually commented. 'We could move in next week, if I've recovered enough, that is.' Anna's eyes flicked up to look at the ceiling. 'But,' whimpered Bella, 'there's still forty pounds owing and since I, a mere woman, cannae get a loan from the bank, I'll have to wait until Gus puts in an appearance.' Bella looked up at the clock as if somehow he was just hours overdue instead of months and added, 'And if he takes too long, the contract he signed will be broken. And as if that's not enough to worry me, the builder says he's got a waiting list of people who want to buy.'

'Forty pounds?' exclaimed Anna. 'That's a king's ransom. Near a half year's wages for most men about here, that is.'

Forgetting how weak she was trying to appear Bella loudly retorted, 'Auntie, I know that fine!'

However, before the discussion could go further, there was a loud knock on the door and Sandy entered, attired in his funeral uniform and mandatory mourning face.

'Look,' he began, ignoring the fact Bella was in bed and Anna was cleaning up after the birth, 'can either of you two come down to the shop – I mean funeral parlour – and help out?'

'Come in and help you out?' exclaimed Anna.

'Aye, you see this flu? Och, they're still drapping like flies and since I've got, let's say, a bit friendly with the night porter in Leith Hospital I'm getting more work than I can handle – and that's even if you two were at work.'

Licking her lips Anna winked at Bella. 'Sure, Sandy, it's the talk of the Walk and the Kirkgate an all.'

'What is?' hollered Sandy.

'How Leith Hospital's night porter and you have a very profitable arrangement,' Anna shamelessly provoked.

Sticking out his neck and running his finger around his stiff white collar Sandy gulped before saying, 'I don't hold with lying gossip. I just help the laddie out.'

'Oh, talking of helping out. Bella here needs a loan of forty pounds until Gus gets back.'

Sandy's eyes popped and his mouth gaped. 'You're no suggesting that a struggling undertaker like me would hae forty pounds lying about.'

'Your money would be safe.'

'How?'

'It would all be done legal. Oh aye, Sheils & Macintosh, the lawyers in Charlotte Street, would draw up a deed.'

'Naw. Naw,' Sandy muttered, quickly heading for the door.

'Oh. So you think it would be better if I told the matron how many corpses the night porter dispatches your way?'

The door banged shut. Sandy turned and leant against it. 'You wouldn't. It would cost the laddie his job and I'm no wanting any trouble either.'

Anna shook her head. 'Aye, you mightn't want trouble, Sandy, but...'

'Aw right. Aw right. But the minute her

man returns,' he spat, signally toward Bella with his thumb, 'I want repaid – with interest.'

'Fine,' replied Anna. 'And so you can *liaise* with your business associate the night, I'll come in and attend to your silent customers.'

Sandy had just left when the door opened and Rachel entered.

Jumping towards her, Anna cried, 'Are you not a sight for sore eyes? And let's look at you. What a swank!'

Dressed in a mid-calf lilac swagger coat that was set off by a cheeky head-hugging many-coloured hat, Rachel approached the bed. 'So your wee one's arrived,' she stated, smiling broadly. 'Boy or girl?'

'Girl,' replied Bella proudly. 'And I'm going to call her ... Bluebell.'

'Bluebell,' queried Rachel, 'and why are you not calling her after Auntie Anna and yourself?'

Bella sniffed. 'Suppose Annabella ... wouldn't exactly be out of place when we go up in the world ... but – no. Bluebell it is because it sounds so classy.'

Rachel did try to think of an answer to that but as none was forthcoming she turned again to Anna. 'Miss Fraser, Eugenie...'

'See what I mean? Eugenie, Bluebell. Names like that just reek class,' simpered Bella.

'Well, Auntie,' continued Rachel, who chose not to reply to Bella, 'I think she means to stay down in Melrose until her father passes over.'

'Very ill is he?'

'No. It's just that he likes having Eugenie fuss over him.'

'So that means you'll be staying down there too.'

'Yes. I do like it down there. And I'm...' she now waltzed about the room, before going on. 'Oh, Auntie, everyone down there thinks that I'm Miss Fraser's companion and not her maid!'

'So that's why you're dressed up like the Queen of Sheba.'

Rachel had just circled to the door when it abruptly opened and she was sent flying across the room. 'Sorry,' exclaimed Robert, helping her to her feet. 'You know, you must be psychic. Just ten minutes ago I was telling Bud here all about you and how I knew you'd soon be finding the pathway home.'

Everyone's eyes were drawn to the young man who had accompanied Robert into the house. He was fair and tall, with eyes that twinkled when he firmly grasped Rachel's hand when Robert introduced them. However, it was his broad, engaging smile that completely mesmerised her – turning her legs to jelly.

No one in the room that day could have

been in any doubt that, between Rachel and Bud, there was an immediate compelling chemistry. Indeed, he held on to her hand for so long that Robert contemptuously hissed, 'Here, Bud, you cannae take her hand with you so why don't you put it down.'

Blushing with embarrassment Rachel pulled her hand abruptly from Bud's. She then went on to quickly remove her hat and run her fingers through her hair before looking directly at him and asking, 'Are you a workmate of Robert's?'

'Me? Labour in the docks?' exclaimed Bud, laying his instrument case on the floor. 'Well, no I don't. But he and I are both in the Leith Brass Band and tonight's rehearsal night.'

'You play in the brass band?'

Bud was now rocking with laughter. 'You sound so like my mother. She thinks because we now live in Trinity and I was educated latterly at the Royal High School I should play rugby and be a virtuoso on the violin – but you see I prefer football and,' Bud paused, to pretend by extending his right hand backwards and forwards to be playing an instrument, before emphasising dramatically, 'th–the trombone.'

Anna had to suppress her amusement. She knew Bud Watson's mother well from when she'd lived in West Cromwell Street and worked at Bond Nine. Then she was known as Big Bessie who wasn't to be tangled with. Having graduated, however, to Trinity with an inside lavatory, she was now a leading light in Wardie Church and only answered to Eliza. Sighing, Anna admitted Eliza and her Bella had a lot in common. Somehow they thought that a private house with facilities for their exclusive use and a back green to hang their washing in somehow made them a cut above all the rest of the world.

Without trying to conceal her pride Anna's thoughts strayed to Rachel, who she thought had innate intelligence, grace and charm, and acknowledged to herself, 'Oh aye, those two with bought houses might be a cut above some, right enough, but never my Rachel – any fool can buy a house and dress in fine feathers but the one thing you can't buy is *class*.'

Unaware of her aunt's meanderings Rachel asked, 'So you two play in the Leith Band but what about Freddie? He can blow a trumpet too?'

'Oh, you mean, our dear brother who's had stars in his eyes ever since he met sweet Violet Stobie?'

'Courting, is he?'

'Aye, winching he is – and by the time he's eighteen she'll hae him up the aisle.'

Anna quickly interjected, 'Robert! They're just bairns.'

'That right, Auntie? Well, they might well

be but right now Bud and me have to be on our way or we'll be late for band practice.'

'Are you home for long, Rachel?' Bud asked as Robert steered him towards the door.

'Just for a couple of days,' she replied hurriedly before adding, 'but I'll be home for a weekend every...' She didn't get time to add 'month' because as Bud and Robert left Johnny came in.

'You here to see Bella's new baby?' Anna asked Johnny.

Blushing, Johnny stammered, 'No-o-o really. I heard Rachel was home and I dashed over to say hello.'

His eyes now reluctantly left Rachel to stray towards Bella. 'But I'm pleased about you and the baby – what is it?' he managed to ask.

'A girl and her name is ... Bluebell.'

Johnny made no comment to Bella about the baby's name but he did manage to turn and say to Rachel, 'You've changed.'

'I have?'

'Aye. You're even more – don't you think so, Auntie?'

Anna nodded. 'Come on then – you two sit on the fender stool here. And let's be hearing about what you've both been up to.'

Johnny and Rachel exchanged bemused glances with each other and laughed. 'Me?' Rachel began. 'Well, just working and being trained...' she now leaned over to pat Johnny's knee and laughter rippled from her before she added, '...to be a fine lady.'

'And you are that already.'

'You think so?' laughed Rachel. 'And now, Johnny, what have you been up to?'

Blushing deeper Johnny hung his head and mumbled, 'I've signed up to do three years in the army. My dad says it'll make a man of me.'

'What?' shrieked Anna. 'And how many laddies?– Och. The man's a menace. And when is he expected home?'

'Mammy says he should be back before I leave next month.'

The day Johnny was due to leave for his army service coincided with Rachel being home. She was already in 18 Couper Street when he came in to show his auntie how handsome and smart he looked in his Black Watch uniform.

'Now, Rachel,' crooned Anna, 'have you ever seen such a good-looking man? And know something? Some day a lucky lassie will capture my Johnny's heart. It's true she might, like us right now, not always having something to eat, but she sure will always have something to look at.'

'Auntie,' stammered Johnny, 'you're no half-giving me a stotter. Sure, Rachel, any man that gets you...'

'Will have to get over Auntie's dead body,' interrupted Bella, who was changing the baby's nappy. 'And by the way, Johnny, when you get back you must remember we're related by *blood* so you'll always be welcome at Lochend Road.'

'So you're moving in?'

'Aye,' replied Anna. 'Bella was a wee bit short, but Sandy and I have always had good business arrangements and he insisted on lending her the forty pounds she's needing.'

'He did?' blurted Johnny, 'But my mammy says Sandy wouldnae give a worm to a blind hen.'

'Rubbish!' chuckled Anna, reaching for her coat. 'He's always happy to put his hand in his pocket. You just need to ask him in a language he understands.'

16

THE AMALGAMATION

A cold Antarctic blast engulfed Leith on 21 October 1920 when the Town Council met for the last time. The people rightly felt that their wish to remain independent from Edinburgh, which had been granted to them in the Reform Bill of 1833, had been ignored.

Since the adoption of the Reform Bill, the port had known outstanding success. Trade had expanded and businesses, large and small, had thrived. Skills that had been perfected in the shipbuilding industry were also keenly sought after by many companies outside Leith. One such enterprise saw four hundred men leave Leith by train each day, bound for work on the construction of the Forth Railway Bridge. Public services and transport were envied by Edinburgh who (Leithers felt) always had their greedy eyes on the flourishing port and were constantly pushing for amalgamation on *their* terms.

One of the gains from the First World War was the delay of any further action on the proposed union between Edinburgh and Leith – an outcome which true Leithers did not want.

By the end of 1918, however, the subject was raised again. The people of Leith were outraged and to quieten their resistance it was suggested that a plebiscite be held. With lightning speed this attempt at giving the people their say on the proposed union went ahead. So great was the anger against the amalgamation that 36,000 people out of the 39,000 entitled to vote did so. The result was 5,500 in favour and 30,000 against. A resounding victory for true Leithers – but all too soon they realised the plebiscite had just been an appeasement.

Despite their forthright rejection of an amalgamation with Edinburgh, it went ahead. To rub salt into the wound an enquiry was held on the legality of the union but all to no avail. The enquiry decided that as the amalgamation had gone ahead and, angry as the people were that their democratic rights had been ignored, there was no point in changing things back.

Anna and Rye, who were vehemently against the amalgamation, were always at the forefront of every protest. Their large banner, which they proudly carried between them, read:

LEITH for EVER.
WE PROTEST AGAINST
AMALGAMATION

On arriving back from their last futile demonstration, Anna and Rye, weary, dispirited and swamped by a feeling of betrayal, flung their banner into the gutter.

They had just entered Anna's house and already Anna was busy making the tea when Rye stated, 'We've been robbed.'

'Robbed,' hissed Anna. 'Aye. And in daylight with violence. Mark my words! Green-eyed Edinburgh will suck us dry and we'll be nothing but the poor relation. We, a prosperous, flourishing port, will be reduced to begging Edinburgh City Chambers for our rights and will get fobbed off with the crumbs from their table.'

'Suppose you're right,' replied Rye, stirring some sugar into her tea. 'I mean, hasn't poor Portobello gone down the drain ever since Edinburgh took it over?'

The women were still at the table drowning their sorrows in Melrose's best tea, courtesy of Ratty, when Rosie came in and joined them.

'Just heard it's all done and dusted,' Rosie said, taking out her snuffbox and, after inhaling a good dose, she offered it to Anna.

'No thanks, Rosie. I'm despondent right enough but not quite suicidal,' replied Anna, who detested snuff. Be that as it may, she silently conceded that in Rosie's case she must thole the disgusting practice, as it was preferable to her falling back into alcoholism.

Sensing Anna's disapproval, Rosie ran her index finger under her nose and sniffed. 'Know you dinnae like it, Anna. But see. A wee sniff now and then keeps me sane, so it does.'

'Talking of your sanity, is your Ella really gonnae get hitched to that school janitor?' asked Rye. 'Sure he looks a real gawk, so he does.'

Still sniffing and now sneezing, Rosie, who

was expert at averting controversy, looked up at the gaslight. 'Here, Anna,' she said, deliberately ignoring Rye's remarks. 'Do ye ken your mantle has a hole in it?'

Anna looked up at the gaslight. 'Aye. Robert broke it a couple of nights ago. Gonnae replace it on payday, he is.'

An uneasy silence followed until a rap on the door had them look from one to the other. When the door opened Jack McIntyre in full police uniform entered with a holdall in his hand. While he placed the bag on the floor Rye took the opportunity to lift the tea caddy from the table and secrete it on the mantelpiece.

'Long time since we saw you, Jack,' remarked Rosie, rising to leave.

'Aye,' he replied. 'Been back up north ... burying,' he now adopted a sorrowful and mournful look before shaking his head and continuing with, 'my poor old mother.'

Rye now advanced to join Rosie at the door. 'Hope she was really dead because any time in the past when I saw her, I thought she'd already gasped her last,' she whispered while playfully nudging Rosie.

'Rye!' was the only reply an indignant Rosie could utter.

The women were now in the passageway. 'Well,' commented Rye, 'haven't you and I been praying for years for the good Lord to take her up beside Him. But Him, up till now, no brave enough to give her house-room.'

The door had just closed and Jack was now sitting at the table facing Anna. 'Sorry I didn't get the chance to tell you that my mother had caught the flu and – well, she was just too old.'

Anna remained mute.

'Don't know how she got it because I kept her away from everybody.' Jack stopped and Anna could see he was still puzzling over the problem. 'But, like yourself, she was devout – never banged a tambourine though – but was always insisting on going to her church. The last time we went out together was three weeks ago.' Anna still made no comment and, unaware of her lack of interest, Jack continued. 'Now you wouldn't think God would let you pick up flu in the Wee Free Kirk.'

Still staying silent, Anna thought that the Wee Free Church was so dull and austere that nothing, including the flu virus, would venture in there.

'Anyway,' Jack lamented, 'like she wanted, I took her back home and buried her there. Lovely service it was. You should have heard the mouth music.'

A deep sigh escaped Jack before he pulled his chair closer to Anna. 'Now,' he said, taking Anna's hand in his, 'sad as it was to lose my mother, who said the only thing she had against you was you not being one of us, I have to be consoled by the fact it leaves me free to ask you to marry me.'

Still there was no response from Anna but the look of horror on her face spoke volumes – as did the pulling of her hand from his.

'Oh,' Jack went on, picking up his bag from the floor and pulling a package from it. 'Nearly forgot. This here is a haunch of venison,' he said as he laid his courting inducement in front of her. 'Slaughtered a stag, they did, for my mother's farewell tea and I asked for them to put a rear end by for me to bring down. And who else would I be giving it to but my ... wife to be?'

Still choosing to ignore Anna's indifference, Jack bent towards her and began patting her left hand, which was stroking her chin. 'Know it has all been such a big surprise to you, but you'll get used to it,' he coaxed. 'And don't forget forbye you landing me there's a three-roomed flat with kitchen and bathroom, and electricity just about to be put in at 103 Easter Road and that's in addition to my regular policeman's pay every week.' With a nod and a wink Jack stopped to emphasise the advantages. 'And,' he added with a smile, 'I'll be quite generous with your housekeeping. Mind you, you'll need to give up the Salvation Army and come back and worship with me at my church.'

'That right?' Anna slowly responded whilst looking up at the broken gas mantle. 'Well, know something, Jack. I like biding here at 18 Couper Street with my two laddies and two lassies and all my pals. And know something else? I would rather have this,' and she now pointed to the five oat-meal-coated herring, 'for our tea, a broken mantle and bang a tambourine than the luxury you're offering!'

Jack's mouth gaped. He was obviously in a state of shock and could only stutter, 'Perhaps my dear departed mother was right in saying that...' he paused, sniffed and snorted before continuing, 'I should have given Shona Nicholson all the attention I've lavished on you.'

'Shona Nicholson?' gasped Anna before raucous laughter overtook her. 'Now when did I ever think I'd agree with your mother? Oh yes, my dear Jack,' she added, going over and patting him vigorously on both cheeks, 'what you justly deserve is to be sentenced for the rest of your life – to your mother reincarnated in the form of Shona Nicholson!'

Without another word Jack stood up, pushed past Anna, grabbed his bag and headed for the door. It had just banged shut when he flung it open again but Anna well knew why he'd so hastily come back, so before he could ask for the return of the venison, the haunch hit him squarely in the chest.

No one had told the audacious influenza virus that it was to remain in the towns and cities, so when it invaded Melrose and the surrounding countryside everyone was caught ill-prepared. Sir Charles was the first in the house to fall ill, then one by one members of his personal staff. Before long only Eugenie was left. Eugenie had worked tirelessly to nurse her father through the worst of the illness but the old gentleman was too frail. He had only been laid to rest in the family crypt when Eugenie announced she was going back to Moray Place.

However, they had just arrived back in Edinburgh when Eugenie herself became ill with a chest infection. In addition to a doctor calling in daily Rachel tried all the remedies she'd seen her aunt use. Plenty of water to drink. Tepid washes. Camphor chest rubs and steam inhalations. Eventually Eugenie did recover but she was very weak.

Taking her doctor's advice, Eugenie arranged to go to Switzerland to recuperate. Before leaving she sent for Rachel who was surprised when Eugenie said, 'Rachel, my dear, you won't be accompanying me to Switzerland. You see I am so incapacitated now I require the services of a trained nurse companion.'

Rachel's face fired and she bowed her head to hide her disappointment.

'Now, now,' Eugenie continued. 'Please accept that my decision is no reflection on you. Believe me when I say I've so enjoyed the time we've spent together that I'm going to furnish you with a year's wages. Now,' she stopped to take a slow breath. 'The money is meant to keep you until you find suitable employment. And I mean *suitable*. Please do not become fodder for the factories of Leith.'

The smell of crisp fried herring not only wafted through Anna's house but also drifted into the passageway.

'See when you've worked yer guts oot aw day in the docks it's just great to come home and get your bones thawed at the fire and your belly filled. And,' Robert added through a packed mouth, 'I just love boiled tatties and fried herring.'

'I'm glad about that,' responded Anna while serving up Freddie's tea and putting it in the fireside oven to keep warm. 'And here was me feeling guilty about passing up a roast venison dinner for you.'

Robert stopped eating to look quizzically at Anna. 'Naw. Too rich, venison is. Mind you, I do long for Hogmanay – the only time we might be lucky enough to have the dosh to buy a nice steak pie swimming in plenty of that "Ah! Bisto" gravy,' enthused Robert before loudly sniffing the imaginary aroma of that beef delicacy.

He barely stopped his daydream when Freddie walked in. 'Do you know? I smelled what was for the tea down at the dock gate. And look who chased me up the stair.'

'Rachel!' Anna and Robert shouted in unison.

'Hope there's some tea for me,' remarked Rachel as Freddie laid down her two suitcases.

Eyeing the luggage, Anna asked, 'Looks like you're gonnae be staying a while?'

'How about for good?'

'Been sacked, have ye?' queried Robert, as he got stuck into his second fish.

'No,' replied Rachel, turning to face Anna. 'Auntie,' she continued, 'Firstly Sir Charles is dead...'

'So Eugenie's back,' responded Anna with delight. 'But she must be devastated at the loss of her dad. Nice man, he was – and they were so close. I'll go and see her first thing tomorrow.'

'Sit down, Auntie,' coaxed Rachel.

Obediently Anna sank down on the fender stool and Rachel joined her there before saying, 'Eugenie's been *very* ill too and she's now gone to be nursed in Switzerland for at least six months. It's the only hope she has.'

No one spoke. They all knew Anna's relationship with Eugenie was a special one.

It had been forged when they'd met on the suffragette marches. Eugenie had never visited Couper Street but they had kept in touch over the years by meeting occasionally for afternoon tea at Moray Place.

'Auntie, I'm sorry to bother you,' Freddie whispered, 'but I'm meeting Violet. We're going to the last showing at the Palace Picture House, so can I get my tea?'

Anna nodded and fetched the plate out of the oven.

'Still going with Violet? Must be serious,' teased Rachel.

Freddie humped and hawed before admitting, 'We've got plans. Saving up we are.'

'Aye. But still happy to squander a bob or two at the pictures.'

'Look, Robert, I'm only going because Violet is desperate to see Mary Pickford in *Poor Little Rich Girl*.'

'Would you no be better to wait another two weeks and then take her to see that John Barrymore playing *Dr Jekyll*...' Robert was now pulling gruesome faces and throwing his hands about, '...*and Mr Hyde?* Real horror film, that is.'

'And why should I take Violet to see a picture like that?'

'Because she'll be so scared she'll jump up on your lap and then...'

'That's quite enough out of you, Robert,' snorted his aunt, giving him one of her famous warning glares.

'Och well, Auntie, see the way Freddie, Johnny and Bud all drool? Makes me want to boak.'

'Here, Robert, what's Johnny and Bud got to do with Violet and the pictures?' demanded Rachel, prodding him in the shoulder.

'Just that when you're here,' continued Robert, dodging away from Rachel, 'Johnny and Bud run around you like lovesick parrots.'

'But Johnny isn't here. He's in India and won't be home for another year. And as for Bud, he's so in love with himself he's not able to court anyone else,' mocked Rachel, giving Robert another poke in the shoulder.

Running footsteps stopped at the door and Robert quipped, 'And talking of the late Bud, that'll be him now.'

It was Bud and he was breathless and even more so when he saw Rachel.

'We need to get a move on, Bud,' urged Robert.

'Aye. Aye,' replied Bud. 'But surely I've time for a wee word with Rachel. After all, it's nearly three months since she was home.'

Quickly Rachel recounted to Bud why she was now home. 'So you see,' she announced, 'now that I'm unemployed I've got to get myself a career.'

Freddie burst out laughing. 'Oh dear, here's another one that's lost it. But tell me, what's wrong with just finding a job?'

'Nothing. But if you think I'd be happy bottling whisky in the bonds, packing biscuits in Crawford's or putting walnuts on top of the walnut whips in Duncan's – you're quite mistaken.'

'Good for you,' Bud encouraged. 'So what would you like to do?'

'Write a few letters to the big stores up town and try to get into their ladies fashion departments.'

'Oh. Oh. Oh!' mocked Freddie.

Three long weeks passed. Rachel had written to a dozen top-class stores and ten had replied by return of post, stating that there were no vacancies in their shops. She knew this was a lie and that she must be doing something wrong.

On rehearsal night Bud asked if she'd been successful in finding work. She explained just how difficult it was before adding, 'I can't even get an interview.'

Pondering earnestly for a minute, Bud ventured to suggest, 'It's not your experience or your references that are the problem. They're all first class. But,' he hesitated and looked directly at Anna, 'I think it's your address!'

Anna stopped her treadle before demanding, 'And what's wrong with 18 Couper Street?'

Swallowing hard and shrugging Bud muttered slowly, 'Nothing. That is, if you want to work in the factories around here. But look, the likes of Jenners and Greensmith Downes are looking for "ladies" to promote their image. And they have a mistaken idea these "ladies" won't be found in...' Hesitating, he tried to find words more acceptable than, 'A slum like Couper Street'. Eventually he managed to mumble, 'The port of Leith.'

'See,' snarled Anna, wagging her finger. 'That's exactly what I prophesied about this unholy amalgamation. The snobs in Edinburgh think we're all like the working girls that frequent places like that notorious Standard Bar on Parliament Square. Forever creating bloody havoc, they whores do. Especially when they're that full of Red Biddy that they cannae even stand.' She stopped, took a deep breath then exhaled with a grunt. 'And if they Edinburgh business folk know what's good for them, in no way should they class my Rachel along with them.'

Bud ignored Anna's outburst. 'Look, Rachel,' he advised, 'next time you write a letter, head it up with my address. And, believe me, you'll get the right reply.'

'No need for that. Our Bella has a better

address than you have and Rachel will use that,' countered Anna.

When Rachel arrived at Bella's house in Lochend Road, Bella, her chosen sister, was delighted to see her.

'I was expecting you,' crooned Bella.

'You were?'

'Yeah, your mother told me to expect you today. She also suggested I get in a couple of chuck-out cakes from the store bakery.'

Rachel was not at all surprised by Bella's claim that she had been speaking to her long-dead mother. Anna had told her that Bella had been driven mad by Sandy forever demanding to know when he would get his forty pounds back. In desperation Bella had gone to a spiritualist meeting to see if the lady medium knew where Gus was and when he would be likely to come home. The clairvoyant, like the shipping agent who Bella badgered on a weekly basis, had no news about Gus, except to say he would eventually turn up somewhere alive or dead. This statement had left poor Bella quite despondent until the medium said she felt convinced that Bella was one of the few people who had the gift of being able to talk with the deceased and that she should cultivate the talent. Anna had given a sly wink to Rachel when she concluded, 'And ever since, on a daily basis, our Bella communes with the dead. And that's fine by me because she really doesn't have the gift of being understood by the living.'

Not wishing to upset Bella by being sceptical about her powers, Rachel began, 'And did my mother tell you why I would be coming?'

'Of course she did. And there's enough hot water for you to wash your hair and have a bath. Hope you brought your own soap and towel.'

Before Rachel could respond to this bizarre question Bluebell toddled over to her. Picking the child up, she smiled. 'But my, are you not a bonnie bairn? And Bluebell suits you because your eyes are as blue as they are.'

'Aye, Gus is missing the best of her. She's long gone one and I'm wondering if he'll put in an appearance before she's two.'

Looking about the room Rachel asked, 'And where's Nat?'

'Feeding the ducks in Lochend Park with Mrs Grant, he is. You know the auld busybody that bides next door.'

After thirty minutes had agonisingly passed Rachel began to wonder if she was ever going to get Bella told the real reason why she'd come. It was annoying her that Bella was forever turning to speak to those in the spirit world and passing on messages to her from deceased relatives she didn't know. When she could take it no longer Rachel suddenly screamed, 'For goodness sake. Bella, will you shut up and listen to me? I'm here because I need your address so I can get a good job in one of the department stores up town.'

'Edinburgh! And what's wrong with Leith?' replied a miffed Bella. 'Don't you realise ... the only way we can survive this enforced amalgamation with pride is for us to stay loyal to Leith!'

'But Bella, can you see me working in a factory?'

Scratching her head while looking Rachel over, Bella began to wonder if sending her to Eugenie who, like Anna, saw her as the refined daughter she'd never had, had been a good thing? No way could Rachel survive in the Roperie where a number of lassies smoked pipes, snuffed and whose idea of enjoying themselves was to get blotto on Red Biddy in any jug bar that would serve them.

Time ticked slowly by before Bella said, 'Not in the factories ... but how about trying to get into our braw new Leith Provident Department Store? As good as any in Princes Street, it is. And that's on any day of the week.'

Rachel pondered. Why hadn't she thought of writing there? 'Look, Bella, thanks for that. I'll write to them tomorrow but to be on the safe side, could I use your address?'

'Aye, on the condition you do some watching of Nat and Bluebell which would let me go back to do nights in Sandy's funeral parlour.'

Since Rachel had left for Bella's, the pendulum wall clock had been checked every fifteen minutes by Anna. After an hour not only did she look up at the clock, she also craned her neck to look out from the kitchen window. 'What's keeping her?' she asked herself over and over. Bella had been strange of late but she was a good lassie. And for sure weren't Rachel and she like sisters? Hadn't she reared them that way? So no matter what Rachel asked, Bella would do it. But why wasn't Rachel back home to tell her all was fine?

Rising again to peer from the window she was surprised when the draught from the front door being opened hit her back. Turning quickly and skipping over the floor, 'Rachel,' she crooned hopefully, but instead she was faced with her guid sister Rosie. Her delight was quickly extinguished.

'Don't say you're pleased to see me.'

Recovering, Anna patted Rosie on the shoulder. 'Of course I'm pleased to see you. Whenever am I not?' Anna peered behind Rosie. 'But where's Davy? You never come without him.'

Rosie didn't reply but she took a seat at the kitchen table. Anna, perplexed, sat down opposite her. 'What's wrong?' Anna asked, leaning over to grasp Rosie's hands that were drumming ceaselessly on the table.

Swallowing hard Rosie replied, 'Anna, you know I'm not a gossip.'

Anna nodded. 'Is there a problem with our ain folk?' she asked. Rosie shook her head.

'Well if you've come to tell me that there's something seriously going on between Freddie and Violet – I've already guessed.'

'There is a problem – but not with your Freddie and Violet that I know of,' emphasised Rosie, shifting in her chair.

Anna quickly realised how uncomfortable Rosie was but she said nothing.

Suddenly Rosie spluttered, 'You do ken Mona's...'

'Dead. I know. I laid her out and boxed her.'

'Naw. Naw. Listen. What I trying to say is Mona's sister Gladys – well she's chapel, like me.'

'Aye, she turned when she married her man.'

'Oh, Anna, just listen and hold yer wheesht till I tell ye.' Anna nodded. 'When we were coming out o' benediction last night she took me aside and told me – and I swore I wouldn't tell anybody else but I feel I have to...' Rosie now crossed herself and appeared reluctant to go on.

'Share the secret?' Anna suggested. Rosie bit her lip. 'Oh, come on, Rosie. What did she tell you?'

'Just that Ratty goes to see her every week and this week he said – well – he's got married again!'

'He's what?' shrieked Anna.

'Aye, he has, and in the Leith registry office at that.' Rosie crossed herself again. 'And I was thinking what a shock it's going to be for that guid soul Rye. Her feeding and doing for him.' Rosie paused. 'But here – maybe she kens.'

Anna shook her head. 'No,' she vehemently replied. 'She was in two hours ago and all she could speak about was making him some soup.'

'And that's no the worst of it.'

'There's more?'

'Aye, you ken how moaning Mona always said that she'd no bairns because Ratty was a Jaffa...?'

'A what?' questioned Anna.

'Ye ken – seedless.'

Anna's shoulders heaved up and down as she tried to suppress her laughter. 'No I didn't know that but then I'm just a gossip.'

The women looked earnestly at each other before Anna added, 'So what you're saying is someone's been ironing his shirts and she's now in trouble?'

Rosie nodded. 'And Gladys says he's over the moon. Even had the gall to suggest if it's a laddie he'll teach him to catch rats and take over from him.'

Just then the clip of Rachel's high heels was heard in the passageway and Anna signalled to Rosie to say no more.

Before Anna could drop the Ratty bombshell on Rye she had good and bad news from her children. She was delighted that Rachel was going to try for a job in the Leith Department Store and she'd just made a celebration pot of tea when Freddie took the opportunity to disturb the peace.

'Auntie,' he began as he supped his soup and dunked a crust of bread in it, 'see Violet and me ... well...'

'What?'

'Well, we think since Leith's finished we should emigrate to Canada or America.'

'And why suddenly do all you bairns think there's something wrong with Leith?'

Playing for time, Freddie mopped up every drop of gravy from his plate with a chunk of bread. Still searching for the right words, he popped the bread into his mouth and slowly wiped his chin with the back of his hand. 'Not us,' he said diffidently before dropping his eyes, 'you.'

'Me?' exclaimed Anna.

'Aye,' continued Freddie, gaining confidence. 'Ever since the amalgamation with Edinburgh was bulldozed through you've said the port's finished. Besides, even if it isn't, people have always been going in and out of Leith.'

'You do what you think is right for Violet and you, Freddie,' Rachel suggested, to Anna's annoyance.

Getting up from the table Freddie looked about the shabby room. Adding to the picture of wretchedness a mouse was fearlessly jumping all over the bunker. 'Look at that,' he stated and all stared towards the mouse but only Rachel shrieked and backed away.

'This hoose is a breeding place for mice, rats and bugs,' he went on. 'Honestly, they're so sure this place belongs to them and no us that they boldly send us cowering.'

Opening the window further and then with one swipe of a tea towel Anna sent the mouse hurtling down two floors onto the pavement. 'Can't understand why they come in here, I don't,' she mused. 'Surely they know we've hardly enough to feed ourselves, never mind them.'

Before she'd fully recovered from her fright Rachel looked directly at Freddie and stammered, 'And when were you thinking of emigrating, Freddie?'

'Right now,' he replied confidently, 'if we could gather thegither another thirty pounds.'

'Just the one thirty?' asked Anna, who just couldn't understand why the children she'd reared spoke about forty and thirty pounds as if they weren't a king's ransom.

Rachel, who had long realised that Freddie always blamed her for their mother dying young and Robert and himself being sent away to the Industrial School, always felt that, if ever she could, she would help Freddie one day in the hope he would feel better about her. Biting her lip she said, 'Look, if I get a job in the Leith Provident Store next week I'll lend you not thirty but thirty-five pounds.'

'And where did you get that kind of money?' demanded a breathless Anna.

'Eugenie gave it to me so I could take my time to find a job that I wanted to do. And it will just be a loan. When our dear Freddie makes his millions he can pay me back with *interest*.'

Freddie jumping gleefully about the room hollered, 'Is this no dandy? We can now escape while we're still young!'

Two hours later Anna at last found herself on her own. She should have felt relieved but she knew before she could lay her head on a pillow tonight she had to speak to Rye. However, Rye was down at Ratty's feeding him and tidying up. Anna therefore asked Jamie to tell his mother that when she did

222

eventually get back she was to come over to Anna's house as there was urgent business to attend to.

By the time Rye put in an appearance Anna had just finished sewing up Betty Burgess's wedding dress.

'Sorry I'm so late but I just got back and Jamie said you urgently needed me to help you,' drawled Rye, who was looking so happy and relaxed.

'Rye,' Anna began as she pushed the sewing machine into the corner, 'it's not me that's needing help.' She hesitated. 'It's bad news that I've got for you!'

'Me?'

'Aye.' Anna now wished that Rosie had never told her. That way she wouldn't have to caw the feet from Rye. But she had told her and Anna, although it was paining her, knew she must tell Rye. 'Look, it might just be gossip, but it is reliable gossip.' Rye frowned. Searching for the right words, Anna shifted uneasily. 'Look, Rye,' she gulped before going on, 'you've been led up the garden path by Ratty – he's gone and got married again!'

The peal of Rye's laughter ricocheted off the ceiling.

'You've heard the same rumour and it's no true,' chortled Anna as relief seeped in.

'Oh, but it is true. Got himself hitched last week in the Leith registry, he did.'

'You know that and yet you're still doing for him?'

Rubbing her hand under her nose and sighing Rye looked directly at Anna. 'Look, I was going to tell you but you – well – you're always banging your tambourine and so against so many things.'

Anna was astounded. 'Like what?'

'A wee bit slap and tickle if you're no churched.'

'So you're saying, you know he's got some feckless young lassie into trouble and you think there's nothing wrong with that?'

'Believe me, I'm no some feckless young lassie!'

Wishing the floor would open up and swallow her Anna remained speechless.

'Can ye no see? He was lonely. I was lonely. I'd made him a clootie dumpling to die for and well – one thing led to another. And with me believing that I was through the change and he was…'

'Seedless,' whispered Anna

Rye nodded. 'But we've put things right.'

'So why are you still staying next door and him in his house on the bottom landing?'

'There isnae enough room next door – wouldnae be right for the bairns to hear – and he needs privacy – he's a shy man.'

Anna knew she should now be shunning Rye. She couldn't. Rye was one of these people that you just couldn't help liking and putting her out of her life would be a price too high for Anna to pay, so all she said was, 'And is Ratty happy with the situation?'

'No really. But now I have a man to sign the missives I can get the Edinburgh Corporation to rent us a house out o' here.' Rye became pensive. 'And ken what we'd like? One o' they newly built nice tenement fiats in Restalrig or Redbraes.'

Anna knew what Rye was saying was true but the thought that this slum, which was her sanctuary and that of the bairns she had fostered, would be turned to dust was more than she could bear right now.

'Come on, Anna, smile or bang your tambourine,' said Rye, going over and putting her arms about Anna. 'Look at the pluses. Me who thought I was past it will need you to deliver this bairn. This precious gift.' Rye lovingly patted her stomach before going on, 'And Ratty, me and the bairns will be the first to get out o' here. Say goodbye to the rats, mice and bugs.'

Anna shook her head.

'Och, Anna, no matter what, you ken they're coming in with the bulldozers in the next few years. We all hae to accept,' Rye looked about her, 'that these hovels are no fit for human beings. We deserve better. Our men died in that blooming war so we could hae better.'

17

THE UNANSWERED QUESTION

By the spring Rachel had been employed in Leith Provident women's fashions for three months.

When she'd left 18 Couper Street to hand in the letter asking if she could be considered for an interview Anna had put her hands behind her back and secretly crossed her fingers for luck. Of course, if Rachel was to be granted an interview then the letter would arrive at Bella's address. No such invitation by letter would arrive.

Rachel had walked into the store with her usual air of confidence and the manager, who was on the shop floor, sidled up to her, 'Can I help you?' he asked as he appraised her.

Hesitating, Rachel reached in her handbag and pulled out the letter. 'I'm just here to hand in this letter.'

Taking the communication that was addressed to himself, the manager opened the letter. Rachel smiled and turned to leave, stopping suddenly when he said, 'Wait. Please come into my office and take a seat.'

Half an hour later Rachel had been offered a position. She was, of course, to be the junior, who each morning and afternoon had to make the tea and tidy up the staff room. Rachel, although reluctant to clean up after anyone, readily agreed to these conditions and as the manager was escorting her to the door he hesitated.

'Look. I have an idea.' The manager purposely strode over to a model, which was dressed in an ocean blue wool coat with an astrakhan collar, and he removed it. 'Now, Miss Forbes, take off your coat and put this one on.' Rachel was bewildered. Why was this man giving her a new coat? 'And what I would like you to do,' he continued, strutting over the floor, 'is go with me to millenary and we'll get a matching hat and then all you require to do, for just half an hour, is walk about the store, with the same superior air you came in with. Every so often you must go out the main door into Great Junction Street and come back in the side entrance round in Taylor Gardens.'

Rachel thought the man was quite mad. Not so. Every time she paraded about either a coat or two hats were sold.

Naturally part of her daily duties was to select some of the expensive clothes and model them. One day Rachel even had to wear a musquash fur coat. Very slowly she allowed her hands to stroke the luxurious pelts. Sauntering about the store she felt every inch a lady; however, when emerging into Great Junction Street three rugged returning whalers wolf-whistled at her before one had the audacity to suggest, 'You might be pricy, hen, but after three years away in the frozen Antarctic I'll let you thaw me out and I dinnae care how much it costs!'

It was true that a ship carrying wealthy whalers – or they thought they were when they were paid off – had docked but so had a few other merchant ships that day.

So when Gus opened the door and walked in, Anna wasn't surprised. Looking at his kitbag that he'd just dumped down, she smirked. 'You'll just need to pick that up again because Bella bides up in Lochend Road now.'

'How come? We were a good few quid short,' Gus pointed out, giving his bulging wallet a few good slaps.

Anna explained about the loan from Sandy. 'I best be off then. I'm just dying to see Nat again.'

'Afore you rush off...' Anna was about to say 'And what about Bluebell', but then she realised that Bella had warned her she wanted it to be a great surprise for him. Hard to believe but she'd never told him about his daughter. Swallowing hard Anna quickly changed tack and blurted, 'And I hope now you've a braw family you'll be going up north to show them off to your kith and kin.'

Gus snorted and seemed unnerved by Anna's remark. He was looking at her but somehow he seemed lost for an answer but eventually he managed to drawl, 'Naw. I'm dead as far as they're concerned.'

Anxious for an explanation Anna deliberately waited for him to continue. The pause gave her time to study him and she could see his thoughts were far, far away. After first running his fingers through his hair and then drumming them on his chin he looked directly into Anna's eyes before menacingly stating, 'And best for all concerned if it stays that way. Is that clear?'

Gus had just departed when Anna sat down to think. What was it that Gus had done that was so heinous it was still to be kept secret? The problem of finding the answer to this riddle was still causing her a few sleepless nights. She was so obsessed with it that every opportunity she was afforded she tried to get an answer. A sly smile played on her lips when she thought back to three months ago when her brother Andy had returned from a long voyage.

After he'd spent time greeting Rosie and his children he, accompanied by young Davy, had come to visit her, his beloved sister. 'Guess what?' he said, putting down a parcel. 'This'll surprise you. Knew you wanted one. So I spent quite a lot of time doing this for you.'

'Oh, so you've written up the story about why you were able to blackmail Gus Cochrane.'

Andy stopped untying the parcel. 'Why would I do that, woman?'

Anna shrugged. She knew when her brother called her 'woman' she'd over-stepped the mark. Davy, sensing the growing tension in the room, looked from his father to his aunt, 'Something wrang?' he anxiously asked.

'Naw,' his father replied, staring at Anna. 'It's just your auntie sticking her nose in where she shouldn't.'

The parcel was then completely untied and Andy brought out a ship in a bottle. The voyage before he'd made one for Rosie and Anna had so admired it that he had silently vowed next trip he would make one for her. Anna now glanced at the ship that had pride of place on her mantelshelf and wondered if she would ever know the answer to the Gus enigma.

She rose and, going over to the calendar nailed to the wall, she ticked off nine months, thinking, *Oh, aye. As the New Year's heralded in so will Bella's third.*

18

THE *JEANIE WILSON*

Gus surprised not only himself but everybody else when he decided to give up going on long voyages – or, as Rye guessed correctly – two- or three-year whaling trips.

The two excursions to the Leith Whaling Station in Antarctica's South Georgia, where he had even done the punishing over-wintering, had given him a degree of financial security. This meant he was now in the happy position of being able to house himself and his family outwith the slums of Leith.

The security, however, had been bought at a heavy cost. It was not just the long hours of back-breaking work in intolerable conditions, nor the stench of boiling whale oil which would forever live in his nostrils – it was the self-imposed separation from his infant son that had cost him dearly. Deeply he regretted that no matter what, he could never buy back those years when he wasn't at home to see Nat take his first steps or hear him say his first words. It was a loss he could never right but it had taught him not to make the same mistakes with Bluebell.

Another reason for giving up the lucrative whaling trips was that by the end of the second trip Gus, for the first time in his life, began to feel his age, reminding him he was mortal. Nonetheless he was still driven by insatiable hunger for security. Still he had to earn money at any price, just so long as it provided a better life for his son and of course, his beautiful dainty daughter. He could still remember the joyful exhilaration he'd felt when he first held her in his arms.

Before his children arrived he hadn't really cared if he lived or died. Continually he had consoled himself by thinking death had advantages in that all outstanding debts would be cancelled. Now, however, all he wished to do was live to spend more time with what he thought he'd never have or value – his family. He also looked at Bella in a different light. Hadn't she put her shoulder to the wheel and helped to pay off any debt attached to their home in Lochend Road?

The change in Gus left Anna dumb-founded. His obsession with his children and Bella was quite revealing and, she thought, quite out of character. Vividly she remembered how he had to be blackmailed into marrying Bella and now they appeared to be a true love story with him cosseting and nurturing her at every opportunity.

He'd been home three weeks when he'd

told Bella he was going to search for a job. There was no doubt Gus had insight and he knew it would have been asking too much of himself to give up the sea completely. So on a blustery Friday afternoon he found himself patiently awaiting the return of the local fishing fleet to its home in Newhaven.

As each boat tied up he surreptitiously studied the crew. He knew Newhaven was a close-knit village community and each trawler was a family business. Marriage to anyone outside the village, especially to anyone from the neighbouring port of Leith, was not to be encouraged. 'So,' pondered Gus, 'just how am I, a foreigner married to a Leith woman, going to get a foot on board one of these vessels?'

The Carnie family boat had just anchored when he became aware of two distinctively dressed women walking purposefully along the quay. The several-layered skirts of the women were of mid-calf length and hitched up on either side, exposing the distinctive Newhaven fisher-wives' striped working dress. In contrast, their heads were adorned in unique Flemish-looking frilly caps. Gus also noted that to keep out the cold and rain – and also, he suspected, any admiring glances – they wore thick hand-knitted stockings and stout, neat shoes, which further emphasised their strong, healthy figures.

It was obvious that the industrious, thrifty

women were mother and daughter. The older woman was the first to take up a dominant stance. With arms akimbo and right foot forward she stared towards the open sea. The second woman, although younger (Gus judged her to be early middle-age), pointed to an inward coming trawler. The advance of the boat made both women relax and nod to each other.

The trawler, which Gus noted was called the *Jeanie Wilson,* quickly came alongside the quay but the women didn't move. It was very obvious, however, that they had business with this craft.

When a muscular young lad jumped from the boat and onto the harbour to secure the trawler the women again nodded to each other, indicating their pride and relief. The other five crew members followed the young lad onto land but the oldest, a man evidently too old for trawling, was not as agile as the rest and the women winced as he laboriously climbed down.

While the crew and women spoke, wily Gus approached an old man sitting on a capstan and engaged him in what appeared to be a casual conversation. In between puffs of his clay pipe and spitting into the water the aged fisherman told Gus how the trawler was owned by one of the Wilson families. He went on to softly confide that the skipper of the *Jeanie Wilson,* the husband of the younger woman, had recently died of a heart attack. This unfortunate happening meant that the young lad had been taken out of school to join the crew, and to make up for his inexperience the older man, his grandfather, had come out of retirement.

The women, who were sole traders, should have been out selling part of their menfolk's fishing harvest. In the younger woman's case, vending from her creel, no less than one hundred and twelve pounds' weight of fish, round the doors of Edinburgh. The older woman, now obviously too old to carry such a heavy creel, could normally be found sitting at the bottom of Leith Walk selling her wares from a barrow.

When the men climbed back on board to unload their good catch, Gus sauntered up and asked if they'd like a hand. 'And why would we need that?' the bemused old fisherman asked.

Gus pointed out to the horizon. 'Because a storm's brewing and I can work twice as fast as you.'

The aged man's laughter echoed round the harbour. 'Just twice?' he mocked, hoisting another box of fish on before signalling to swing the load onto the quayside. 'When I was your age, I could work the like of you to a standstill.'

Without uttering another word, Gus jumped aboard and suddenly the loaded hoist was flying off and on the boat so quickly the old man couldn't hide his astonishment.

Once the unloading was completed and most of the catch had been dispatched for auction, the old man came forward to Gus with an outstretched hand. 'Thank you, mate. I'm Charlie Wilson.' Gus nodded and Charlie continued, 'That unloading was quite a spectacle. But know what I'm wondering?' Gus shook his head. Charlie, silently contemplating, took off his hat, scratched his head and spat into the sea, then added, 'Just where you were taught to work as hard and as fast as you do?'

Warmly shaking Charlie's hand Gus replied, 'How about on two long harsh trips to very jaws of hell.'

Standing back, Charlie took a good look at Gus. He knew from the first handshake of his shovel-like hand that Gus was a no-nonsense bloke – a grafter – who was hungry for a job. Keeping Gus under constant scrutiny, Charlie wondered if hiring this tall, dark, muscular man would be what his family needed right now? He was sure he was right to consider this break from tradition by hiring someone from outside the local fishing community. After all, what his family immediately required was someone of Gus's experience who would be more than able to deal with any emergency that occurred at sea.

He knew he should be offering Gus a job but something – he didn't know what – was telling him all was not as it seemed with Gus. He paused to mull over the dilemma. *Why,* he asked himself, *would a money-hungry man, not afraid to graft, be looking for a much lesser-paid job than whaling?* Charlie was convinced that the deep knife gouges he'd felt when he shook Gus's hand told him he'd once been a whaler. Also why did he go twice to whale? For most men one trip was more than enough. 'So you were a whaler,' Charlie stated with emphasis.

'Retired.'

'That so. But why haven't you high-tailed it back up Peterburgh way where you hail from?'

Gus, unnerved that Charlie, by listening to his accent, could place him within ten miles of where he'd been born and raised, decided not to contradict him. Indeed he knew there was no advantage in saying he hailed from the far-flung Hebrides. But he also judged it was time to play an ace and, engaging Charlie with a smile, he replied, 'Married a lowland lassie. A Leither, to be precise.'

The mention of Leith brought about a change in Charlie's demeanour. 'Don't say we don't like Leithers,' he drawled. 'It's just that they're hard to thole. That's right, Daisy, isn't it?' he went on, turning to his wife for confirmation.

Daisy, aware that her husband was no longer fit enough to be back out fishing, took her time to answer. She knew people, like herself, just had to look at her husband to see his old bones were stiff and gnarled by a lifetime coping with his heartless mistress, the sea. Looking lovingly at him she wondered what use he would now be in a time of crisis. She accepted he wouldn't be able to react quickly enough and therefore he would be a liability – a liability that could compromise the safety of the other family members. The foregoing being the case, she looked quizzically at Gus before asking, 'Where about in Leith does your wife come from?'

'Lochend Road. You know the new houses,' replied Gus when he could see Daisy was no longer preoccupied.

'But I asked you where in Leith your wife comes from?'

'Couper Street. 18 Couper Street.'

Daisy face softened. 'You wouldn't know an Anna Campbell?'

Gus laughed heartily. 'Know her? She's the bane of my life. None other than my bossy mother-in-law.'

'Is she now?' replied Daisy, nodding her head. 'Aye, but one Bonnie Fechter, she is.' She gave a contemptuous sniff before elaborating, 'Just like us Newhaven wives, she rules the roost.'

'Aye, but at what price?' Gus paused and waited vainly for Daisy to respond. 'Left you speechless, have I?' he chuckled. She remained impassive so he added, 'And that's exactly what Anna does to all men! Oh aye, none of them are allowed to have an opinion.'

Daisy's head shook from side to side. 'You,' she said, pointing to Gus, 'and all your feckless cronies might think that – but I ken it sticks in your craw that, like the Salvationists she belongs to, any bairn that's wanting or homeless she takes in. Believe me, never a soul that has needed tending or feeding has she ever turned away.'

Gus pondered. 'You're right,' he conceded. 'My Bella's one of the bairns she's fostered.' He now realised that Daisy's admiration and respect for Anna could be the thing that could assist him to negotiate a job on the trawler.

Instinctively he knew Daisy Wilson needed him. She being, like Anna, a Bonnie Fechter would, no matter the consequences, do what was best for her family. She was well aware that her husband was too old to master the *Jeanie Wilson*, and her grandson – well, what would a green laddie know about how to read the signs of where the fish were? Not to mention his lack of knowledge of tides, reefs and winds. And when the weather changed to the fishes' advantage, would he be wise enough to head for shelter or foolish enough to chase them and flounder?

She had read Gus well. He was desperate for a job on a fishing vessel. But not having kith or kin in Newhaven, he would only get one if she gave the word to her menfolk to hire him.

At the conclusion of the deal Charlie had asked Gus to join him for a pint in the Anchor bar. As was the custom, Gus signalled to the barman just as soon as Charlie's pint glass was empty that he should serve up another round.

By the time Gus left the bar he had downed six pints and by the time he arrived home an irate Bella was waiting for him.

'Kept wee Nat up well past his bedtime, I did,' Bella loudly hissed. 'And all because, stupid me, believed you when you said you wanted to build up a relationship with him.'

'And I do,' lisped Gus. 'Now listen. I'm going back to work.'

Bella visibly relaxed. 'Oh, so you went to Leith Hospital to see about that porter's job that Sandy told you about?'

'No. The sea's in my blood...' he spluttered, staggering towards the table.

'Oh no. Don't tell me you've signed up for another two years?' wailed Bella, swallowing hard. 'I mean, what about the bairns? What about me? How am I going to manage?'

Bleary-eyed and still not steady on his feet, Gus threw himself down on a chair. 'What are ye talking about?'

'I know my auntie Anna told me never to argue with a man who's had his feet in the sawdust but I just have to have my say,' bawled Bella before whacking him with a dishtowel.

Gus shrugged then waved his hand to indicate she'd his permission to continue. 'What I would like to know is how you expect me to cope with two bairns and another on the way while you sail the seven seas?'

Gus rose and tried to grab hold of Bella who expertly evaded him. 'You're having another one?' he chuckled. 'That's just great!' Looking in the mirror he pointed his thumb back at himself before saying, 'Eat your heart out Dr Glaxo.'

'Well,' corrected Bella slowly, 'I don't know for sure. But as I explained to you that the lassies in Crawford's told me, that if I didn't want another baby for a couple years, which I don't, it would mean you getting off at Haymarket.'

Gus nodded and giggled. 'But as I didn't know where Haymarket was – didn't I, steed that I am, just gallop straight on to the Waverley.'

'Precisely,' hissed Bella. 'But in case I'm no away you can sleep in that chair until you go away to South Georgia.'

'But the *Jeannie Wilson* just trawls in the North Sea. No way could she make it to Antarctica.'

'What are you talking about?' Bella demanded, flashing her eyes upwards. 'Oh Lord,' she pleaded reverently. 'Please grant me patience.'

'What I'm trying to tell you is this: Daisy Wilson, a pal of your auntie's, gave the thumbs-up sign to her man to give me a job on their trawler. Oh, Bella,' he pleaded again, seeking to get hold of her, 'the sea's in my blood and this way I'll be happy and I'll be home every weekend.' He stopped, flashed her a wolfish smile, licked his lips, winked and whispered, 'And I might even try getting off at Haymarket, if you really want me to.'

Bella couldn't subdue the irritation in her voice. 'If you know what's good for you don't you dare talk to me like that,' she warned.

'Oh, I see, you were brought up by a Bonnie Fechter and now you think you're one as well.'

Opening the living room door Bella inhaled deeply before saying, 'Do me a favour. Go to bed and die there!'

The family had been up for two hours before Gus came back into the land of the living.

Sauntering into the kitchen he was surprised that Bella withered him with a hostile stare. Scratching his head, Gus muttered, 'Was it something I said or … maybe did?'

'No. It was the gallons you drank!' replied Bella, banging a plate of cold porridge in front of him.

Lifting a spoon and plunging into his breakfast Gus tittered when the spoon stayed upright in frozen solid offering. 'Aye, now where was I?'

'Well, when you remember perhaps you could let me into the secret too,' replied Bella in a voice leaden with sarcasm.

Blowing out his lips Gus was obviously having problems remembering and then slowly he brightened as his memory returned. 'Did I no tell you? I took myself to Newhaven.'

'Aye well, they mustn't be as particular as they used to be,' spat Bella, as Gus donned a quizzical look. 'Oh aye,' she further informed. 'Not any Tom, Dick or Gus do they allow to cross the bridge from George Street.'

Gus ignored Bella's comments on how the Newhaven folk kept themselves to themselves and proudly announced, 'And I got myself a job on a trawler.'

Bella sniggered. 'In your dreams.'

Going over and, trying to put his arms about her but unable to do so as she ducked behind the table, Gus announced with gusto, 'But I did get a start. So first of all I must get down to the shore and buy the clothes and gear I need.'

Bella, who was still stiff with anger and resentment, didn't respond so Gus then decided to change tactic and threatened, 'And that'll include a nice big gutting knife that might come in handy at home too.'

'Gus,' a contemptuous Bella answered, 'there is no way any skipper in Newhaven will share out the earnings of a boat with any stranger – especially one that bides in Leith.'

Sniffing Gus replied, 'You're right. But I've bargained with them and for half of what a Newhaven bloke gets paid they offered me a job.'

'Have you lost your marbles? How will we live on that?'

'I thought about that but I still agreed.' Gus went over and closed the door to the back garden. Raising his finger to his lips he signalled that they must not be overheard. 'You see I can work better and faster than any of them and I also have better knowledge and respect for the sea. So I'll go on a few trips for the pittance on offer.' He stopped to savour the moment. 'Then when they find out that they cannae do without me ... I'll put in my notice and...'

Bella, a true Leith woman, was now grinning. 'Renegotiate,' she shouted, punching the air.

'Precisely,' replied Gus, grabbing Bella and dancing her round the room.

Suddenly he stopped. 'But until the proper money comes in I was thinking – you know how the lassies working with Rachel are always asking her if you'll tell them their fortunes?' Bella, who was delighted her fame as a medium was spreading, nodded and Gus continued, 'Then why don't we put the word about that, if anyone crosses your palm with silver, you'll tell them their future in our front room on a Thursday night?'

Bella preened. It was not just the thought that she would be known as a fortune-teller in Leith, it was the fact that Gus believed she had the gift! 'Well, why don't I do it two nights a week and maybe a Saturday afternoon as well?'

As if he could push that idea away Gus raised his hands. 'No. One night only – and always when I'm at sea. Don't want people to think the hoodwinking of daft lassies has anything to do with me. No. No. I'll be your silent partner.'

Crestfallen Bella replied, 'But that means I'll still have to do shifts at Sandy's.'

'And that's good.'

Bella looked bewildered. Gus took her hand in his and gently stroked it before adding, 'But can't you see your gullible customers will think that when you're washing and dressing the dead you're also talking to them and getting the gen.'

Bella's mouth gaped. 'What are you talking about? Of course I talk to the dead when I'm washing and dressing them. It would be...' she paused, 'un–unfeeling to heave them into a wooden crate without a word of good luck and goodbye!'

19

DANCING UP A STORM

Rachel, firmly clutching the dress bag in her hand, emerged from the centre doors of the Leith Provident Department Store. As her heels clipped swiftly along the road her excitement grew. Bud had actually picked up the courage and asked her to accompany him to his firm's annual dinner dance to be held on Friday night. He'd also told her the orchestra had been instructed to play some modern dance music at the function. This was great news for Rachel who'd never been keen on the old-fashioned Victorian group dances where all you seemed to do was point your toe and pass behind your partner's back and emerge to curtsey to another man. She squirmed with delight as she thought of the modern dances – waltzes, foxtrots, tangos – all the type of dancing where you and your partner were afforded the opportunity to hold hands and dance cheek to cheek.

To add to her excitement, Bud had said there was to be a Charleston dance competition. She knew she was in with a shout to win this because, at every possible opportunity, she had perfected her routine. Added to her expertise of the dance she, unlike some, would be fittingly dressed with the dress and headdress that were secreted in her bag. Of course, to finish off her ensemble she'd invested in a long imitation pearl necklace that she would twirl and twist as she circled.

While nonchalantly swinging the bag it brushed against her leg, which reminded her of just how much she'd handed over to buy the necessary creations. Craning her neck until it hurt she wondered what Auntie would say about her reckless expenditure. It wasn't only the dress that had nearly broken the bank but the cost of the shoes, gloves and headdress had also been crippling.

She had asked Bella when she'd come into the shop to buy a maternity smock what she thought she looked like when she adorned her head with the feather creation and was somewhat put out when Bella replied, 'A demented hen!'

Rachel was now turning into Couper Street and half-turned when she heard someone call out, 'Wait a minute, Rachel. I've something to tell you.' Turning around completely she discovered there was no one to be seen. 'Rachel,' the disembodied voice called out again before Robert hobbled into view.

'Why are you limping?'

'The sole's hanging off my shoe. I'll need to get mending them,' replied Robert, lifting his leg so Rachel could view the problem.

Rachel sighed. Robert, who had been taught cobbling in the Industrial School, had been going to repair his shoes for over a week now and if he didn't carry out the necessary work soon they'd be too far gone to do anything with, but then that was Robert – everything would be done tomorrow. Trouble was, tomorrow never came.

Sensing his sister's disapproval he sidled up to her and whispered, 'But never mind my shoes ... I've got something to tell you.'

'And what might that be, Robert?' Rachel asked kindly because she remembered what an awful life her brothers had had until Auntie had taken them in.

'Well, to be truthful, three things actually. First is, did ye ken Johnny Campbell's home on demob leave?'

Rachel shook her head.

'Well, he is. And secondly,' Robert looked

about to make sure they were not being overheard, 'your pal Rosa's no got someone to chum her to Bertram's ball.'

'But I thought she was madly in love with that buffoon who's the projectionist in the Palace Picture House.' Rachel paused. 'And she's so crazy about him she thinks she might even consider marrying him – and that would be with or without her mammy's permission!'

'Ah well, after darling Mammy got her lamps on him she telt Rosa to give him the bum's rush. And Rosa, who has the backbone o' a jelly fish, gied the poor bloke the heave ho.'

'She did?'

'Aye,' confirmed Robert. 'And no only him but the twa others that followed.' Robert stopped when Rachel began to giggle.

'Now who were they?' asked Rachel, feigning ignorance.

'Don't start, Rachel. I ken fine you're the only one that doesn't find it impossible to keep up with Rosa's love life.'

'That's where you're wrong. Ever since she got employed as a clerkess in Bertram's engineering, where men outnumber women a hundred to one, I can't keep the head count either.'

'I asked Bud about her flirting madly at work,' Robert hunched his shoulders, 'and all he said was, right enough they worked beside her, but all she was trying to do was get one of them to partner her to the dance.'

'Well,' explained Rachel, who was trying to find an excuse for her friend's improper behaviour, 'she could hardly turn up un-escorted.'

'And why for no? Ye can at the Corner Rooms.'

'But it's okay to do that in a public dance hall in Leith – but it's not the done thing at the posh Edinburgh Assembly Rooms.'

Robert pondered. 'That's probably the reason she even asked Bud to take her. But he said he couldnae as he'd asked you. And then when Bud found out about Johnny being home he came up with the brilliant idea of getting Rosa to ask Johnny and then everybody would be happy – even Bud's mammy.'

Rachel, who had lost interest in her brother's banter, suddenly interrupted. 'What did you say about Bud's mammy being happy?'

'Well, Rosa says his mammy is like her mammy, and they dinnae think their bairns should get chummy with us Couper Street folk. Anyway, it seems Johnny's going to be asked to take Rosa, so what do you think of that?'

'The more the merrier,' quipped Rachel, thinking it would be nice to see Johnny again and more so for Auntie Anna who just adored him. 'And,' she continued, wishing to forget that Bud's mother didn't approve of her, 'what's the third thing that you're burning to tell me?'

'Just that,' Robert stopped, scuffing his shoe along the pavement before blurting, 'I've met this bonnie lassie from Bowling Green Street. Bunty Rankin's her name.'

Rachel's laughed out loud and clear. 'Robert,' she reminded, 'you met each other when you both started at Couper Street Infant School.'

'Och, I know that. But she's changed.'

'Changed? Are you saying that in fourteen years she's no longer a snotty-nosed, under-sized cry baby?'

Robert ignored Rachel's sarcasm. 'She's wee and dainty,' he whispered, putting his arm through Rachel's. 'And she says she needs a strong man like me to help her.'

'Do what?' demanded Rachel, pulling herself free from Robert.

'Like climb up into her house when she lost the key last week,' spouted Robert.

'Oh, sugar,' exclaimed Rachel, looking in disbelief at her brother. 'Robert. Robert. Please don't tell me you risked your life by climbing up a crumbling wall to a first-floor flat in Bowling Green Street?'

'Of course I did. And why shouldn't I?'

'Because, like us, they've nothing worth stealing so they don't lock their doors!'

Robert had to think before he responded. It was true what Rachel had just said. He vividly remembered how breathless he was after climbing up the wall. His hands and fingers were all scraped and bleeding from gripping the rough stones as he scaled. The hardest part of his escapade had been trying to prise open the window that had obviously not been opened for months – probably years. Eventually he managed to get the window and sill to grudgingly part for him to lever up enough space to allow him to wriggle into the room. On setting his feet down he was conscious of a cloying, stuffy unventilated smell that would never have been tolerated by Auntie, who was a firm believer in fresh air. That was not, however, the worst of it because when he got to the door he discovered it was open and there was no lock on it!

Anxious that his sister would think well of Bunty, he giggled before saying, 'She fancies me, she does. And it was all a ploy to get me to notice her.'

Rachel stayed non-committal, but she did think she would have to be careful, as she didn't wish to be like Bud's mother and judge people by where they were housed.

Entering the house they were surprised to see Johnny Campbell seated at the table, drinking tea. 'Well, are you not a sight for sore eyes?' he exclaimed, getting up and greeting Rachel and ignoring Robert.

'And I'm here too, Johnny,' remarked Robert. 'And I think she might need her hand to eat her tea – so you can put it down now.'

An embarrassing glow started to run up Johnny's neck and to his face. Rachel coyly smiled as she noted the flush deepened his bronzed skin. Allowing her gaze to linger on him she was pleased to see how muscular he'd become. Evidently the time spent in India had made a man of him.

With reluctance he let go of her hand when she asked, 'And are you really on demob leave, Johnny, or are you going to sign up again?'

Johnny shook his head to and fro. 'No. I really did enjoy the army and all the places I got to see.' He hesitated. 'But, you see, I was never in a war zone and I now know my conscience would never allow me to kill or maim another human being.'

'Here, Johnny,' exclaimed Robert with disdain, 'does your heid button up the back?'

Johnny, shaking his head from side to side again, looked quizzically at Robert.

'I think it does,' Robert announced. 'Because anybody who joins up to be a sodger surely kens they'll have to fire their rifle and if their aim's guid somebody will land up deid.'

Johnny was about to explain his reasoning

to Robert but Rachel, who could see that if an argument developed it could end up in fisticuffs and blood on the floor, interjected, 'Where's Auntie? And what's more important, where's my tea?'

'Your stovies are keeping warm in the there,' Johnny said, nodding towards the fireplace oven. 'And Auntie is playing midwife to Jessie Tate and Eva Green and in between delivering the bairns she's also going to be laying out auld Bert Souter.'

When Robert rescued their tea from the oven, Rachel's eyes espied an orange glass creation on top of the kitchen dresser. 'And what's that?' she asked, going over to inspect the sparkling object.

'Can you no see?' asked Johnny, lifting one of the small drinking glasses that were attached to the bowl by a hook. 'Bet all the posh houses you've been in hadnae a crystal punch bowl as grand as this. And see they wee things attached, Rachel, well they're eight wee drinking goblets.'

Rachel could have said that not only had she seen many punch bowls but that they were all more tasteful than this one, but not wishing to burst Johnny's bubble, she just smiled.

'The minute I saw it in a market in Calcutta,' he explained with a knowing nod to Rachel, 'I just knew that Auntie would want to own such a beautiful...' he stood back to let the late rays of the sun dance off the bowl and as the rainbow of colours circled the room he murmured with gushing pride, 'handsome crystal creation.'

Without taking her eyes from the bowl Rachel began to wonder if it was true that the sun was so hot and bright in India that it could affect your sense of reasoning. It was bad enough that Johnny hadn't realised that soldiers were expected to kill the enemy but surely he could not have forgotten that 18 Couper Street was a condemned slum? And it was only now that she and Robert were bringing in a bob or two that Auntie didn't have to be quicker than the seagulls and get any fish that fell off when the trawler men unloaded their catch onto the quayside in Newhaven. 'So when, dear Johnny,' she silently asked, 'do you think Auntie will throw a party and serve punch in those dainty glasses to the likes of her dear pal, Rye, who since she married Ratty drinks stout from heavy metal tankards and her loyal sister-in-law Rosie who likes nothing better than a good sniff of snuff?'

Rachel was still thinking about the ornate monstrosity (as she saw it) when Auntie came in.

Knowing Rachel as well as Rachel knew herself, Anna was aware that the punch bowl was just too ostentatious for Rachel's refined taste. Worried in case Rachel would say something out of turn about Johnny's present, Anna, feigning delight, picked one of the little cups off the bowl and handed it to Rachel for examination. 'Have you ever seen anything quite so ... so exquisite?' she simpered.

Taking the cue from her aunt Rachel responded, 'No. I'm quite jealous.' Before replacing the small goblet she turned to Johnny and, adopting a dazzling smile, she asked, 'And did you bring anything as handsome for me?'

Anna, realising that Johnny had only brought something for her, his adored aunt, quickly interjected, 'Yes. He brought his handsome self.'

Rachel, who had taken up Bella's offer of a long soak in the bath at Lochend Road, was now standing in Robert's room getting herself dressed for the dance. Pulling on her very expensive, pure silk stockings she thought how much nicer it would have been if Bud had just been calling for her on his own.

For years she'd dreamed of him picking her up and then they would go off to spend a romantic night dancing with each other. 'Huh,' she exclaimed out loud before going back to her reflections, 'all because of the snobbery of Bud and Rosa's mothers they were going as a foursome. Bud would call in for Johnny and then they would come for her and lastly they would pick up Rosa. Only Bud, who was to pretend he was taking Rosa to the dance, would ring the bell and bound up the stairs while Johnny and Rachel hid in the doorway of the Leith Provident Department Store.

Emerging from the room Rachel felt she was the personification of sophistication, that was until Anna looked up from her sewing and gasped, 'Oh, good heavens, you're not going out in a dress that's only half there. Tell me you're not?'

'Auntie, I know you like skirts to be down to mid-calf but this is now the Roaring Twenties and the Charleston can't be danced with your legs hampered in long petticoats.'

To demonstrate her reasoning, Rachel began to dance a wild Charleston. Soon her legs were flying in all directions and as she swung her mandatory long string of beads Anna at first was horrified but as Rachel pivoted on her toes she began to relax and enjoy the spectacle.

'Like your mother, you are. Just a daredevil too and you *do* look so good,' commented Anna before quietly adding, 'but be careful, lassie. Don't be like your mother and throw yourself away on a waster!'

The dance exceeded Rachel's expectations. The grandeur of the two dance halls, which meant you could choose between conventional ('decent' as Anna would say) or modern romantic dancing, coupled with the magnificent banquet which had been served by waiters in tail coats who were expert at silver service, had left her speechless. She became mesmerised by the dresses of the ladies. Most of the designs were so fashionable just now – simple elegance and yet so comfortable to wear.

Rachel had seen the designs in magazines that Eugenie had passed on to her and she would not have been surprised if the now-famous couturier, Gabrielle Chanel, had walked into the ballroom with one of her now-famous evening scarves, of which Rachel owned an imitation of, draped around her neck. The men were attired in evening dress, mostly hired for the evening as Bud and Johnny's suits were.

Always she would remember how she felt that she was in a fairytale when, for the first time, Bud waltzed her round the floor. She just couldn't believe that all her dreams seemed to be coming true. Everyone who looked at them could see that they were madly in love – instinctively they looked as if they belonged together. This fact was not wasted on Johnny, who could only think that, for some, dreams never materialise.

When the competition for the Charleston was announced Rosa had grabbed Bud and dragged him onto floor. Johnny then approached a crestfallen Rachel. 'Know I'm second-best but would you give it a try with me?'

Rachel laughed. She so enjoyed doing the Charleston that rather than miss doing the dance she would have been happy to accept Jack the Ripper as a partner. Johnny thankfully was not a creepy, back-street murderer. In fact, when they took the floor she thought he was as handsome and charming as Douglas Fairbanks, her favourite film star – and she had noted that his latest film, *Robin Hood,* was to be shown in the Palace Picture House next week and she would be first in the queue!

As the music took hold of her, thinking of Douglas Fairbanks was pushed into the background and she didn't need to wait for the judges to ask the other contesting couples to leave the floor as they all stopped, one by one, to watch and admire her and Johnny, who danced so well together that they could have been mistaken for professionals. Indeed their expertise was such that no one could have blamed the judges for thinking they'd practised regularly together instead of them just being naturals who instinctively danced expertly together!

20

MISTAKES MADE RIGHT

A year ago Rye had been re-housed in a three-bedroom luxury (as Rye saw it) corporation tenement flat in Redbraes, just beyond Bonnington Road, but as far as Anna was concerned, a far-too-long fifteen-minute walk away from Couper Street.

Rye's going had left a void in Anna's life. Rachel wondered why because it was a funny week that Rye didn't visit at least three times and she always dropped everything when Anna needed her to help as an assistant unqualified midwife or undertaker.

Rachel and Robert had just left for work when Anna had time to think about the bombshell Robert had dropped last night. The stupid laddie had managed to get Bunty Rankin in the family way and now her father, if he ever got sober that is, was threatening to … well if he did do what he threatened it would have a hidden bonus in that his Bunty's expected bairn would be the first and last to be fathered by Robert.

Sighing, Anna looked up at the ceiling. 'Sorry, lass,' she said to Norma, her late friend. 'I did try to steer your bairns right but...' Still pondering she rose, took the boiling kettle off the fire. 'Well,' she continued, 'once Bunty got her hooks in him there was nowt I could do. And I know you'll be disappointed because he'll do the decent thing and marry her and then it will be bairn after bairn and he'll never get out the bit. Poor soul will be so weighed down with debt and...'

'That's no you speaking to Norma again?' a shrill voice interrupted.

Turning Anna was relieved to see Rye. 'Aye, just telling her about last night and wondering if she'd any comments.'

'Oh, so you know?' Anna nodded. 'Well,' enthused Rye before sitting down, 'they might make a go of it – plenty of us have. Look at your Bella.'

Anna quickly masked the tea and brought it over to the table. Pulling out two chairs she sat on one and indicated to Rye to sit down on the other. 'I know that you're a good friend, Rye, and want to cheer me up but looking at Bella right now will only make me want to throw myself off the swing bridge.'

Fishing in her bag Rye brought out two bran scones. 'I buttered them afore I came over. And eh, what's up with your Bella now?'

'She's away again.'

'Och, that'll make five she'll have. Quite a

261

handful for her.'

'I know that. But she says I've no to worry as, and you've to keep it secret too from the men and the church,' Anna leaned closer to Rye and whispered, 'a woman doctor is starting one of those Maria Stopes-type clinics in Edinburgh's south side. You know that woman who advises women about ... birth control.'

'I know about some of they methods. Ratty and I tried the rubbers twice last week. And they do work.' It was now Rye's turn to bend over and whisper to Anna. 'But Ratty says it's like chewing a caramel with the paper on. So we just ... anyway since wee Duncan came along I think I'm well ye ken ... past the change.'

Anna got flustered. 'Oh, my Bella was only saying she might get fitted with a Dutch cap.'

'What?' exclaimed Rye. 'And what use would there be in going to bed with a frilly hat on yer heid?' She let out a bawdy chuckle before spluttering, 'And you have to admit that frilly caps have no done much to keep the family sizes doon in Newhaven, have they?'

'No. Not a frilly hat for her head, a cap for putting...' Anna's face was burning with embarrassment and she blustered, 'you know,' as she waved her hand over the top of her legs.

Rye was stunned into silence. She knew Anna claimed she was still a virgin but surely with all the bairns she'd delivered she realised that putting a cap on down there would do nothing but get in the road.

Realising there was no use in trying to further explain the objective of the Dutch rubber cap, Anna changed the subject. 'But Rye,' she confided, 'birth control's no the real worry – hasn't Gus gone and lost his place on the boat.'

Rye gasped. 'Eh. But I thought he was the one keeping them aw afloat?'

'Now,' said Anna, nodding in agreement, 'I'm no, as you know, his biggest fan but he did sort out all their problems. And okay, after a year went by and he knew they realised they couldnae do without him he demanded and got a full share of the profits. But him being so efficient, well... did it no stick in the craw o' their young grandson they'd given the title of skipper to.'

'Right enough, it's one of the Wilson family boats he was on and always their skipper is related by blood.'

Anna nodded. 'And the young buck thinks he knows it all and no way was he having Gus getting all the credit.'

'So he sacked him,' gasped Rye. 'What a stupid, blinking laddie. But here, what's his granny, Daisy Wilson, saying about all this?'

Anna shrugged. 'To tell you the truth, I'm

surprised she's done nothing – especially when her kinfolk could be riding out a gale-force ten with a naïve hothead at the helm.'

'Right enough.'

'Aye, and here was my Bella going to give up the job with Sandy and I was quite happy about that because – och, my eyes Rye.' Anna vigorously rubbed her forehead. 'I just cannae see to do the intricate small sewing any more and so I could do with working full-time for Sandy.'

'And for sure,' chortled Rye, 'the dead'll no notice if you've stitched them up with ower big tacking stitches.'

'Naw. They never give you any grief, the dead don't,' was Anna's despondent reply.

Sipping slowly from her cup, Rye pondered. She was trying to think of something that was going right for Anna just now. But she conceded there was nothing really except ... Rachel. 'Here, is there no sign of your Rachel getting engaged to that Bud guy? They've been going steady for a while now and he's nuts about her.'

'We know that. And if Bella is to be believed, she says the spirits know that too and they've told her a big surprise is coming our way.'

A rustling of paper followed by a soft knock on the door caused both women to shudder and look expectantly at each other.

'It cannae be the rent man – I paid him

yesterday,' whispered Anna, drawing the sugar bowl nearer to her. 'And I hope it's no some poor cratur needing a sugar poultice put on a carbuncle,' she went on as she shoogled the bowl, 'because there's nowt but a couple of spoonfuls in there.'

Rye rose and before crossing the floor she asked, 'But is this no the night Sandy pays you your wages?' Anna nodded. 'Then if it's a poultice that's needed they'll need to come back the morn.'

When the door opened Anna could see that Rye was perplexed. 'Problem, Rye?' she asked.

'Naw. It's some old fishwife and I think she wants to sell you some fish but as you're skint...'

Before Rye could continue the woman brushed past her and Anna was surprised to see Daisy Wilson sling a pauchle of fish on the table.

Anna being at least a foot shorter than Daisy attempted to add to her stature by pulling herself up. 'If that's a peace offering,' began Anna, pushing the parcel back towards Daisy, 'then it's no here you need to deliver it.'

'No. This fish is...' Daisy paused. She knew she was not what anyone would call diplomatic and she would need to walk a tightrope here so she warmly smiled before adding, 'For you. Because I ken how you've always had a sair time making ends meet and feeding awbody that's starving.'

'Maybe so, but I don't need charity,' was Anna's hostile retort.

'Och, woman, it's no charity. If you dinnae want a couple o' haddies and a few herring then toss them out the window to the gulls.'

Grabbing hold of the pauchle Rye lifted the fish to safety. 'That'll be right. And thanks, Daisy. And believe me. Nae bird'll stuff its gob with this fish as long as yin bairn in Couper Street needs a feed.'

Anna considered putting Daisy in her place but hadn't Rye become Daisy's unlikely ally. This meant Anna could be at a disadvantage and was not sure to come out on top. In fact, any confrontation could result in her falling out with one or maybe both of them. And that wouldn't do. So graciously she indicated for Daisy to sit down. 'Will you wet your thrapple with us?' she asked, pouring a cup a tea for Daisy.

Rye's raucous laughter echoed. 'And if we had any scones we could have offered you one on jam,' she was now laughing bawdier, 'that would be if we had any jam – but we've nane of that either.'

'Daisy,' began Anna, lifting her cup to sip from it, 'my head doesnae button up the back. So, thanks for the fish, but if the real reason you're here is to get me to mediate in the row between your laddie and my Bella's man – well you've backed a loser.'

Rocking her head from side to side Daisy chuckled. 'Naw. Like you I fight my ain battles. All I want is his address. I ken he bides in Lochend Road but I can hardly walk the length of it shouting, 'Caller herring', in the hope that he'll recognise my dulcet tones and come out.'

All three women were now laughing. 'He bides in the main door just next to the store,' a relieved Anna advised.

'The Leith Provident shops on the corner of Lochend Road and Hermitage Park?'

Anna looked quizzically at Daisy. 'You've already been up there searching for him.' Daisy said nothing so Anna continued with her theory. 'I just knew leaving that unholy mess for a month just wasnae you. Aye, Daisy, there's no many up afore you in the morning.'

Daisy nodded. 'But rest assured. Settled this day the mess will be, or my name's no Daisy Wilson.'

'Hope you're right, Daisy,' a pensive Anna replied. 'But like you he can be quite cussed. Even *I* have to walk round about him as if I was walking on egg shells.'

Anna was surprised when Daisy winked and confided, 'Aye, but when you go into battle with the likes of – what's your son-in-law's name again?'

'You losing it, Daisy? Ye ken fine his name's

Gus Cochrane, or on a Sunday Angus Cochrane, and he hails from the far-flung Hebrides.'

Rising Daisy nodded but Anna was not convinced Daisy wasn't on a fishing trip of her own. She was just about to try and find out what she was up to when another rap came to the door.

Putting on her shawl Rye said, 'I have to get going.' She turned to speak direct to Daisy. 'No offence, but an hour ago I've left my eldest lassie to care for my baby. She's good with him but my wee Duncan likes his mammy best.' Turning back to Anna she continued, 'I'll get the door on my way out.'

Throwing the door open wide so Anna could see who was standing there, Rye shouted, 'Oh, it's yourself, Mrs Rankin. Come away in. I think Anna's just dying to have a wee word with you.'

Before Anna could say a proper goodbye to Daisy she'd taken her cue from Rye and left. She didn't need to be Sherlock Holmes to realise Mrs Rankin had serious confidential business she required to sort out with Anna.

The minute the door closed Mrs Rankin, wringing her hands, whined, 'I'm real sorry, Miss Campbell, about the trouble that's been brought to your door. I mean it must be very hard for you, a Salvationist, holding your head up after what your Robert's done.'

'No,' replied Anna, clearing the table. 'And Mrs Rankin, it's *your* daughter that's in trouble, not my chosen son.'

Humiliated, Mrs Rankin was suddenly filled with rage and she quickly spat back, 'Aye, but my Bunty didnae go into your Robert's trousers and help herself!'

'She didn't?'

Mrs Rankin was now on her feet and heading for the door. 'My Bunty,' she screamed, 'was an innocent until your Robert took a loan of her. Without question she does everything he tells her to.'

The door firstly was flung open and Mrs Rankin disappeared into the lobby before it was forcibly banged shut. Within minutes the door creaked open again and Mrs Rankin's head peered sheepishly round it. 'Look, Miss Campbell,' she whimpered. 'I didnae come to argue about who was to blame. I just wanted to know how many of you will be at the church next Saturday for the wedding and if you all like Dickson's mince pies?'

Anna was grateful for the peace that had settled in the house since they'd all left. Remembering the happenings of last night and this morning she felt as if she had been put through a wringer.

Allowing herself the luxury of a mischievous titter she remembered Daisy and the fish. It was true she'd not been down to Newhaven to do battle with the seagulls for two years now. At the start it had been because Gus, or to be correct Bella, always made sure she got more than a fair share of his pauchle. But now Gus was no longer trawling that meant she did need to be standing waiting for trawlers landing their fish and hoping some would fall off. Sadly she looked down at her hands and flexed them. The truth was there to see. Her fingers were so rickety and twisted now she couldn't even fight a sparrow and win, never mind a seagull. She tittered again and rubbed her lower back and thought, *And if I did fall down there's no guarantee I'd ever get up again.*

Squinting up at the clock she sighed, thinking, *Is that the time? Och, I cannae believe I should be up on my feet and out to Sandy's. Thank goodness the dead make allowances for you being slow and clumsy.*

She was buttoning her coat when another knock came to the door. Thankfully it was the postman with a letter from Freddie. She was pleased to read that they liked Canada and although things had been difficult at the start it looked now as if things would work out for them.

Being one of the few in Leith who could afford a pram – and a Silver Cross coach-built one purchased from the Scott's pram shop in Yardheads at that – Bella took every opportunity to show off the vehicle by proudly pushing it down Lochend Road. Today there was the baby at the top of the pram and two toddlers sitting in the bottom.

She was just struggling out the front garden gate when she saw Daisy Wilson coming up the road, but before she could challenge her Daisy had disappeared. But to where? Bella shrugged. She had wanted to give Daisy a piece of her mind, and she would eventually, but as Rachel was with her she decided perhaps today was not the day, so she didn't go in search of Daisy.

Daisy, who had jumped into the store butcher's shop, discreetly watched as Bella and Rachel crossed Hermitage Park and then sauntered down the street until they disappeared. Quickly declining the butcher's offer of some fine sausages, she skipped from the shop in Hermitage Park, danced round the corner into Lochend Road and then up the pathway of Gus's house.

With Bella and the children gone Gus had settled down to read his paper when the front doorbell summoned him.

Through the stained-glass panel he was able to make out that it was Daisy Wilson. Before opening the door he composed himself by inhaling deeply. He also counselled himself that his feeling of injustice was in no way due to her actions. Nonetheless, it did rankle that he'd been sacked by a green whipper-snapper who thought he was Neptune and could control the waves. The result of all this was he, with all his maritime experience, was labouring like a coolie in the dust-laden hemp store of the notorious Roperie in Bath Street.

Daisy was surprised to find Gus grinning from to ear to ear when he opened the door to her.

'Looking for to sell me some fish?' he teased.

Daisy shook her head. 'No. Just think it's time for you and me to talk about the fine kettle of fish we're all in.'

Gus blew out his lips in a contemptuous puff, hunched his shoulders and began to close the door. Daisy quickly prevented this by sticking her foot in and her warning stare told him not to jam the door any further on it. 'As I've already said – we need to talk.'

Opening the door further Gus, with a curt nod of his head, bade her enter and was surprised she hesitated before saying, 'No. I won't come in.'

Daisy's reluctance bewildered Gus who then asked, 'So you won't come in. Then why in the name of heavens are you...?'

Daisy, who appeared not to have heard

Gus speak, slowly continued, 'You see, I feel I would be at a disadvantage in your house – so definitely not here.' She again paused to think before saying, 'Would be best for us to meet on neutral ground.' He nodded. 'You know Mother Aitkin's Roadhouse at the end of Leith Links? I'll meet you there in half an hour,' she suggested with a knowing nod.

Shaking his head Gus gave a series of half laughs. 'And why would I run to your beck and call? Just go, eh.'

'Oh, you'll come. You see, I knew you might be stubborn so I wondered what would move you and ... Murdo...'

The colour drained from Gus's face and she could see a look of exactly what? Terror, anger or was it even some sort of relief in his eyes before he nodded and closed the door?

Mother Aitkin's was an old-fashioned type of roadhouse where, in addition to selling good ale that the dockers and workmen drank greedily to quench their thirst, it also provided good wholesome food.

By the time Gus arrived Daisy had ordered up two plates of soup along with chunks of home-baked bread. Bowing her head Daisy said, 'Dear Father, for what we are about to receive we give you our grateful thanks.'

Gus smiled to himself. He'd forgotten fisher-folk always thanked God before eating. Lifting his spoon he started to lazily stir his soup round and round. 'And, Daisy,' he said, lifting his eyes to stare directly into hers, 'what exactly are you dishing up? Perhaps something I might thank God for?'

Daisy pushed her soup to the side and leaned forward on the table. The determination he knew she was capable of was clearly stamped on her face. 'This is the deal. You come back to work on the *Jeanie* this Monday as assistant skipper.'

'That'll be right,' snapped Gus. 'If you think I'm going to let your grandson tell me what to do.'

Sticking her tongue in her cheek Daisy sniffed. 'Oh, I think you will when you hear the rest of what I have to say.'

'You think so?' he replied with a 'huh', before rising. 'Well let me tell you,' he went on vehemently, 'the day I work with your grandson again there'll be two suns in the sky!'

Daisy, emotions completely in control, just sat with a smug smile on her face. This complacent attitude only served to further infuriate Gus.

Through gritted teeth he then hissed, 'Don't you realise, woman, it's just a matter of time until your precious grandson is not only at sea but is also in it!'

'And don't you think I'm well aware of that and that's why I'm here today? So sit down.'

'Why should I?'

'Because Gus, it's true what Bernard Shaw says in *Pygmalion*. There are those, like my Charlie, who can listen to a person's accent and place them within a few miles of their place of birth. In Charlie's case he only requires to hear another fisherman speak and he can pinpoint to within ten miles of where he hails from.' Daisy paused, stuck her tongue out and licked her lips before confidently going on. 'And he says that you hail from around Peterhead!'

'He's mistaken. And if all you have is his notion that my accent tells him I come from the northeast and not the far northwest, well ... good-day and goodbye.'

'I'm no fool. We fisher-folk have a network and I made enquiries and it seems there's a tale that's regularly told up Peterhead way about a young lad called...'

Gus didn't let her finish. 'Okay. So you think you can blackmail me?'

'No. I'm just going to talk to you in a dialect you'll understand.'

'Dress it up as you like, Daisy, but in my book no matter how you say it – it's nothing but stinking, sinister blackmail!'

Daisy, in no way intimidated by Gus's outburst, relaxed. 'You will still get your fair and whole share of the profits, Gus,' she began. 'But you must agree to take on my grandson and make him the best skipper to sail out of Newhaven.'

'Huh,' responded Gus, without attempting to conceal his scepticism. 'And who's going to make him take heed of me?'

'I've already counselled him and he knows the score. He respects you and he stays skipper of a happy trawler. If he doesn't...' She inhaled deeply which heaved up her ample bosom and this action assisted her to summon the courage she required to say, 'Then against all our traditions I'll make you skipper and arrange a transfer for him to gut, day in and day out, in Croan's fish house.' She allowed a long pause to hang between them before sagely adding, 'Pity the young always have to be taking on the old stags but, as *you* well know from experience, Gus, the rutting season does eventually pass.'

Gus nodded. He'd forgotten that Daisy, wily old bird that she is, was well educated and he knew she wasn't only talking of the grief her grandson's impetuosity had caused – but also his.

'I'm a fair woman, Gus,' she continued, patting her chest where she kept her money hidden, 'so I promise you I'll never mention Peterhead to anyone. Your secret is safe with me.'

They were both looking directly into each other's eyes and she hoped he could read that she was a woman of her word. From what she'd said he knew she was guessing about his troubled past. Fortunately, the whole sordid story was only known to himself and Andy Campbell – and it was not in the interest of either of them to ever divulge it to another living soul. However, he would allow Daisy to think she had him in her pocket because he wanted back to the fishing where, in vibrant clean air, he could earn the good money he required to keep his family.

'Look, I accept your assurances,' he drawled, 'but please believe me, my wife and my family mean *everything* to me and anyone who would try to destroy that ... well, now you've managed to contact the old wives in Peterhead...' He didn't finish his menacing warning – he didn't require to – all too well she understood the terms of their bargain.

Before rising to leave she put her hand over Gus's and further promised, 'I will also give you, in cash,' again she patted her bosom, 'a yearly bonus, on the understanding that it is a personal deal between you and me.'

Gus was astounded. This was an indication of how far Daisy would go to make sure she didn't lose her precious only grandson to the sea. 'Give me your word,' Daisy further demanded, 'that you won't divulge our arrangement to anyone – even your wife.'

Gus and Daisy both nodded their agreement. 'And I also guarantee,' Daisy whispered, 'if you keep your part of the bargain, that for as long as you wish I promise you'll always have employment within my family businesses.'

21

AN UNLIKELY PROPOSAL

As the year drew to a close Anna sat reminiscing. She thought it had been an eventful twelve months. The changes, she acknowledged, had begun even before the year started. Anna inhaled as she relived the relief when Gus and Daisy had been able to find acceptable solutions to their mutual problems. Indeed, hadn't peace descended on the *Jeanie Wilson* with the truculent skipper and his assistant appearing to be always willing to bend with the wind?

Bella had then given birth to her fifth child. Little Annabella had been delivered, not like her other siblings by Anna, but by a doctor.

Anna allowed herself a slight laugh. Rye had thought she'd have felt slighted by a doctor doing the delivery but Anna had reluctantly admitted she wasn't as able as she used to be, so rushing up Lochend Road in the middle of the night was no longer an option. The other reason why she was pleased was that Bella and Gus were prospering and therefore could afford a doctor's extortionate (in Anna's opinion) fee.

Now that her memories were in full flight she thought about Robert who, when Bunty had gone into labour, had flown along Great Junction Street and on to Couper Street just to have Anna and no one else deliver his daughter. The most pleasing thing about the birth was that Robert insisted that his daughter be called Norma.

Looking out the top of the window at the storm clouds chasing across the sky, she grimaced. Most things hadn't been too bad this year but... Hesitating, her thoughts now strayed to Rachel and she was wondering what was wrong with Bud? For years he'd strung Rachel along and as the lassie was approaching twenty-one and no ring on her finger it was becoming embarrassing. Anna suspected his mother, who had always considered a lassie brought up in Couper Street, round the corner from where she'd been reared, to be inferior to her son was to blame for Bud's reticence. But how could Bud's mother look down on her Rachel? In Anna's opinion, Rachel was the best and most tastefully turned-out lassie, not only in Leith but Edinburgh as well.

You never saw her with a scarf around her head. No. When Rachel went out she was always wearing a small head-hugging hat of some description. Anna knew she favoured the small hats because they allowed her long, now nearly black, glistening hair to be shown off to advantage.

Thinking of Rachel always brought a smile to Anna's face. Today as she beamed she thought back to how easy it had been for her to request that she take her from the orphanage to rear her as her own. Tears flooded her eyes as she acknowledged they were meant to be together. There was no doubt she loved Bella and all the boys dearly but Rachel from the start had been the daughter of her heart.

Anna's head shot up when a pounding on the door disturbed her. She shuddered and alarm bells rang in her head. The panic was not because of the pounding on the door but from the guttural tirade spewing from the drunkard's mouth.

Rising quickly she wrenched open the door and Gabby reeled in. Kicking him until he finally rolled over and was therefore no longer an obstruction to preventing her closing the door, she hissed, 'And what the blazes do you want?'

'Aaah, aaah,' he slavered, grabbing hold of the end of the wax table-cover which he managed, along with the contents of the table, to pull down on himself.

'Be quiet, you drunken sod. I've got neighbours and I have to live here so I don't need you giving me a showing up.'

Gabby was now sitting upright and brushing precious sugar from his hair and knives from his overcoat. 'Anna, I need yer help, hen.'

'You what?'

'Aye, you see, the sadistic buggers have chucked me oot.'

'Are you saying you've lost your job and you're expecting me to give you a handout?'

'Naw. I'm still yin of the best riveters going. Aye, aw the shipyairds would like to employ me.' Gabby blew out his lips with pride before uttering another throaty moan. 'Naw, you see Anna. It's my house – I've been chucked oot.'

'So what's that to do with me? If I'd been your landlord I'd have sent for the sanitary to dump you on the street years ago.'

Gabby ignored Anna's tirade. 'And I thought, you being a good Christian woman who takes in all sorts of strays needing a hame, you'd welcome me noo ye only have Rachel.' Gabby continued to slaver profusely and attempting to wipe his chin with the back of his hand he only managed to make the mess worse. 'Noo,' he earnestly continued his plea, 'we could baith benefit. I'm willing to take ower yer back room and you'd get the turn of a bob or two rent off me.'

Taking the opportunity to give him another kick, Anna responded, 'That back room of mine has been used by Rachel ever since Robert left.' Anna now pointed to the back bedroom. 'Rachel sleeps in there with all her stuff round about her and I sleep in,' she now pointed to the bed behind her, 'in there. So sir, there's no way I would allow you to disrupt Rachel's life!'

Rocking backwards and forwards Gabby appeared to be deep in thought. Slowly his demeanour changed and making a grab for Anna's leg he pulled her down beside him. 'Oh, Anna,' he exclaimed as he imprisoned her chin in his right hand. 'I didnae ken you cared.'

Shrieking, Anna struggled to be free but he managed to get hold of her mass of hair that she'd imprisoned in a chignon on the top of her head. Rolling over the floor together her now pure-white hair cascaded over her face. 'What in the name of heavens are you talking about, you drunken buffoon?' she managed to splutter.

Gabby released Anna and they sat facing each other. 'Just that you,' he said, putting out his hand to cover hers, which made her promptly wriggle further away, 'don't want to put me in Rachel's room because you want me to share *your* bed!'

As panic gripped her Anna tried desperately to crawl away out of Gabby's reach and towards a chair. She was still endeavouring to lever her unyielding arthritic frame up when thankfully Rye burst in.

'I heard the screams,' stammered Rye while trying to take in the situation. 'Oh my goodness. What in the name of all that's holy is going on in here?' she cried, assisting Anna up and onto the chair.

Through her uncontrollable sobs Anna whimpered, 'That pig wants to come and stay here with me and not only that he even had the nerve to...' Anna's head trembled and sobs racked her. There was no way she could even utter the obscenity that Gabby's suggestion was to her.

Putting her arms around Anna all Rye could utter was, 'There, there. You're not alone. I'm here.'

By now Gabby had struggled to his feet. 'Look, Anna,' he spluttered, 'if it's us no being churched that's the problem then ... mind you ... against my better judgement it would be, but...'

Breaking from Rye's hold Anna lifted a plate from the bunker and swiftly broke it over Gabby's head. 'Me, marry you?' she spat. 'I'd rather throw myself into hell's burning fire!'

Gabby shrugged. 'Look, you'll need to take me in. For if you dinnae I'll need to go into the lodging house in Parliament Street. Is that what you want?'

Reaching for the mantelpiece Anna retrieved her purse and taking coins from it she flung them towards Gabby. 'Here. There's the price of your first week's lodgings. Now get out of my sight.'

Rye's eyes were darting between Anna and Gabby and she found herself trying to swallow her fist to stem her laughter when Gabby, picking up the coins from the floor, asked, 'Am I right in thinking, Rye, that Anna here doesnae want me as a husband?'

The store had been closed for fifteen minutes before Rachel and two of her workmates emerged into Taylor Gardens.

Rachel had been reluctant to transfer to the newly opened chemist part of the store. Nonetheless she had been persuaded to leave women's fashions, where she was still a junior, by being offered a senior shop assistant's post in the make-up department.

She had really blossomed in the job and had become quite expert in her knowledge of cosmetics and perfumes – Ponds, Yardleys, Coty travellers were soon courting her in an effort to get her to promote their merchandise. Of course, she had also to attend to the less glamorous side of the business – cough cures, chest rubs, bunion pads, pile ointment, etc.

As the door closed behind the young women, Rachel noticed Bud loitering on the corner. 'Look girls, there's my boyfriend,' she said, skipping towards Bud. 'See you all tomorrow.'

'Rachel,' chorused Bud as soon as they were alone. 'Our luck has changed. I've just been asked by my boss if I'd like to go, for two years, to our sister company in America.'

'Oh,' was all Rachel could utter.

'Look, let's sit down on that bench over there,' Bud continued while propelling her over to Taylor Gardens. 'Now what that means is since we have an understanding we could get married right away and I could take you with me.'

Trying to keep her excitement in check Rachel muttered, 'We have an understanding?'

'Well, I understood that you understood that we had an understanding,' blustered Bud. He then stopped and waited for a response from Rachel but her attention seemed to be far away so he went on, 'Surely after all this time you knew that one day we would get married.'

Reminding Rachel of just how long she'd waited for him to ask her to marry him brought all the resentment she felt about his mother to the surface. Rachel knew that Bud was deterred by his mother always spouting, 'Surely you're not going to throw yourself away on a lassie from Couper Street. And remember, Bud,' she would add with feigned maternal concern, 'I'm not saying there was a ... let's say "unseemly" reason ... but as everyone in Leith knows there never was an acceptable one as to why her saintly auntie wheeled her in a *fish barrow* away from her father's house in Coatfield Lane!' She then would allow a long silence to hang before simpering sweetly, 'Not telling you what to do, son – just asking you to look at the lassie's father and then consider what you're taking on.'

Rachel's mouth was dry when she asked, 'But what will your mother say?'

'Darling,' enthused Bud, 'that's just it. We'll get a special licence and get married and take off.' Rachel seemed perplexed. Unperturbed, he continued, 'Can't you see if we make a go of it in America, and just think we might never come back, so what my mother thinks is irrelevant.' Bud was now down on his knees in front of her, 'Darling, I love you. I always have. Please say yes, and let's spend the rest of our lives together.'

Hot scalding tears cascaded down Rachel's cheeks as she nodded her consent.

After saying goodbye to Bud an hour had passed before Rachel was walking up the stairs to her aunt's house.

She smiled inwardly as she recalled every word of Bud's proposal. She'd just consented when he said he'd need to get home, as his mother would have his tea on the table. Rachel, still awash with emotion, felt she needed time to compose herself, time to tell someone her great news.

Being in Taylor Gardens it was only natural to think of confiding in her long-time friend, Rosa, who lived in one of the flats round the corner from the department store in Kings Street.

Vigorously ringing the bell she waited impatiently until Rosa's mother, Mrs Liston, stuck her head over the banister and called out, 'What do you want?'

'Just to speak to Rosa, Mrs Liston. It's important.'

'She's not in.'

Before Rachel could thank Mrs Liston for her information Rosa's head appeared alongside her mother's and she yelled down, 'Don't listen to my mother. I never do. Hold on, Rachel. I'm just coming down.'

Rachel had just opened the door when she became aware that Uncle Andy and Aunt Rosie were in the house and Anna, her face whiter than a ghost's, was propped up in bed. 'What's happened?' she asked, advancing towards the bed.

Andy, who had a soft spot for Rachel, placed a comforting arm around her shoulders. 'She's just had a wee shock.'

'Oh, please not a stroke.'

'Naw. Naw, lassie. Someone, and I don't think they meant to, gave her a wee fright. But she'll be right as rain in the morning.'

'Who?'

Rosie and Andy didn't answer but they did look at each other before shrugging.

Rachel inhaled. The stink of alcohol, mixed with vile scent of body odour that invaded her nostrils told her exactly who the culprit was. Hadn't that cocktail of odours always turned her stomach? So much so that now it was fashionable, when you were out socialising, to have a wee port and lemon or a sweet sherry she never did. Like Auntie, she was strictly teetotal.

Sitting on the side of the bed she took Anna's hand in hers. 'Why did my father come here?'

Andy drummed his fingers on his chin. 'It seems the poor crater,' he now grimaced before going on, 'needs somewhere to bide ... but, no offence, lassie, who's going to have him?'

Patting Anna's hand Rachel replied, 'Certainly nobody in here! This is my sanctuary – my home!' She then ran her hand over Anna's face before emphatically saying, 'Yes, this is Auntie's and *my* home and never ever will there be room for *him*.'

'Oh, lassie,' cried Rosie, wringing her hands, 'he's your father and it's un-Christian to turn him away. Remember what the Bible

288

says, "Honour your father and mother".'

'That right? Well, Auntie Rosie, you honour him because I can't – I can only thank him for the grief he's always caused me and for nothing else.'

Rosie was about to speak again when Andy spoke. 'That's enough, Rosie,' he warned. 'He wasn't turned away without being given food and the price of a bed for the night.' Turning to Rachel, his tone softened. 'And heed me, lassie, that's all you, as his daughter, will ever be required to do. Now we'll get going. But we'll send Johnny over in a bit in case you need anything doing.'

The door had just closed on Rosie and Andy when Rachel was able to give full attention to Anna. *Why,* she wondered, *hadn't she noticed how old and frail she'd become? When was it her frame had shrunk and her head had become permanently bowed by dowager's hump?*

The realisation of the deterioration in Anna couldn't have come at a worse time for Rachel. She'd danced up the stairs eager to tell Anna the glad tidings, that Bud at last had asked her to marry him, but how could she now? Anna couldn't earn enough to pay the rent of the house, buy coal to keep her old bones warm or nourishing food for her belly.

Laying her head on the table Rachel wept bitterly. *Why is it,* she thought, *that you longed and prayed for your dream to come true and when it did you had two choices: either to run with your dream or do the decent thing and realise it was payback time!*

By the time Bud reached home in Trinity he'd rehearsed over and over again what he was going to say to his mother. However when he got into the house his mother was like the sullen dame in Robert Burns' 'Tam O'Shanter', nursing her wrath to keep it warm.

'What time of night do you call this?' she hissed, unable to keep her anger in check.

'Wait 'til I tell you, Mum.'

'Tell me what exactly? That you've been dilly-dallying with that man-crazy bitch from Couper Street?'

Bud's father, who was trying desperately to stay out of the escalating row between his son and his wife, lowered his paper and said, 'That's enough, Eliza. You can't go about slandering people...' He sighed to give himself time to pick up courage and go on. 'Especially as all you're alleging would appear,' he lifted his hands and pushed them towards his wife, 'and I say again *appear* to have no foundation.'

Eliza's mouth dropped. Was she hearing right? Her husband, who she thought hadn't an opinion on anything, was taking sides against her. 'So that's how it's to be?' she sniffed. 'You, his father, don't care if he takes on a totally unsuitable slum-dweller as his wife?'

Buoyed by his father's brave stance Bud said, 'Look, Mum, what I have to tell you is this: the firm is sending me away to America for two years.'

'Good. That might bring you to your senses and you might meet up with more suitable girlfriends there who come from decent families like ... like...' Eliza paused to think and both Bud and his father howled with laughter when she spluttered, 'The Rockefellers and Carnegies.'

'Mum, we're just like Rachel's family – working class. Now what I propose is that Rachel and I marry before we leave for America.'

'You're taking her with you?' spluttered Eliza, clutching her breast.

'Yes. And that'll give you two years to get used to the idea of us being husband and wife.'

A long silent pause hung in the room. Eliza was obviously thinking of her next move and Bud and his father were surprised when she said, 'Okay. Two years will let everybody calm down but...'

Bud looked at his father. 'I just knew there would have to be a *but*...'

'Before you go, why don't you get Rachel a nice wee engagement ring? She deserves that,' Eliza simpered. 'But don't tie yourself down with a wife until you come back.'

'Och, Mum, you don't know Rachel. She wouldn't go off with me to America unless we were married.'

Eliza smiled sweetly. 'I know that. What I'm saying is, promise yourself to her but tell her you want to be fair and not rush her ... but as soon as you get back wedding bells will chime.'

Bud looked at his dad who shrugged his resignation. That hunch of his dad's shoulders told Bud he'd lost his ally and that he'd have to take on his formidable mother on his own. He was resigned to capitulation.

Rachel had sponged Anna down and fed her some soup by the time Bella came to visit. 'The spirits have already told me how things are but just in case I didn't get the message quite right...' Bella asked, looking over her shoulder, 'How is she?'

Rachel sank down on the fender stool beside Bella. 'It's really the arthritis. Every movement is so painful for her and each day she gets stiffer and stiffer.'

'Aye, she's certainly been failing of late,' Bella said, looking directly at Rachel. 'But I feel, and so does your mother, that forbye Auntie there's something amiss with you.'

Rachel nodded. She and Bella had always shared confidences and it was a relief tonight for her to tell someone all her worries – and who better to trust than Bella, a bosom friend who'd never let her down?

Without hesitation Rachel poured out the story about Bud asking her to go to America with him and how she felt about Anna and the enormous burden of indebtedness she felt. Bella had the sense to remain silent. After Rachel had finished speaking, Bella lifted the poker and lazily stirred the embers of the dying fire.

Eventually Bella leaned forward and took Rachel's hand in hers. 'Look,' she said, 'you're not the only one here that owes Auntie. I do too. So you go to America and promise to be as happy as Gus and me. And I'll take Auntie up to bide with me and look after her there.'

The stiffness from the stress she was under visibly melted from Rachel's shoulders. 'Oh, Bella, would you really do that?'

Bella nodded. 'Now let's make some tea. And seeing as Auntie's sleeping, I'll have two sugars in mine.'

The young women were drinking their tea when the door opened and Johnny crept in. 'Here, Rachel,' asked Johnny, with a wink. 'Is there a cup in the pot for me?'

Bella was disappointed that Anna didn't awaken before she left. She had wanted to stay but the bairns would all need to be bedded. 'Johnny,' she tentatively asked, 'you're no in a hurry?'

'Naw. You get going. If it's needed I'll bide aw night.'

Rachel, after throwing a large shovel of coal on the fire, had decided it would be better for Anna if she didn't light the gaslight and she and Johnny sat comfortably together just looking at the pictures that were thrown up by the firelight.

'What do you think we should do?' Johnny asked in hushed tones.

Rachel was about to answer when a soft tap on the outside door caused her to rise. On opening the door, she was surprised to see Bud and, like Bella, she could be instinctively intuitive and something was telling her to go into the passageway to speak to him.

'My aunt's not well,' was the excuse she offered for keeping him in the lobby.

'Oh, well,' he spluttered. 'It's just that I want to arrange to take you out on Saturday afternoon to buy you an engagement ring.'

The relief that he wasn't here to tell her he'd changed his mind, or had had his mind changed for him, caused her to relax and fall against the cold damp wall. 'Bud, are you sure? Should we not be keeping as much money as we can? After all, we don't know how things are going to be in America. I mean, will I get a job right away and things like that?' she babbled on.

Searching for her hands, he kissed them before saying, 'Now listen. Nothing's changed. I will marry you,' he emphasised, 'but ... not until I get back from America.'

The euphoria visibly drained from her. His mother had won again and Rachel, at this present time, had no desire or reserve left to fight her.

'Well, Bud,' she said, rising from the wall, 'isn't it a funny thing. Here was me trying to pick up courage to tell you I don't really want to go to America.'

Taken aback, Bud stammered, 'But I *am* coming back for you. Please tell me you'll wait?'

'Rachel.' Anna's feeble cry caused Rachel to open the door and say, 'Just coming, Auntie. I'm just saying goodbye to Bud.'

Turning to go inside Rachel was surprised when Bud grabbed her. In a tear-laden voice he murmured, 'Darling, you haven't said you'll wait. I need to know you'll wait.'

She chuckled. 'Oh. Is that all you want? Then off you go, Bud, with the memory of me saying, no matter how long it takes, I'll wait until Mister Right sweeps me off my feet.'

Three days later, to Bella's surprise, Anna was up and about. 'What are you doing out of bed?' Bella asked, dumping her shopping bag on the table.

Anna looked about the room and then out of the window. 'Saw the clouds chasing each other so I thought it must be a good drying day.'

Bella nodded. 'Aye, for them that can get stuck into a washing.' Bella was now fishing in a paper bag. 'But let's face it,' she pointed out in a kindly tone, 'the only thing you can get stuck into the day is this well-fired store roll.'

Anna gripped the tabletop and was starting to rise to her feet when Bella placed a hand on her shoulder and lowered her back down. 'No. I'll make the tea. You're just going to take it easy.'

'Bella,' Anna began tentatively, 'do you know what's going on with Rachel and Bud?'

Bella shook her head. 'No. I can only guess.'

'Look, I'm not an idiot,' protested Anna. 'And I should be told what's going on in my own home.'

'All I know is that Bud's going to America for two years. And...'

'He's never going to leave Rachel behind?'

'Not exactly,' drawled Bella. 'He wants them to get engaged right now and they'll get married...'

'Bella,' Anna interrupted in a croaked voice, 'are you saying they'll marry before he leaves?'

Roughly massaging her cheeks, Bella tried to think of how she could tell Anna the truth. There was no easy way so she blurted, 'No. All Rachel said was, and I swore I wouldn't tell another living soul so I'm only telling you...'

'Because I'm half dead?' suggested Anna.

Ignoring Anna's comment, Bella finished by hurriedly saying, 'She doesn't want to leave ... right now.'

'Are you saying,' queried Anna, running her fingers through her hair, 'that she's not going with him because of that wee spat I had and she now feels she's to stay to look after me?'

Bella looked down at the floor but when the door opened she managed to say, 'As she's just come in – why don't you ask her yourself?'

'Ask me what?' Rachel enquired, looking from Anna to Bella.

Rising Anna went over to Rachel and took her hand in hers. 'Look, lassie,' she began, 'you mustn't pass up the chance to go to America with Bud because of me.' Rachel didn't respond so Anna felt she had to go on. 'It's the chance of a lifetime. And you owe me nothing. Neither does Bella, Freddie or Robert,' she gulped back the tears, 'and my two laddies who've gone before me, Rab and Jimmy.'

Rachel and Bella sat down as they waited

for Anna to get everything out of her system. 'You see,' she told them between frowns and mutterings, 'I was lucky to be on hand when you were just bits of bairns and needing a mother – a roof over your heads.' Anna paused to deliberate on other memories that rushed to the surface. 'Never told anyone ... nobody's business but mine. But you see ... I couldn't have my own bairns and I wanted bairns ... so wasn't I lucky I was able to rear, or help rear, my four God-sent laddies and you two? And you've all done so well. Believe me I couldn't be prouder of you, not even if you'd been my own flesh and blood.' Anna stopped. There was no need to elaborate further.

Bella, emotionally drained, couldn't speak. Rachel, on the other hand, knew she had to say something. Here she was facing Anna, the only mother she'd ever known, and Bella, her chosen sister, so she accepted she had to tell them the truth and she also knew they would keep her confidence.

Inhaling deeply she bowed her head and before raising it again she prayed she would have the courage to tell them what they had a right to know. 'Auntie,' she began, 'there are things you should know. Firstly, I do owe you.' Anna began to protest but Rachel silenced her by raising her hand. 'And if I had stayed because you needed nursing it would have been because I wanted to out of love – not obligation. Bella, who also loves you dearly, was willing to make it easy for me to go by taking on your care. But...' Rachel stopped. She seemed reluctant to go on, however, she swallowed hard and picked up from where she'd left off, 'And it's a big *but* – you see Bud's again doing what his mother tells him to do. So as a sop, I've to get an engagement ring and in two years his dearest mother may – and it's a big *may* – be willing to have a Couper Street lassie as a daughter-in-law. Huh. Doesn't she realise I know she's hoping he'll meet someone in the next two years that'll measure up to her standards?'

'Her standards?' queried Anna, brushing her lips with her hand. 'And whatever are they?'

Shrugging, Rachel finished by saying, 'I don't know what they are – but what I do know is they're in no way good enough for any mother-in-law that I would be prepared to accept.'

22

THE WISE WOMEN

The preliminaries to the 1926 General Strike in support of the miners whose war cry was: 'Not a penny off the pay – not a minute on the day', had been grumbling on for months.

For over a year now Andy, who felt he was too old for long sea trips, had been labouring in the shipyards. Naturally working ashore hadn't changed his political views – only entrenched them. So it came as no surprise that he was at the forefront of the support being offered to the miners by the shipyard workers.

Rosie, who again would have to work to keep the household stocked in food and a roof over their heads, this time scrubbing stairs in Easter Road, took delight in pointing out to Andy that the support he was enjoying from his workmates was not so much because they identified with the strike but because there was not much work in the yards anyway.

People were on the streets vehemently voicing their objections to shortages of food and also demanding an upgrade to the allocation of one bag of coal a week for each household. Rosie and Anna had chuckled when they heard this because if another bag of coal was to be put on offer in the dock area of Leith nobody would have been able to find another two shillings and nine pence to buy it!

Fortunately May was the chosen month for the strike and as Andy thumped the table he proudly pointed out that God was on the side of the strikers as He'd sent down pleasant clement weather. Andy's euphoria however was nipped in the bud when he, having been identified as a ringleader, was arrested, along with another ninety-one people, by the baton-charging constabulary.

Immediately after Rosie became aware of the arrests she ran to tell Anna.

'Calm yourself, Rosie,' commanded Anna.

'How can I calm myself when that idiot brother of yours has not only got himself banged up in prison but...'

'But surely he'll get off with a fine,' Anna interrupted. 'He usually does.'

'A fine? Oh aye, he got that right enough but unfortunately you have to be able to pay it before you're allowed out to make a nuisance of yourself again.'

'Right enough. He's not had much work of late. Oh, Rosie, I'd like to help but I've just no been able to pull my weight of late. It's

Rachel who keeps this place going.' Anna looked around her humble home. 'Sure if it wasn't for her I'd end up in the Poorhouse.'

Rosie tutted. 'And do you think I would allow that? Nae chance.'

Anna smiled, 'But here, Rosie, there's a bonus in everything.'

'And what's that?'

'Just that our Andy'll no be on his soapbox at the Foot of the Walk tomorrow spouting, "Down with the aristocracy and bring on the guillotine!"'

Rosie cackled. 'Look, Anna, you've side-tracked me. What I came to tell you is that Johnny's been brainwashed by Andy and he's also been arrested,' she sighed wearily, 'and it looks like he'll need to do time.'

'Oh no. That means he'll no be able to take Rachel to the dancing. Real disappointed she'll be.' Anna huffed. Rosie shook her head. 'Aye, going dancing thegither is the highlight of the week for them.'

'Here, talking about them always being thegither, do you think anything's going to come of it?'

Glancing up at the clock Anna glibly said, 'If Bud doesnae hurry and come back from America ... it just might.'

Rosie too was looking at the clock as if it was somehow going to tell them how long they would have to wait for an answer when she drawled, 'Don't want my Johnny to get hurt. And I certainly don't want him hitching up to Rachel and her thinking he's second-best.'

'Johnny second-best!' exclaimed Anna with a chuckle. 'Might be to some but never to a mammy's boy like Bud Watson. Besides, he's yesterday's news.' The words had just left her mouth when she knew she'd said too much.

'Yesterday's news?' Rosie was quick to query. 'Since when?'

All Anna could do was give a half-hearted shrug. Had she not been so poorly of late she might not have forgotten that only she and Bella had been taken by Rachel into her confidence.

The three of them, Bella, Rachel and herself, had been sitting round the table having a good blether. Those were precious times Anna treasured, especially now when she was so frail. During the conversation Anna noticed Rachel was not joining in the banter as much as she usually did. Then without warning, Rachel decided to break the news that her best friend Rosa Liston, who had gained a reputation for herself as being 'easy', had been dispatched by her mother to relatives in America – Texas, to be exact.

'Oh,' interrupted Bella, 'but is that not where Bud is?' Rachel nodded. 'Bet she met up with him.'

'Anyway,' Rachel had continued, 'Mother

Liston hoped that in Texas, where Rosa's infamy wasn't public knowledge, she'd find herself a "good" husband and settle down.' Rachel had allowed a long pause before announcing, 'Within three months she'd done just that.'

'Oh so, all's well that ends well,' exclaimed Anna.

'Not really,' Rachel had said with a shake of her head. 'You see, the gullible candidate found out that he'd require, for the sake of the expected baby, to do the honourable thing and marry Rosa.' Rachel breathed in deeply before adding, 'And she's now the respectable – Mrs Bud Watson!'

Anna also remembered, with more than a hint of satisfaction, how four months later Rosa had achieved the miraculous and given birth to a nine-pound baby girl who was a whole five months premature!

Rosie, unaware of Anna's dilemma, did as she always did when faced with a problem: she took out her snuffbox and inhaled a large pinch from it. 'And,' she briefly hesitated to give herself time to sniff and meditate, 'I suppose when she finds out my Johnny's been bunged up and will do time, as I havnae got the price of his fine, he'll be Mister Yesterday too.'

'Right enough,' still pondering, Anna said more to herself. 'But why did Johnny allow himself to be influenced by his father?'

Shrugging, Rosie replied, 'Like father like son. And you know fine, Anna, how Andy keeps going on about a better deal for working folk. So along with Andy's views and that of his mates' in the union, Johnny's now convinced that the only way a working man will ever get his voice listened to will be through a forceful trade union.'

'So Johnny went on the march to support the miners?'

'Anna, don't you realise he's a bigger hothead than Andy now? He speaks better. The men listen to him. Everybody but me thinks he makes sense and is the way forward.' Rosie stopped to take another pinch of her instant composure before adding, 'And not only did he lead the march, he was the one carrying the banner!'

Anna could only look at Rosie and shake her head.

The long silence between both women continued until Rachel's entrance broke it.

'What are you doing here at this time of day?' Anna managed to splutter.

'I got time off...' Rachel abruptly stopped as she spied a letter propped up on the mantelshelf. 'Look, it's for me. It's from my brother Freddie in Canada.'

'Hope he's no needing another handout because he's had it. Oh aye, none of us hae a brass bean,' Rosie grumbled under her breath.

Tearing the envelope open Rachel sank down to read her letter, which she held in her right hand while grasping the other contents in her left. 'It says here, Auntie, Violet and Freddie are very well. And at last they've a wee place of their own.' Rachel started to laugh and cry at the same time, 'And I've also got twin nieces and, Auntie, you won't believe it but he's called them Norma and Anna.'

Not only was Rachel crying, but so were Rosie and Anna.

Through smiles and tears Anna managed to ask, 'What else is he saying?'

'Oh, just that he's doing so well that,' Rachel started to wave the other piece of paper high above her head as she danced around the room, 'here is a postal order for half of the money that he borrowed from me to get to Canada!' She stopped dancing to throw her arms around Rosie and looking directly at Anna she chuckled. 'And now do you doubt the power of prayer?'

'What are you taking about, lassie?'

'Just this, Auntie. I asked for time off because I heard my Johnny had been arrested and I came home here to beg you to let me sell or pawn that punch bowl set and your pendulum clock...'

'You've got to be joking,' a horrified Anna challenged.

'No. You see I need four pounds ten shillings so I can pay Johnny's fine or he'll be locked up for a month.' Rachel's shoulders dropped with relief. 'And here at home waiting for me was the answer to my prayers.' Rachel now kissed the warrant before brandishing it in the air again. 'So I'll hightail it along to the post office and get them to cash this for me.'

'No matter how fast you run, Rachel,' Anna warned, 'you won't be able to get the order cashed and then get to the court in time to pay the fine.' She sighed before adding, 'So it looks like our poor Johnny will need to spend the night behind bars.'

'Aye, well,' chipped in Rosie, 'maybe a night in the cells will cool his heels.' She paused and scratched her head, adding sulkily, 'And I suppose my Andy will be left to rot there on his own.'

'Auntie Rosie, you're a right wet blanket the day. Do you think seeing there's seventeen pounds ten shillings here, I'd let Uncle Andy rot in jail and not pay his three-pound fine?'

'Just a minute,' intervened Anna. 'Why has Johnny, on his first march, got a bigger fine and custodial sentence than Andy who's a habitual…'

Rachel sighed. 'Seems they think, and I'm afraid I know, that Johnny is a rabble-rouser – the foremost union leader now. But look, forget all that. After we get them out we'll still have ten pounds clear to tide *all* of us over.'

'Aye, and with most of the trawlers being laid up, even our Bella's feeling the pinch,' croaked Anna.

The following day when Rachel paid for Johnny and Andy's release she'd achieved quite a lot.

With great satisfaction she recalled how she'd just cashed in Freddie's Godsend of an order and was skipping down the steps of Leith's General Post Office when she noticed Eliza Watson coming up the stairs. 'Good afternoon, Mrs Watson,' Rachel said in a voice dripping with honey.

'Eh. Eh,' stammered Eliza. 'I'm just posting a letter here to my Bud.'

'Congratulating him on becoming a father? And you must be thrilled to be a grandmother.'

Eliza swallowed hard as her face fired. 'I know what you're thinking, and everybody else is saying, that the wee lassie's red hair is the same shade...' Eliza continued through muffled sobs, 'as the Palace Picture House projectionist.'

Rachel so wanted to humiliate Mrs Watson and say, 'Oh, but as I come from Couper Street, Mrs Watson, would it not be pretentious of me to think I could think?' But she vividly remembered what Eugenie had taught her, that you should never, in public, lose your temper or dignity. 'When you manage to keep your cool,' Eugenie had counselled, 'you get a great feeling of superiority and satisfaction.' Rachel could have continued with, 'But know this, Mrs Watson, when I wed I'll be dressed in white because I'll have the right to do so and my children will never require to question their lineage.'

Eugenie's words were still ringing in her ears when instinctively she laid a comforting hand on Mrs Watson's arm and said, 'Believe me, I'm so very sorry, Mrs Watson, and could you return this to Bud for me.' Fishing in her handbag she brought out the small box containing the engagement ring Bud had given her before he'd left for America. Lifting Mrs Watson's hand she then dropped the box into it. 'And be sure to tell him, all I'll remember are the good times and I wish him a long and happy life.'

Rachel was not standing outside as some other friends and relatives were when the prisoners, whose fines had been paid, were released.

She felt that one afternoon off work, without pay, sorting out Johnny's problems was quite sufficient and she still had ambitions of furthering herself. Besides, both Auntie Anna and she needed the money she earned just to survive.

Emerging from the store at closing time she was surprised that Johnny was not waiting for her. Although feeling angry she conceded it was not like Johnny to treat her like this. In fact, there were times she wanted to scream at him that she was capable of looking after herself and could he accept she didn't like being molly-coddled.

By the time she got to Couper Street the fatigue from working a ten-hour day was beginning to take its toll and it was easy to allow the feeling of resentment about Johnny not being there to thank her to creep in.

Wearily climbing the stairs she became aware of an eerie silence that seemed to envelop her. Hushed whispers seemed to be urging her to remember Bella's warnings. Inwardly she winced as she recalled Bella's voice saying, 'Your mother is coming back. You know that where Auntie comes from they believe that when it's your time to pass someone from the other side, who loves you very dearly, comes back to show you the way.'

Tentatively turning the door handle of her aunt's house, Rachel's apprehension grew and turned into frantic panic when she stepped over the threshold. There, standing in room, was everyone connected to Anna's life – Uncle Andy, Aunt Rosie, Bella, Gus, Robert, Rye, Johnny, Ella, Davy, Sandy. Only she was needed to make up the complete congregation.

Rachel's eyes were now drawn to the bed bedecked in the pristine linen Anna kept specially for the laying out of the dead. Her dry throat contracted as she looked on the peaceful face of her beloved auntie. Today in the big bed Auntie looked even smaller, in fact quite dwarf-like. Trying hard to control her hysteria and really being terrified to ask, Rachel could only manage to stammer, 'What happened?'

'Took a wee turn for the worse, she did,' Rosie replied. 'And with you keeping back some of Freddie's money for a rainy day...'

'And I decided Auntie being ill meant it was pouring,' interrupted Bella.

'So it was only right to pay for a doctor to come in,' emphasised Andy.

Rachel nodded her thanks.

'And,' Rosie continued, 'He said ... it's now her heart too. So Rachel, you've got to be brave.'

Violently shaking her head, Rachel blurted, 'But there must be some hope.'

'Of course there is,' Andy replied, withering Rosie with a hostile stare. 'All she needs is a good rest and she'll turn the corner.'

'Och, Andy, be realistic. She's in God's hands now,' Rosie huffed before turning to Johnny and Ella. 'Right,' she instructed, 'as there's nothing else for it – us three will get down on our knees and pray.'

Rye crossed over to the bed and placed her

hand on Anna's brow. 'I don't like it when they're burning yet shivering with cold. No a good sign.'

Bella then looked over her shoulder and inhaled deeply before announcing, 'That was Norma, your mother, Rachel, and she says she's now in control and we have–'

Rachel suddenly jumped into the middle of the floor. 'No she's not, Bella. She gave up the right to control anything when she left us all to get on with it. And all you who are down on your knees, either get up or get a pail and some water and scrub the floor.' Stopping momentarily to catch her breath she then proceeded to voice her ultimatum. 'Now, unless you're here to help me pull Auntie through then I would be pleased if you'd just go and take your woebegone attitudes with you!'

Anna had rallied and at two o'clock in the morning Rachel found herself and Johnny staring into the flames of the fire.

'Rachel, now that Auntie's crisis has passed I want you to know I am so very grateful to you for paying my fine.'

Rachel, face cupped in her hands, just shrugged.

'I was wondering,' continued Johnny, who then briefly hesitated as if afraid to go on, 'if you ... went to the bother because maybe you've began to ... think seriously about me or was it because you too want to join in the fight for a bigger share of the country's wealth going to the shop floor workers?'

Although there was no verbal response from Rachel, she was thinking. Hadn't Johnny always been part of her life, ever since she'd come to stay at Couper Street? Never when she needed him had he let her down. She remembered so vividly how distressed he'd been when Auntie had sent her barefoot to beg Gabby for money for shoes. He'd even offered her his boots. She knew he was in love with her. Much to his sister Ella's annoyance, he'd never had any other girl friends. The biggest plus for her in marrying him would be how delighted Auntie, who adored him, would be.

Rachel gave a little laugh as she remembered Auntie always saying that her Johnny's wife may not always have something to eat but she sure would always have something to look at. It was true Johnny was entrenched in the union now and, even though joining it was not for her, she admired his commitment. He was, she accepted, the nephew of Anna and the son of Andy, who had always been champions of the poor, sick, downtrodden, overworked and depressed, so it was only natural that he would follow in their footsteps.

'Rachel,' Johnny interrupted into her thoughts. 'I need to know ... is there any chance for me?'

Acknowledging to herself that she loved him – she really did. But she also knew it was not the burning passion she'd had and still felt for Bud. Her love for Johnny was an enduring love – a love that had grown throughout the many years of friendship and trust. Nodding, she accepted she'd need to settle for that because that was the best there was ever going to be. 'Please, God,' she silently prayed, 'let it be enough to see us our whole lives through.'

Taking his hand in hers she said, 'I do love you, Johnny. I always have and we will marry but...' Both she and Johnny now looked over to the bed and were relieved to hear the quiet gentle rhythm of Anna's regular breathing.

'I know,' Johnny responded gently while squeezing her hand, 'you have to see her safely over to the other side before we wed. I understand that and I wouldn't have it any other way.'

Rachel reached up and took down a letter from the mantelshelf. 'Haven't told her about this yet,' she said, scanning the letter again.

'Aye, they say they're gonnae demolish Couper Street,' Johnny looked up at the ceiling as if it was about to crash down about their heads. 'But they havnae said when. Just sometime in the near future.'

Biting her lip, Rachel pondered before suggesting, 'Aye, but seeing it's the Edinburgh Corporation that could mean we could have maybe a year or two.'

'Or three or four,' suggested Johnny, who was torn between his urgent desire to marry Rachel immediately and his wish to hang on to his beloved Auntie for as long as possible.

Still in reflective mood, Rachel inhaled slowly before thinking out loud. 'Whatever, but it will be far more time than she's got and we have to be thankful that she won't see this place where she reigned as queen reduced to a pile of rubble.' She sighed and had difficulty holding back the tears before saying, 'Don't know how I'd feel if this place, without Auntie in it, was no longer here. I remember the day I came here. I wasn't her flesh and blood. She was under no obligation to take me in and provide for me.' Rachel gave a sly snigger. 'And yeah, there were times I could have run away when Auntie would wander back to her crusade to get even with Gabby. But she kept me safe – gave me standards. Made me what I am today. Oh aye, I knew she was always here to run back to. The door to this house was always open.'

'Yeah, no matter the problem, or who had it, she'd find an answer or help out,' Johnny added wistfully. 'She is the very best and she brings out the best in everyone around her. And sometimes all she had to support her in her quest to carry on was her undying faith.'

'Johnny, do you think that when we set up home there'll be helpful folk around us like there's here in Couper Street?'

'Of course there will. There's an Anna, a wise woman, in every tenement here in Couper Street, Admiralty Street, East and West Cromwell Street and all the other streets. It's a Leith thing. The poor and downtrodden helping each other along and we've all learnt from those wise women. They've taught us well. And when our bairns come along we'll teach them that no one's an island – we all need each other. And the best way to survive is being part of a community where we care for and support each other. That way we'll keep faith with all the aunties, like Anna, and go forward and claim what is rightfully ours – a better and fairer society.'

Rachel didn't respond. She was thinking that listening to Johnny's rant was like listening to his father on his Saturday soapbox. What if Johnny was like his father and Anna? Would he sacrifice his immediate family's wellbeing for the good of the community? Could she live with that? Bella had prophesised that she would have many children but she wasn't Rosie. Oh no, if she was forced to scrub stairs it would be to put food in her own children's bellies – they would always be her uttermost priority.

She had just decided to voice her concerns to Johnny when Anna called out, 'Rachel.'

Immediately the urgency to challenge Johnny was lost and any doubts she had were forced to the back of her mind, and she earnestly prayed that she would *never* be given cause to resurrect them.

The publishers hope that this book has given you enjoyable reading. Large Print Books are especially designed to be as easy to see and hold as possible. If you wish a complete list of our books please ask at your local library or write directly to:

Magna Large Print Books
Magna House, Long Preston,
Skipton, North Yorkshire.
BD23 4ND

This Large Print Book, for people
who cannot read normal print,
is published under the auspices of

THE ULVERSCROFT FOUNDATION

... we hope you have enjoyed this book.
Please think for a moment about those
who have worse eyesight than you ...
and are unable to even read or enjoy
Large Print without great difficulty.

You can help them by sending a
donation, large or small, to:

**The Ulverscroft Foundation,
1, The Green, Bradgate Road,
Anstey, Leicestershire, LE7 7FU,
England.**
or request a copy of our brochure for
more details.

The Foundation will use all donations
to assist those people who are visually
impaired and need special attention
with medical research, diagnosis
and treatment.

Thank you very much for your help.